spells & sorcery

The Lexie Carrigan Chronicles

S. Usher Evans

Line Editing by Danielle Fine

ISBN: 1945438037
ISBN-13: 978-194543835

Contents

Dedication

To Jo,
For creating the world
where I learned my

Magic

One

You have magic.

One sentence, three words, four syllables. Enough to change my life forever.

(And I'm not talking about the whole spells and sorcery thing.)

The day before my fifteenth birthday was so painfully normal, I probably wouldn't have noticed even if something were amiss. My kindergarten teacher used to say I was a little old woman in a little kid's body. Ten years later, I was still more Golden Girl than Party Girl. Between the Advanced Placement, dual enrollment, and honors courses jam-packed into my schedule, it was enough just to get through each day without adding more complications.

"The northeastern colonies were settled less out of economic necessity and trade, and more for those seeking religious freedom. But as the population grew, more secular colonists began to settle amongst them, increasing the rift between the two communities. It should come to no surprise the majority of those accused during the Salem Witch Trials were the more wealthy, secular colonists."

I jotted down a note about the cause and effect. Mills had mentioned there would be an essay test soon, and I wanted to be ready. Plus, being the uber-nerd I was, I actually liked seeing the narrative unfold as each event directly impacted another. It was one of the reasons history was my favorite subject.

Mills was one of those guys who'd been teaching the same subject the same way for thirty years, and enjoyed every day of it. Unlike the rest of the school, which had moved on to whiteboards and overhead projectors, Mills hand wrote a section of his bulleted history of the United States every morning on the chalkboard, which stretched over three of the classroom walls.

"Many of the women accused of being witches were actually widows of means, meaning they had more economic power than the men." Mills paused to chuckle. "But most of the hysteria ended when someone accused the Massachusetts governor's wife of being a witch."

I snorted, and glanced around to see if anyone else was laughing, but they all wore the same glazed-over expressions. As usual, I was the only one paying attention in our last-period history class. Our schedule rotated each day so as to give a different class the post-lunch doldrums. To boot, it was Monday, so the attentiveness was already in the toilet.

Mills must've caught my snort, or he knew I was the only one actually awake, because he asked, "Lexie, can you explain about how the end of Puritanism resulted in the Salem Witch Trials?"

I looked down at my notes and flipped back a page to read

what I'd written down. "Because of the rise of trade, and the shift of power from religious leaders to the merchant class, it created a power vacuum. The witch trials were a backlash of the change toward more secular holdings of power."

He praised me and I kept a smile to myself as he moved on, quizzing another student who was much less prepared than I was. But that student was saved from answering any more questions, as the bell rang. Groaning and rubbing their faces, my classmates woke from their stupor and began talking about their plans for the afternoon—jobs, sports, and whether the nearby Gulf of Mexico would be tame enough for some stand-up paddle boarding.

My little high school fit the Florida beach town I'd grown up in. I'd known most of those in the sophomore class since kindergarten, though I wouldn't call any of them my good friends and we didn't really hang out. Then again, most of the school was nose-deep in trying to survive honors and college-level classes, while maintaining jobs, volunteer hours, and extracurricular activities in the hopes we could all get big fat scholarships at the colleges of our dreams.

I stopped at my locker to grab my things, and crouched down to the bottom level to work the lock. In the eight weeks we'd already been in school, I still hadn't figured out how to get it open on the first try.

"C'mon you...son of a..." I mumbled, swirling the lock around. I'd nearly gotten it when someone bumped into my hand with their foot, knocking the dial out of alignment.

I glared at the offending leg. Callista was one of those girls who exuded confidence. Smart, athletic, and usually always with friends, or her boyfriend, Joel. He was in some of my advanced classes, and he was on the football team in the fall, the soccer team in the winter, and the baseball team in the spring. They were all right, except that when they started making kissy-faces at each other, they forgot that other people needed to get into their lockers.

"Can you please...?" I asked, shoving their feet as they bumped into me again.

I saw the eye roll from Callista and ignored it. I didn't have time to get into it with her. With a grunt, I pulled on my too-heavy backpack and hurried out the front doors of the school into the sweltering fall afternoon. My sister wasn't above leaving me if she got to her car before I did. But I spotted Marie's cherry red convertible and breathed a sigh of relief that I wouldn't have to walk home.

I had no earthly idea how Marie convinced our aunt to buy her something so absurd and unnecessary, especially since Marie and Jeanie fought like cats and dogs. Then again, Marie was so used to getting her way, I wouldn't have been surprised if she'd flashed her smile to a car salesman and he'd handed over the keys.

I didn't have to wait long before Marie walked out the front doors of the school, her best friend Charity by her side. Blonde, flawless skin, long tanned legs thanks to the nearby beach, together, they were a picture of teenaged beauty. But, I frowned, if Marie was giving Charity a ride, we'd spend an extra half an hour at Charity's house so Marie could flirt with Charity's brother.

And that meant me stuck in the car until Marie decided to drive me home.

I tried not to look too upset when they approached the car. That would only give Marie cannon fodder.

"And I swear, I don't remember anything about his mother," Marie said. "Do you?"

"Was she even in the play?" Charity asked. "God, Shakespeare is so boring."

"Right?" Marie gave me a once-over but said nothing to acknowledge my presence. That, at least, was preferable. I climbed into the backseat and pulled out my copy of *To Kill a Mockingbird* to start reading the assigned chapters, more to drown out their conversation than to get a head start on homework.

Our little town was small, so it only took Marie five minutes to reach our neighborhood, and another minute to swerve through it until we reached Charity's house.

When Charity left the car, Marie finally turned around and said, "Walk home."

I glowered at her. "Marie, that's not fair."

"I'm sorry, I don't care."

Growling and muttering about how I was going to tell Jeanie about this, I stuffed my book back into my backpack and scooted out of the backseat, slamming the door shut behind me.

"*Watch it*!" Marie said.

"Maybe you can get your new boyfriend to fix it." I glanced at the car next to hers with a parking sticker of the local community college. "What, so you've worked your way through all the high school boys?"

Instead of retorting, a smug smile grew on her face. "You think you're *so smart*, don't you? Let's see how smart you are after tonight."

I was halfway to a comment about her latest test grade when I realized what she'd said. "What do you mean, after tonight?"

Marie feigned innocence. "Oh, I don't know. Maybe there's actually something I know that you *don't*. Maybe you aren't as smart as you think, little genius."

I glowered.

She looked over my head and flashed a thousand-watt smile at someone behind me. "Hey, *you*!" Then her gaze landed on me again, and it hardened. "Can't wait to chat later when you're losing your shit."

I wasn't sure I believed her, but it was rare for Marie to be so smug. The only thing I could think of was perhaps Jeanie had a surprise for my birthday. In any case, any questions I had were answered by the slamming of Charity's front door.

By the time I heard my oldest sister's car pulling up in the driveway, I was putting the finishing touches on the discussion questions for English. Nicole was a student at the local university, and spent most of her days either in class or at her part-time job at the local pharmacy. Although she could've gotten a scholarship anywhere, she preferred to stay close and help Jeanie with me and Marie, as she'd done pretty much her whole life. And as much as I hated to think of Nicole putting aside her own aspirations for me,

I was secretly glad of it.

Her face, so similar to my own, lit up when she walked through the kitchen door and put her bag down next to mine. "Happy birthday."

"It's tomorrow," I said, quirking my eyebrow. Birthdays weren't that exciting around our house; then again, Jeanie never really celebrated anything with too much flair.

"Yeah, but...happy *early* birthday." Nicole went to the fridge and poked around, before sighing loudly. "We don't have any food. Do you think Jeanie's going to the store?" She chewed her lip. "I should go to the store."

While she fretted over the state of our dinner, I dug in my bag for the last bit of homework that I'd been putting off. "Want to help me with chemistry?"

She glanced at me, then back in the fridge. "I could make a boxed dinner, I guess. But we don't have any chicken—"

"Nicole," I said, a bit more forcefully. "Chemistry? You promised me you'd help me with it when I signed up for the class, remember?"

"Chemistry is easy," she said, moving to the freezer.

"For you."

She offered the ghost of a smile before whipping out her phone. "We've all got our talents, Lexie."

As she texted our aunt, I flipped through my homework. After spending all day in class, and all afternoon doing more work, the chemistry fractions might as well have been written in French.

French! I still had French homework to do. Damn. I wasn't

quite sure how I was going to survive high school if this was what it would be like for the next three years.

"Ni*cole*," I whined.

"Fine, fine." She put down her phone and looked over my shoulder. "Oh, Lexie, this is easy. It's just math. See? The book tells you what to do right here."

"I don't want the book. I want you to show me."

She snorted and crossed the kitchen to check her buzzing phone. "That's a first."

"What?"

"You not wanting a book." Nicole sighed. "I'm going to get food. Want to come?"

I shook my head. "I need to finish this. Would you at least check my chemistry when you get back?"

"That I can do."

The house went silent again, and I struggled through chemistry, cursing Nicole and her suggestion that I take it over an easier science. She'd said it was the easiest class she'd ever taken, and that she'd help me with it, but most of her help had been "Just read the book." Normally, that was more our aunt's teaching style, which probably explained my penchant for the local bookstore.

I'd finished three questions before I heard a car in the driveway again. But instead of Nicole, Jeanie walked through the door. Thirty-something, with short, spiky brown hair, she'd been in her early twenties when she'd taken us in. She'd never been the nurturing type, but she kept us clothed, fed, and happy, so I supposed that was all I could ask for in a guardian. Although Marie could probably quibble with the "happy" part...

"Hey, hey," she said, spotting me at the kitchen counter.

"Hey," I said, closing the chemistry book. "How was work?"

"Good. How was school?"

"Good."

We stared at each other for a moment, which piqued my curiosity. Jeanie usually high-tailed it to her bedroom when she got home, returning just in time for dinner, and spent the evening on her computer or phone.

"What's going on in the news lately?" she asked, taking a seat at the table. "What's happening in Washington?"

"Um..." I blinked at her. While I was an avid follower of the political news sites, Jeanie couldn't tell the difference between a Democrat and a Republican. "You hate politics."

"Okay." She blew air out through her lips. "What are you studying in school?"

I glanced at my history notebook. "Salem witch trials?"

She snorted but didn't respond.

We descended into silence, and again, Jeanie's behavior drew my curiosity. "So...what's up?"

"Birthday tomorrow, right? What do you want to do? Go out to dinner?"

"S-sure..." I said, slowly. "Is something going on? You're acting really weird."

"Where's Nicole?"

"Getting dinner, like you asked."

"Hm." Jeanie ran a hand through her hair and glanced at the

clock.

Marie's foreboding words earlier came back to haunt me, and I gave them a little more weight. "Is everything all right?"

"Sure, sure. We just need to have a little family talk tonight."

Family talk—when had we *ever* had one of those? "I'm not in trouble, am I?"

"You? Hardly." Jeanie snorted. "Speaking of trouble, where's Marie?"

I shrugged. "She said she was going to work a few hours ago. Oh, and she made me walk home from Charity's today. Did you know she's trying to date—"

"Lexie, don't even start," Jeanie said, wearily. "There's a list of things Marie needs to answer for when she gets home tonight."

You mean if, I said quietly. I'd heard them arguing the night before. Jeanie had said Marie had never come home. Marie didn't deny it, although she said she'd spent the night at a friend's house on the beach. The conversation had ended abruptly, and Jeanie had been in a stormy mood the rest of the evening. That was actually a nicer ending to most of their fights. Usually, Marie would end it with a hearty, "You aren't my mother" and Jeanie would ground her for three weeks.

Nicole chose that moment to walk in the front door, carrying three bags of takeout. Jeanie stood and helped her get everything out and on the table. There were more than a few furtive glances shared between them, and enough directed at me that I couldn't take it anymore.

"Okay, enough!" I barked, shocking both of them. "What the

hell is going on? Did someone die?"

"Nobody died, Lexie," Jeanie said. "We just... We need to talk to you about something important. About the family. And about you."

I glanced between the two of them, random thoughts and worries spinning through my mind. Were we moving? Had we won the lottery?

Nicole opened her mouth then closed it, looking at Jeanie, who wore an indecisive look on her face.

"Well?" I said after a too-long silence.

"I think we should just come out with it," Nicole said, watching Jeanie.

"I suppose. Lexie, you—"

"Well, *hello,* everyone!"

Marie's voice echoed through the room, making me jump. I'd been too focused on Jeanie and Nicole and hadn't even heard her come home.

She wore a devious smile on her face, which never boded well for anyone. "Did you tell her?"

"Getting to it, Marie," Nicole said. "Go back—"

In front of my eyes, a plate appeared on the counter, seemingly out of thin air—no strings, no hands, nothing actually *placed* it there. And then, a fully-formed ham sandwich with lettuce and tomato and, I assumed, mustard appeared on top of it.

Just.

Appeared.

Then the sandwich was gone from the counter, and in the

blink of an eye, was in Marie's hands. "Wanted to make myself a snack before I went back to work."

And with that, she winked at me and disappeared in a puff of smoke.

My gaze, wide and unblinking, shifted over to Nicole and Jeanie, who didn't look the least bit surprised that sandwiches and sisters were appearing and disappearing all over the kitchen.

I swallowed and cleared my throat. "What the *actual hell* was that?"

"Damn her," Jeanie seethed. "I knew I should've charmed the house before Lexie got home—"

"I'm sorry, *what the actual hell was that*?" I repeated with more fervor.

Nicole tutted, glancing between Jeanie and the space Marie had *disappeared* from. "She's Marie, and she's always going to—"

"*Excuse me!*" My panicked voice echoed in the kitchen. "*Can someone explain to me how the hell that just happened*?"

"Lexie, you have magic," Jeanie said with a heavy sigh.

"M... What?"

"Magic, Lexie, like you see in the movies," Jeanie said.

Nicole, at least, seemed to care that I was on the verge of fainting. "Take a deep breath, okay? It's not really that big a deal —"

"*Not that big a deal*? You're telling me...you're...I've... Wh..." I sank into the nearest chair, feeling lightheaded. This must've been a dream. I must've fallen asleep at the counter. Maybe I was hallucinating, and I'd start seeing chemistry problems floating across the kitchen, too. After all, sandwiches didn't just appear and disappear, and Jeanie and Nicole *couldn't* have been serious.

"Let's start at the beginning," Jeanie said calmly. "Lexie, some people have magic—"

"Right, because *that's* believable." I pressed my head into my forearms and wondered when I was going to wake up. This had to be a dream. There was *no way* Jeanie would ever say something so completely ludicrous.

"It's okay, Lexie," Nicole said, placing a hand on my shoulder.

If I were dreaming, could I feel that? Could I also feel the dull thudding in my brain from a stress headache?

"Maybe I should get the calming draught?" Nicole said.

"Might be a good idea. I think she's about to pass out—"

"*She* is right here," I said, snapping my head up. "And she is...are you...you *can't be serious*?"

Jeanie looked at Nicole and shrugged. Then, with a flick of her wrist and a puff of yellow smoke, a cup appeared in her hand.

"Drink this—"

But I wasn't having any of it. I'd now seen two physically impossible things in this kitchen, and I'd had enough.

"I need some air!"

Two

I ran out of the house as fast as my legs could carry me. I couldn't believe it. I just couldn't...

Magic?

Was real?

Not only was it real, but I had it. So did that make me a witch or a wizard or...?

Or nothing. Magic didn't exist.

But it did, because I'd seen with my own two eyes.

I slowed and looked behind me to see if Jeanie or Nicole were coming after me. I wanted them to rush out and say it was a giant joke and Marie was in on it and "Ha-ha. Happy birthday, idiot."

But as the fall night darkened around me, I heard no voices behind me. Nothing except the random car door slamming or the rumble of a truck passing on the highway nearby.

Perhaps I'd just imagined the whole thing. Maybe I'd had a stroke.

There was a small park in the distance, and I marched toward it, waiting to wake up from this strange dream. The lamplights snapped on, and I jumped nearly out of my skin, my heart thudding wildly. I stared at the orange glow for a moment, taking a few moments to convince myself that the streetlights were on a timer, and not turning on of their own volition.

They couldn't have been turned on by magic, could they?

Could they?

"I'm losing it," I whispered, covering my face with my hands.

I crossed the grassy park, headed for the swing set. I plopped down on the swing and leaned against the chain. After a moment, I began to swing back and forth, allowing my mind to go blank for just a moment. I took a deep breath in and out and stared at the empty suburban streets.

"Yer a wizard, Lexie..." I whispered to myself.

"Rough day?"

My head bobbled up at the sound. An older man stood on the sidewalk. He wore casual khaki pants and a polo shirt, and his salt-and-pepper hair was neatly trimmed. He stood under one of the street lamps, which gave him an almost angelic sort of glow.

"W-what?" I said, realizing he was still talking to me.

"I asked if you were all right," he said, stepping out of the spotlight and closer to the swing set. "You look like you've seen a ghost."

"Have you ever questioned everything you thought was real?" I asked, for lack of anything better to say.

"Once or twice," he responded with a charming smile. "Mind if I join you?"

I shrugged, and he sat down on the other swing beside me. I might have thought it strange, a middle-aged man on a swing set, but I didn't have a clear definition of weird anymore.

"Want to talk about it?" he asked.

"I doubt you would believe me," I said. "I don't believe me."

"That's a tough spot to be in. Let me guess: did they tell you about magic?"

I nearly fell out of the swing. "W-wait, you know? Does *everybody* know?"

He laughed, his few wrinkles deepening with smile lines. "No, of course not. Just those of us who have magic."

"A-and how did you know I have it?"

"We can tell," he said. "You'll get there, I'm sure. But I only assumed—teenage girl, looking the way you did, magical..."

I slumped lower against the metal chains. "I wonder what else people are lying to me about..."

"You know about the Easter Bunny, right?"

I sat up, wide-eyed. A man-sized rabbit *existed*?

"He's not real," the man finished with an amused smile.

"Very funny," I said, clutching my still-pounding heart. "After tonight, I'm pretty sure I'd believe anything is real."

"Magic is real. The Easter Bunny is not. How about we start there?"

"I can't wrap my head around it," I said, looking up at the stars. I might've still been dreaming, but this guy seemed real enough. "I mean, is science really science or is it magic?"

"I'd go out on a limb and say your understanding of science is sound," he said thoughtfully. "Magic tends to stay within magical communities. Not too much gets out into the nonmagical lesson books."

"What about gravity?" I said, lifting my feet from the ground and letting the swing do the work. "Does magic make the earth go 'round?"

"No, the earth rotates due to leftover inertia from when the solar system was created," he said without missing a beat.

My feet thudded back onto the sand and I stared at him. I'd never been out-nerded before.

"Magic is more like another sense," he said, slowly swinging back and forth. "It's like an extra hand you wield with your mind."

"Oh." I frowned. "I don't know what that means."

"Here." He flicked his hand and, in a purple puff of smoke, a thick book appeared in his hand.

My eyes nearly fell out of my head for what felt like the hundredth time that night. "How did you do that? What is that?"

"This," he offered the book to me, "is a primer. It was used in the late seventeenth century for young magicals. Very basic, of course, but the best tutorial I've found to introduce magic."

The most purple book I'd ever seen, it was well-worn, the edges frayed and water damaged. The title, *Spells and Sorcery, Volume 1*, was embossed in a gold lettering that almost *glowed.*

It was one thing to see puffs of yellow smoke and sandwiches, but something about this book was alive, and calling to some ethereal feeling dancing in the pit of my stomach.

I shook my head. Probably indigestion. "This is..."

"Open it."

"I..." Even though I was still in shock, curiosity was starting to take hold. That strange calling grew more pronounced the longer I held the book in my lap. So, almost compelled, I opened the book to the front page and ran a finger along the pressed pages. "Where'd you get this?"

"I'm a collector of old books—specifically magical ones. I'm sort of a history buff." He paused and nodded to it. "Why don't you take that with you and give it a read?"

Something in the back of my mind reminded me of a book that housed an evil wizard. I glanced at the book and shook my head. "I can't possibly take this. It's...I mean, it's so old. Probably worth a lot of money."

"Books are meant to be read, not gathering dust on a shelf. What good is the knowledge in here if I can't share it?"

I stammered like an idiot and fired off a few reasons why I couldn't, but he placed his hand over mine.

"I insist. Think of it as an early birthday present."

I narrowed my eyes at him. "How did you know it was my birthday? I mean, it's not my birthday. Tomorrow's my birthday."

"Magic comes at the beginning of one's fifteenth year," he said, standing. "I only assumed they wanted to tell you before you woke up with it..."

"Would've been nice if they'd told me sooner," I said, running my fingertips down the front of the book again.

"I have a feeling that book will help," he said, nodding once before turning to leave.

"Oh, I'm Lexie, by the way," I called to him.

He paused and turned back around with a curious expression. "That's an interesting name."

I grimaced. Not the first time I'd heard that. "As in Alexis, but...blah."

"I prefer Alexis myself," he said with a smile. "I'm Gavon. Get home before it gets too dark, okay?"

I nodded and opened my mouth to agree but he was gone.

Just...disappeared in front of my eyes *gone*. In a puff of purple smoke.

Purple smoke.

What was it about people appearing and disappearing in smoke today?

I ran my hands over the cover of the book absent-mindedly. My head was starting to hurt from all the new information crammed into it. But I could never say no to a book, especially one which promised to give me the answers I so desperately needed.

When I opened the book, I could've sworn the air tingled around me. Or that could've just been my imagination. But I definitely wasn't imagining the way the pages glowed, giving me just enough light to read the first lines.

SPELLS AND SORCERY
Or
YOUNG MAGICAL'S BEST COMPANION

Containing,

SPELLWORK, CASTING, CHARMING, and MAGICAL INCANTATION, in an easier way than any yet published;

INSTRUCTIONS TO CAST VARIETY OF SPELLS; the history of magic and magical persons;

THE LETTERS OF POTION FOR THE un-MAKERS; a short and easy method of cataloguing the magical ingredients; care and feeding for magical herbs; methods of de-scaling a dragon.

LIKEWISE THE PRACTICAL CHARMING METHODS made easy;

And also prudent advice to young magical users and potion-makers; the whole better adapted to the world of New Salem than any other book of the like kind.

"*Here* you are."

Nicole's voice pulled me from my reading so quickly I nearly fell off the swing. She and Jeanie were crossing the grass toward me, wearing matching looks of concern on their face.

"We've been looking everywhere for you," Jeanie said, running a hand through her short hair. "Don't take off like that, Lexie."

"Are you all right?" Nicole said.

"I don't know," I said honestly. I was feeling less like I would pass out from panic, but there was still a nugget of disbelief in the back of my mind. Gavon, whoever he was, had been helpful, but I still couldn't reverse fifteen years of reality in half an hour.

"Oh, Lexie." Nicole sat down in the swing Gavon had just vacated. "I'm sorry Marie ruined your Magic's Eve."

"She's in big trouble," Jeanie said, before adding with a wince, "when she gets home."

"What's a Magic's Eve?" I asked.

"The night you grow into your magic. It'll happen at midnight."

"Fabulous," I said, slumping. "And what, exactly, will happen at that point?"

Jeanie shrugged like it was no big deal. "We'll cast a few spells. Then you'll go to sleep, because you've got school in the morning."

"Oh, great. When do I pick out my cat and my wand?"

Nicole snorted and a ghost of a smile appeared on Jeanie's face. "Magic's not like that. There are no wands, no enchanted animals...at least, not anymore. To be honest, it's really not all that exciting."

"You *can't* be serious," I said. "It's only changing everything I ever knew about the way the world works."

Nicole put a hand on my shoulder, but said nothing.

"Why didn't you tell me sooner?" I asked.

"Gram forbade it," Jeanie said.

"Gram?" I knew my maternal grandmother as the voice on the

other end of the annual phone calls on my birthday and Christmas. I'd never met the woman, as she lived up in Massachusetts...

Massachusetts. The Salem Witch Trials. The throbbing in my head returned as question piled onto question, and I didn't know which to ask first.

"She's our... Well, what she says, goes," Nicole said, a little helplessly.

"And why did *she* forbid you to tell me?" I asked, my annoyance growing.

"It doesn't matter why, you know now," Jeanie said.

I stared at her like she had two heads. "That's not an answer."

"Look, Lexie, today's been a bit of a shock," Nicole said. "It's a lot to process, so how about we just go home and have dinner?"

"Just like that, huh? You have magic, and let's go home and have some mac and cheese? Business as usual?"

"It is just business as usual," Jeanie said. "I think you'll find magic's just...another part of you. It makes life a little easier, but you can't use it to make yourself richer or anything like that."

"Did *you* just accept you had magic? That suddenly you're Harry Potter?"

Jeanie nodded, but Nicole looked sharply at the ground, and a blush crept up on her face. "It's different for me. I don't have magic like everyone else."

"I... What?" I'd just found out that magic existed, I hadn't gotten around to thinking about all the variables. "What do you mean?"

"Nicole is a potion-maker," Jeanie said. "And she *has* magic, just not the traditional kind."

"Jeanie—"

"Nicole, you do."

"What are you two talking about?" I asked, glancing between them.

"I can't do the," Nicole waved her hands in the air, "spells and sorcery stuff. Just make potions."

"What about Marie?" I asked Jeanie.

Jeanie snorted. "She's a healer."

"A healer? What does that even mean?"

"She can do the," again, Nicole waved her hands in the air, "but her magic can also heal other magical users."

"So, like, if I had a scrape or something, she could heal it?" I asked.

Jeanie nodded. "She *could*, yes."

Her emphasis did not go unnoticed. "But she wouldn't. Because she's a bitch."

"*Lexie*," Nicole warned.

Jeanie smiled. "She's not very good at it."

I glanced down at the book in my arms. "So what am I?"

"There aren't really specialties other than healers and potion-makers," Jeanie said. "Just the usual spells and enchantments. Traveling, summoning, conjuring. But we *can't* do magic in front of the non-magicals, so you're really only allowed to do it at home, all right?"

I wasn't even sure what "doing magic" encompassed, so I

nodded. But a new question had popped into my mind. I chose my words carefully, knowing I was about to step into a minefield. "Did Mom have magic?"

Jeanie nodded. "She was a great magical."

"So how could she have died giving birth to me?"

It was a mystery to me how, in this day and age, a woman in the United States could've died during childbirth, but apparently it happened more often than I thought. But throw magic into the mix, and it seemed even rarer. Not that I knew much about what magic could or couldn't do...

"Magic doesn't mean you don't get sick, that you don't...you don't die, Lexie," Nicole said gently. "Mom had complications and there wasn't anything we could do."

"Even though Marie's a—whatever, healer?" I asked quietly.

Jeanie nodded. "Marie was only a baby herself. She couldn't have done anything...not really. And Mora was... She was too far gone. There's only so much healing magic can do."

"What about Dad?"

Jeanie's face darkened. "Wasn't magical. Didn't know about magic until Mora died. Then he decided he couldn't handle three magical girls and left."

I knew that last part, sans the magical reasoning. I'd never as much as received a birthday card from him. But I'd also never asked for one. Our father had always been a tense subject best avoided at all costs.

We fell into an uneasy silence. I adjusted the book in my lap, which was when I realized neither Jeanie nor Nicole had mentioned it yet. In fact, they both seemed to be looking everywhere *except* the book. Was there some kind of...*something* on this book making it invisible to them?

Jeanie cleared her throat. "Let's go home. We'll have some dinner, I'm sure you have homework to do."

I groaned. I still had half my chemistry questions to finish. *Good luck, Lexie.*

"And tomorrow morning, you wake up and have magic," Nicole said with a too-bright smile. "See? Nothing to freak out about."

I nodded and followed Jeanie and Nicole to Jeanie's car, parked on the side of the street. Nicole promised me we would have a special dinner tomorrow for my birthday, wherever I wanted to eat, and Jeanie attempted to ask me about current events, which she totally got wrong. Still, I appreciated them trying their best to return my life to some semblance of normalcy. But something told me my definition of normal was about to change drastically.

Three

After a quiet dinner of reheated take-out food, I excused myself to spend some alone time in my room and at least try to come to terms with my new reality. The only normal thing I could think of was to attempt my homework, but after an hour of shattered focus, I threw in the towel and went to lie face-down on my bed.

My eyes were begging for sleep but my nerves kept me wide awake, wondering *what exactly would happen* at midnight. Nicole popped her head in a few times to check on me, but I answered monosyllabically enough that she left me alone.

At eleven, I changed into pajamas and shut off the light. My mind ran through thousands of scenarios that might occur in—I glanced at my alarm clock—fifty-seven minutes.

I stared at the dark shape of the book Gavon had given me then turned to the ceiling. I needed to sleep, of course, but I also couldn't seem to stop the pounding of my heart.

Fifty-six minutes until midnight.

I groaned and slid off my bed, padding quietly across the carpeted floor and pulling the magic book off the desk. The pages glowed enough to see them in the darkness, but I read without comprehending, wishing what I read was making more sense.

PREFACE

As to the first step of forming the young Magical Mind for practicing the art of the spell, being acquainted with the Magical Tongue of Latin. It is acknowledged to be due and principal Qualification in casting and understanding Magic, and therefore it is necessary to be well-acquainted.

"And I decided to take French," I muttered.

The preface seemed overly wordy and full of itself, talking about the necessity of magical persons to have a good Hand, to understand the rules of the clan or the guild (whatever that was) and the governance structure, to know the basics of math and science and reading and drawing and economics and how the English king still reigned over the colonies. I quickly grew bored with the basic stuff—after all, I was already fifteen (almost), and I was pretty sure I had a good grip on the basics.

I flipped through the pages, marveling at how brittle they felt and yet they remained as intact as a newly published book, until I found the first chapter.

THE BASICS OF SPELLWORK

Spells are distinguished by their outcome and the object with which the magic has been applied.

A SUMMONING SPELL, then, will present object to the summoner without use of the physical movement.

A CHARMING SPELL will animate an object as if it were alive.

An ATTACK SPELL will cause

A jolt of electricity flitted through my body, wrenching my mind away from the words on the page. I stared at the wall, this new feeling of energy rolling through my veins. My skin was almost *humming* with power, like I'd had three energy drinks in the span of five minutes.

I glanced at my alarm clock.

12:01AM.

I opened my mouth to call for Jeanie or Nicole, but stopped when I looked down at my fingers.

They were *glowing purple.*

I stared at them for a few moments, wondering if I'd fallen asleep. But I *felt* the sparks that shot out of my fingers, I smelled the burning air around me. I could taste the magic on my tongue. It was as if my heart was no longer just pumping blood, but my very essence from the top of my head to the ends of my toes.

The most shocking of all was how much I loved this new feeling.

Smiling, I twisted my fingers and jumped when a lightning bolt of purple left my pinky and a loud *boom* echoed in my room. Then, my nightstand burst into purple flames.

"Shit!" I screamed, jumping to my feet and waving my arms to try and quell the flames. But that only served to make more lightning bolts fly from my hands, igniting my comforter.

"*Help! Jeanie! Nicole! Somebody!*"

The flames exploded, burning everything in sight and filling the room with smoke. I kept screaming, and was soon joined by the pulsing, ear-splitting fire alarm.

"What the hell is going on in here?"

Jeanie came flying into my room, her hair a mess and her eyes wide as she took in the scene of my destroyed bedroom. With a simple wave of her hand, the chaos disappeared, leaving nothing but the blaring fire alarm and my pounding heart.

"What the *hell*?" Jeanie said, glaring at me as if this were all my fault. "You've had magic for a minute and you've already tried to burn the house down?"

I recoiled as if she'd hit me. "I didn't... This wasn't..." My hands began to glow, and I practically felt the magic dripping out of my fingertips.

"Jeanie?" Nicole said, poking her head into my room. "Why do I smell smoke?" Her eyes landed on me and my purple hands and her face grew concerned. "Lexie, what's going on here?"

"*You guys tell me!*" I screamed and more magic exploded from my palms.

"You need to calm down!" Jeanie barked at me.

"I can't!"

"Everybody take a breath!" Nicole bellowed. "Lexie, especially."

I couldn't take it anymore and I began to cry. More sparks crackled around me as I heaved and sobbed, too afraid to move or even *breathe*. Each sob was accentuated by another spark of magic, which only made me cry harder.

Nicole slowly approached me, her hands up. "It's okay, Lexie, just calm down."

"I—*hic—can't!"* More magic, more explosions. And now my books had begun to levitate.

"This is ridiculous," Jeanie said.

Then, as quickly as it had arrived, the magical humming was gone. I released a breath and sank to my bed, lightheaded and dizzy.

"You can have your magic back when you're calm," Jeanie said, not sounding at *all* sympathetic.

I was afraid to move, but at least the fires were gone and I wasn't a human sparkler. Nicole sat on the bed next to me and rubbed my back. "It's okay. I know that must've been scary for you. We lost track of the time, otherwise we would've been up here sooner."

"Where—*hic*—were you?"

"Doesn't matter. What matters is that it's your birthday," Jeanie said. "And now you've got magic. But you'll need to learn to control it."

"Oh, like it's that simple?" I barked. "In case you forgot, I *just found out that magic exists.*"

My fingertips began to glow again and a flash of shock crossed Jeanie's face, so fast I might've imagined it.

"It *is* that simple, Alexis," she said. "A calm magical is a useful magical. Just take a deep breath. You can't hurt yourself or anyone else anymore."

She was right. Aside from the vague glowing that had since disappeared, there were no more explosions or fires. Whatever she'd done to me, it was working. But that didn't mean that whenever she stopped, I wouldn't return to a human flamethrower.

"This is such a big mistake. I don't want magic!" I cried, but I knew it was a lie the moment it came out of my mouth. I wanted my magic more than anything else in the universe—a strange desire considering I'd just found out about it.

"You need rest, Lexie," Jeanie said. "A good night's sleep will clear your mind, and you've got school in the morning—"

"You can't seriously think that I can go to school like this!"

"I do, because you're a smart girl," Jeanie said. "And you're calm and rational. Remember?"

I used to be calm and rational. I also used to not shoot purple flames out of my hands. Things had obviously changed.

"You're still you, Lexie," Nicole tried. "Just you with magic."

"I'm finding it a little strange that you two are being so...so...*chill* about this!" I said, after a moment. "I mean, this is...I...I..." My head hung and I pressed my hands into my eyeballs. "I don't even know what to think."

"We're so *chill*," Nicole smirked at my word usage, "because we're trying to keep *you* calm so you don't have a stroke."

A stroke was low on my list of worries, but at least things had stopped exploding for the moment. In fact, I didn't even feel the strange hum against my skin.

I released my head and looked up at Jeanie. "How are you...I mean...what is..."

"A grounding spell," she said. "Because I'm your guardian, I can take away your magic. At least until you're of age."

"I thought I was of age?"

"You've gotten your magic, but you won't formally..." She ran a hand through her hair. "Eighteen. Gram's rules are eighteen."

"G-Gram?" More questions.

"Jeanie, can you...?" Nicole said, holding out her hand.

Jeanie flicked her wrist and a puff of yellow smoke appeared in the center of Nicole's hand, and with it, a small cup from downstairs. "Here, I made this after you... Well, just in case."

I peered inside the glass at the goopy, silvery mixture. "What. The hell. Is that?"

"It's a calming draught," Nicole said, pressing the cup into my hand. "It will help you fall asleep."

I jiggled the glass; the goop had the consistency of halfway-set Jell-O.

"Drink it, don't play with it," Nicole said. "That was very difficult to make."

"What...does it taste like?" I asked, dipping my pinky into the concoction and watching it shimmy under my touch.

"It tastes like you'd better drink it before I force it down your throat."

Childhood memories of Nicole forcing me to drink cold medicine resurfaced, and I opened my mouth and downed the drink. It tasted of lemon, chamomile, and honey and almost as soon as I'd had the last drop, a feeling of calm and happiness settled over me.

"There it is," Nicole said, taking the cup from me. "Now get some rest."

I lay back and suddenly forgot why I was so upset over magic. Magic was wonderful, it was beautiful, and it was...

The house I stood in was familiar—even though I'd never seen it before, I could recall when I'd purchased each trinket and painting. I busied myself by tidying up the children's toys on the floor, knowing that it was a futile effort with such young girls. But it kept my mind off of the clock, and the worry that he would never show up.

Lightning cracked outside, and it put me on edge. October storms were rare, but it had been unseasonably hot.

Hot? It was always hot in Florida.

I went to the girls' room to check on them, peering in through a small slit in the doorway to make sure their little bodies were still in bed. They'd been able to sense my worry, to know that something wasn't right. But a little bit of magic, and they'd fallen right to sleep. It was a shame I couldn't perform magic on myself to calm down.

I don't have kids?

The clock struck midnight, and my gut told me something was very wrong.

My alarm went off three or four times before I finally had the energy to roll over and shut it off. Even then, my body felt like sludge, achy and unrested. I wanted to sleep for another three hours. I pushed myself upright, staring at the sun streaming into my room, and rubbed my eyes.

Memory flooded back, and I ripped my hands away from my eyes. But my fingertips weren't glowing. Had I dreamed everything last night? I must have, because there was no way that so much could go so wrong in such a short amount of time. Magic and blowing up my bedroom had been just a very bad dream.

"Rise and shine, birthday girl," Nicole said, opening the door.

Bleary-eyed, I blinked at her a few times. "Wha?"

"Oh, crap," she said, crossing the room to my bed. "Did I put too much valerian root in that potion last night?"

"P-potion? *Crap*." I groaned and fell back into my pillow, throwing an arm over my eyes. So much for the it-was-all-a-dream theory.

"Sorry about that, Lexie, I haven't made a potion in...well..." She cleared her throat. "It should wear off in a few hours. I really should've double-checked the measurements but...it seemed right."

I cracked an eye open. "So you drugged me last night?"

"Potioned."

"Same difference." I glanced at my hand, expecting it to start glowing any second. "Why am I not...you know...magicking?"

"Because your magic has settled, I'd guess," Nicole said with a shrug. "And you're calm. A calm magical is a useful magical."

"You've said that a few times already," I said, rubbing my face. "What about a sleepy magical?"

"Hey, loser." Marie's dulcet tones just served to make my mood even darker. "Heard you royally screwed up getting your magic last night."

"Shut up, Marie," Nicole and I said in unison.

I offered Nicole a half-hearted smile, which quickly dissolved into a yawn. "You got any wake-up potions?"

Nicole snorted. "By the time I leaf through my old potion book, you'll already be awake. But I can offer you coffee instead?"

Book—my book. The magical spell book that Gavon had given me. I sat up and my gaze landed on the book sitting on my desk. The letters were still glowing, the tug from my solar plexus was still there. But *no one had said a thing about it.*

Oh well, maybe middle-aged men handing old books to young magicals was expected. Stranger things had happened recently.

I moved slowly and lethargically as I got ready for school. I already didn't put much effort into my appearance—jeans, a t-shirt, and flip-flops were about as fancy as I got, but dressing was even harder than usual. My backpack felt, if possible, heavier, as I pulled it over my shoulders and trudged downstairs.

Jeanie was already in the kitchen, and she offered me a cup of coffee saturated with milk and sugar. "Nicole said the potion hasn't worn off yet."

"I can't believe you condoned *drugging* me," I said, sucking down the sweet mixture.

"Well, I can't believe you set fire to your bedroom, so there's that," Jeanie said with a wry smile. "Now hurry up or you'll be late for school."

I grimaced. I hadn't even considered what life would be like at school. I already felt like an other, and now? Magical? That was the last thing I needed.

"What's that face about?" Nicole asked.

"Just...nervous about school. I mean, based on last night, do you think it's...safe for me to go?" It wasn't that I wanted to skip, but it would've been nice to crawl back under my covers and sleep for a few more hours.

Jeanie turned around and cocked her head, like she was reading me in some way. "Seem fine to me."

"But what if I...I don't know...set fire to the school? Or blow up my desk? What if the government comes for me?"

Nicole and Jeanie shared a perplexed look. "Government?"

"Yeah, like in the movies. I'm a freak, so—"

"You aren't a *freak*," Nicole said with an exasperated sigh. "You just happen to have magic. It's really not that big of a deal, Lexie."

I couldn't believe how unconcerned they were, especially after what had happened to me the night before.

"Wipe that look off your face," Jeanie said. "You aren't skipping school today."

My worry turned into annoyance. "I don't want to skip school because...because I *want* to! I really feel like I'm a danger to people!"

"The only person who's in danger here is you, if you don't get your butt in the car. We're gonna be late," Jeannie said.

"You're taking me to school?" That, at least, was good news. Though I wouldn't say no to being in an enclosed space with Marie, now that I knew I could zap her if she was a bitch to me.

"Yeah, remember? It's your birthday? You asked me to?" Jeanie sucked down more of her coffee, then put the empty mug in the sink. "Now, get your bags, or else I'll make you to go school with Marie."

Four

"Oh, don't look so worried, Lexie. You're going to be fine," Jeanie said as she pulled up behind a queue of cars dropping off students.

"You really can't be okay with me putting all of my classmates in danger?" I asked, for probably the fifth time since we'd left the house. "I set my bedroom on *fire*, Jeanie."

"Last night, you were taken off guard. Now, you're all right. Look," she reached across the car and took my hand, "no magic here."

I retracted my hand and stared at my fingertips. "Yeah, but what if—"

"Lexie, you're one of the most brilliant kids I know," Jeanie said, and I was too shocked at the rare praise to respond. "Magic is simply another part of you, and it always has been. Just like you can use that brain of yours to remember all those useless facts and quotes, you can use your mind to control your magic. If you want to control it, you will."

"Thanks," I said, although I didn't quite understand what she was saying. If I had no idea what I was supposed to control, or how to control it, I wasn't sure how effective my will was going to be.

Jeanie pulled up in front of the school and turned to me. "Before you go, I have two ground rules with your magic. The first is you are *not* allowed to use your magic on anyone. Not your sister, not students, *anyone.*"

I nodded.

"Second, which should go without saying, is that you aren't allowed to do magic at school. And until you get a handle on it, you are not allowed to use it unsupervised."

Again, I nodded, although I wanted to argue that I hadn't actually willfully done any magic since I'd received it.

"Are you picking me up later?"

"Unfortunately, you'll have to ride with Marie this afternoon. I've got a few meetings I can't get out of. But later tonight, we'll go out to dinner for your birthday, all right?"

"Okay," I said, cracking open the door. My stomach was a mess of nerves, but I took some solace in Jeanie's lack of concern. If she thought I wasn't a disaster waiting to happen, then maybe I wasn't.

Still, I stood on the curb for a moment, clutching the straps of my bag and gathering strength of mind and will. Behind me, another car pulled up, and two freshmen popped out, ignoring the driver and each other in favor of their phones. They didn't even acknowledge me as they brushed past my shoulder.

I waited for something to happen—what, I didn't know, but something.

The girls finally noticed me staring at them and gave me a look. "What?"

"N-nothing," I squeaked, taking a step back and waiting for their faces to melt off.

The girls looked at each other, giggled, and walked away. Another car pulled up behind me. Standing outside, staring at the school probably wasn't the best idea, so I adjusted my backpack again and marched inside.

The halls were already filled with students, all of whom paid me no attention. But then again, why would they? Outwardly, I was just another kid. Maybe today wouldn't be so bad. Maybe I wouldn't royally screw things up. Maybe Jeanie was right and if I wanted to control my magic, I could.

A sliver of calm made its way into the raging storm in my head, and I relaxed the tension in my shoulders as I repeated my new mantra. If I wanted to control my magic, I could.

I approached my locker and all serenity went out the window as Callista and Joel stood in the way, making ga-ga eyes at each other. I stepped forward, hoping they'd see me and they needed to move.

Nope. They continued staring longingly into each other's eyes, and I rolled mine. *Get a damned room.*

"Excuse me," I said.

Callista giggled loudly and made some comment on Joel's

sports-ball performance.

"*Excuse* me," I said, a little louder.

Joel said something about Callista's car being a mess.

"*Excuse m—*" My words died on my tongue as a purple glow caught my attention. I stuffed my hands into my pockets before anyone saw them.

"Oh, sorry, Lexie," Callista said, finally noticing me standing there. She and Joel scooted a few inches to the left to grant me access to my locker.

"Uh, never mind!" I said, spinning on my heel and rushing to the bathroom.

There were already girls lined up against the sink, smearing on lip gloss and checking their eye makeup, so I dashed into one of the stalls. Carefully, I pulled out my hands, which resembled Fourth of July sparklers.

"If I want to control my magic, I can," I whispered to myself, willing my sizable reasoning abilities to overpower the panic.

I closed my eyes and whispered the words over and over again, not caring if anyone heard me. After my heartbeat returned to normal, I chanced an eye open.

My fingers had stopped sparkling.

Brrrring!

And I was late for class.

The benefit of having a schedule full of AP and dual enrollment classes was that I barely even remembered I *had* magic in the first place because I was too busy trying to absorb the waterfall of information. My rotating schedule had Chemistry as the first period of the day, where I struggled to understand the solubility of fluoride salts of alkaline earth metals. Second period was math; there, at least, I understood the concept behind the binomial expansion and Pascal's triangle. In third period English, I was just glad to I escape notice because I definitely didn't remember anything I'd read in *To Kill a Mockingbird.* And I spent three-quarters of my graphic design class staring at a blank white screen in Photoshop.

By the time lunch rolled around, my brain felt about as gelatinous as Nicole's silver potion. As usual, I headed outside to eat lunch. There were already other students outside as well, but they didn't pay me much attention. I picked the farthest picnic table away from the rest of them and sat down to eat.

I looked at my hands, thankful that other than a little sparking this morning, they had remained un-ignited. I groaned and took a huge bite of my sandwich, chewing thoughtfully. A gust of wind blew the clouds away from the sun, and I was bathed in warm, bright sunlight. After spending all day inside, I was squinting, and wished I'd had my sunglasses—

Before the thought even left my head, my sunglasses appeared next to my hand in a puff of purple smoke.

I almost choked on my sandwich, glancing both ways to make sure no one had seen it. Fingers trembling, I touched the sunglasses to confirm they were, in fact, real before slipping them onto my face.

"Huh," I said.

I sat back and took another thoughtful bite of my sandwich.

Accepting that magic was real opened the door to a different thought process.

I had *magic.*

Which meant...well, I supposed I could summon sunglasses. I could do probably anything I wanted to. I had no idea what the limits of my newfound powers were—or anything about them, really. But if I could summon sunglasses, I began to wonder what else I could conjure with the snap of my fingers.

My turkey sandwich on white bread was suddenly unappetizing. Glancing around to make sure no one was watching me, I considered what I *really* wanted to eat for my birthday lunch. I envisioned a thick, juicy steak and a baked potato with sour cream and butter and flicked my wrists like I'd seen Jeanie do.

But nothing appeared.

"Well, damn," I said, sitting back.

Okay, so apparently there were limits to what I could do, and conjuring a steak was one of them. Huffing to myself, I reached for the sandwich again. Two bites in, I remembered my magical spell book. If I could summon my sunglasses, maybe I could summon the book, too.

"Uh...bring the book!" I said, flinging my wrists out.

This time, it appeared in that same cloud of purple magic.

I heard laughing, and my heart stopped in my chest. Had anyone just seen what I'd done?

After a few moments, I spotted the source of the laughter. A group of juniors was hanging around one of the tables. They noticed me staring at them and I quickly looked away. I didn't think they'd seen anything, but I wasn't eager to attract their attention.

But now I had the book, and at least a few minutes to read it. I quickly flipped to the first chapter to pick up on where I'd left off the night before.

THE BASICS OF SPELLWORK

Spells are distinguished by their outcome and the object with which the magic has been applied.

A SUMMONING SPELL, then, will present object to the summoner without use of the physical movement;

A CHARMING SPELL will animate an object as if it were alive;

An ATTACK SPELL will cause physical harm to another magical user;

Et cetera.

A Magical's best tool for spell work is a well-crafted mind. Magic is but an extension of the Human Will, and it is as powerful as the mind it inhibits.

While there are certain birth-given limits to the Mind of a Magical, a good Master will improve upon these limits as a sword on whetstone. Daily reading of Latin and classical works, Magical History and Theory, as well as

daily practice in arithmetic will sharpen the Mind for more effective spellmaking.

I chuckled to myself; perhaps this book had never taken an AP class because my brain was mush after a full day of "mind-sharpening."

The first chapter seemed as dull as the preface—more talk about the importance of a basic education. Then again, based on the age of the book, it was probably written in such a time when primary education *wasn't* a given.

A few things struck me as I continued reading the book. First, as Jeanie and Nicole had alluded to, magic was controlled by willpower and mind more than anything else. Which, I supposed, made sense. Second, the book mentioned several times that innate ability was the groundwork, but with practice and discipline, a magical without much power could stand toe-to-toe with someone who had a lot of power but didn't practice.

The one thing I wasn't getting was the concept of a Master. The book referenced it often as a teacher of sorts, but I also got the impression a Master was a parent or a guardian, especially as the book discussed the best foods a Master should feed their apprentice for breakfast, lunch, and dinner.

Just as I finished the first chapter, the bell rang, signaling the end of the lunch period. My own meal was left forgotten, and the book in my hand was too big to hide in my backpack.

"Okay, go home," I said to it. It didn't move from my hands. "Go *home*," I repeated, more forcefully. A particular tingling feeling emanated from the tips of my toes to the top of my head. I closed my eyes and let the new feeling wash over me.

The warmth of the sun was gone, and I cracked open an eye. Everything was dark—I was also still wearing my sunglasses. I pulled them off, hoping when I did, I'd be at school and not...

Nope, I'd somehow magicked not only my spell book but also myself all the way back home to my bedroom.

"Crap!" I said, throwing the book onto my bed and trying not to panic. I could handle this. I could get myself back to school.

"Okay...*go back to school!*" I said loudly.

I waited for the tingling feeling, but felt nothing. My hands weren't even glowing.

"Go back to school!"

Nothing. My heart began to thud against my ribcage. I was skipping school, and I might've had a test in French this period. A test, of course, I'd barely studied for, so was going to fail anyway.

"Not helping!"

I willed myself to go again. And again, nothing happened.

Over and over again, I tried to take myself back to school, but I remained in my bedroom. As the minutes passed, the panic escalated until I was nearly hyperventilating and was now wondering if I'd magicked away my magic.

Was that even possible? I buried my head in my hands. Not only was I skipping school and missing a quiz, but I'd somehow ruined my own gift not even twenty-four hours after receiving it.

I took a deep breath, in the feeble attempt to get a grip. I couldn't have lost my magic. That made no sense.

And yet, I can't even make my fingers glow.

I shook away that thought. Okay. If this had happened before I'd had magic, how would I have resolved the problem? My inner voice taunted me—*I never would've been in this predicament before because I didn't believe magic existed.*

I'd have to call somebody. But who?

Jeanie would probably yell at me.

Marie would laugh, tell all her friends, and hang up.

Nicole! Nicole would understand.

I rushed to the phone and dialed the familiar number, praying she would pick up.

"Hello?" Nicole said.

"Hey," I whispered. "It's me."

"Lexie, what are you... Why are you calling me from home? Is everything all right?"

"No, I'm...I'm home," I said, feeling the tears well in my eyes. "And I don't know how I got here!"

Nicole was silent on the other end of the line, and I started to feel stupid.

"What do you mean, you don't know how you got there?" Nicole asked.

"I was sitting at lunch," I said, my voice gradually growing higher. "And the bell rang, and I...just...appeared at home. And I think I lost my magic."

"Lexie, really," Nicole said, sounding annoyed.

"Can you come drive me to school?" I said. "I don't know how I can—"

"Are you kidding me? You want me to drive forty-five minutes to get you so I can drive you three miles to school? Are your legs broken, too?"

"What?"

"I know you've got magic now, but just because you can't figure out how to transport yourself back to school doesn't mean I have to drop everything and come get you. Why don't you just walk?"

"W-walk?" I said, the concept foreign to me.

"Yes, like you did before you got magic," Nicole snapped before hanging up the phone.

Walking—that made sense. Why didn't I think of that? Stupidly, I shouldered my backpack and rushed to school, hoping I could make it before the test was over.

Five

By the time I made it back to school, I'd missed most of French, and Ms. Benoit wouldn't let me take the test in the last few minutes. I slunk to the back of the room, sweaty, red-faced, and angry. Not only was my magic on the fritz, I was failing French.

Not even Mills and learning about the Rhode Island colony could pull me from my distracted focus. I spent most of the class staring at my fingers and imagining I saw purple sparks. When Mills called on me to answer a question, I stuttered stupidly for an eternity before he chided me for not paying attention and moved on to someone else.

When my day from hell finally ended, I trudged out to Marie's car, praying she hadn't left me. As I waited by her gleaming red car, I wondered if she'd used magic to make it. When I turned sixteen, would I be able to snap my fingers and get a Porsche?

I stared at my fingers and groaned. I couldn't even summon a book; a car was a far-off fantasy.

Marie was alone when she deigned to grace me with her presence, and for that, I was grateful. She and I clambered inside and said nothing to each other for over half the ride home. But my face must've betrayed my mood, because Marie turned down the music and snapped, "What's *your* problem?"

"Nothing."

"Are you pissed off because nobody sang you happy birthday?"

I made a noncommittal noise and looked at my fingers. "So, magic."

"What about it?"

"You have it?"

I felt her side-eye from across the car. "What's your point?"

"I mean, do you have it like me, or do you have it like Nicole? She said you're a healer."

A pause. "Nicole's the only one who can't summon and conjure."

"Oh."

More silence between us. I ran my fingers along the leather on the car door and imagined how Marie might've created it. "So did you click your fingers and this car appeared or what?"

"Oh my God, Lexie, you're such an idiot," Marie said with a giggle. "You can't just *make stuff appear*. Don't you know anything?"

I bristled. "Considering no one had the courtesy to tell me about magic before two days ago..."

"I know, and it was *so much fun* to do magic around you,"

Marie said, twirling a lock of her hair. "You were such a moron."

I didn't take the bait.

"I can feel you practicing magic, you know. Wonder if Jeanie would want to know about it..."

"Come on, Marie, you know I can't control it."

"And why not? It's *so easy*."

"Oh yeah?" I said, lacking a better comeback.

Marie knew she'd won this round, and smiled smugly. "I thought you could do everything."

"I never said I could."

"Sure act like it."

"Well, I can't do this, obviously."

"Obviously."

We spent the rest of the drive in silence. I shouldn't have expected Marie would help me, but it pissed me off that she'd been so...herself. For once, couldn't my sister be a bit more selfless?

She parked in front of our house, and I couldn't get out of the car soon enough.

"Hey," Marie said, rolling down the window. "Tell Jeanie I won't be home for dinner."

"Okay."

She glared at me. "Don't you care?"

"Why would I?"

"Because...it's your *birthday*? Don't you want us to go out and have a big family dinner?"

I shrugged and marched into the house. After dropping my bag next to the staircase, I went straight to my room to lie down on, thankful for the quiet and the dark. I had homework, I had things to read and prepare for tomorrow, but I was drained. I wasn't sure how long I lay there, feeling sorry for myself. Eventually, a car door slammed below and the stairs creaked as someone walked up them.

Jeanie opened my door, looking not-too-happy. "Nicole told me you decided to take a field trip today," she said, before I could open my mouth.

"I didn't mean to," I said. "I was...trying to send something home and *I* ended up going home and—"

"And why were you using magic at school in the first place?"

"Because...because I don't know. It just happened?"

"Magic doesn't just happen, Alexis. Magic happens because you will it to. And obviously, you're lacking in the willpower department."

"Jeanie, my magic's gone! I don't know what happened to it—"

"Your magic isn't *gone*," Jeanie said, pinching the bridge of her nose. "But it will be if you don't quit acting out. There were two ground rules. What were they?"

"Jeanie—"

"What were they?"

I groaned loudly. "Don't use magic on another person, and don't do magic at school."

"And what did you do?"

"I...I didn't mean to!"

"You aren't listening to me, Lexie," Jeanie said. "Why were you even using magic at school? *Especially* when you have so little control over it."

I didn't have a good response to that. It was true some of my magic happened uncontrollably—the glowing fingers—but I'd made a willful decision to summon my book to me. Hindsight being twenty-twenty and all...

"We're going out to eat for your birthday," Jeanie said, sounding more like she didn't want to. "Where do you want to go?"

"I'm not really hungry," I replied, picking at my comforter.

"Fine, if you're going to be like that, we won't go anywhere." She slammed the door behind her and I jumped a few inches from the sound. I hated being the object of Jeanie's disappointment, and I hated it even more so because I felt caught between knowing the right thing to do, and needing to break the rules to sate my own curiosity.

A few tears fell down my cheeks, which I wiped away. Sitting around and crying wasn't going to do any good. I had the rest of the afternoon and evening to figure out what was going on with my magic. I had a really old magic book, too, so I snatched it off my desk before marching down the stairs.

"Jeanie?" I called but there was no answer.

That was a bit of a relief. Jeanie seemed on edge and might jump down my throat if I asked for her help. And if I were truly being honest with myself, Jeanie's track record with teaching wasn't the best. It was only thanks to Nicole's patience that I ever learned how to ride a bike.

She was the one I needed. "Nicole?"

No answer again. I knew I'd heard her earlier, and both her

and Jeanie's cars were in the driveway. So where could they have—

"Oh yeah."

It was going to take me some time to default to remembering that everything inexplicable happened because of magic. I didn't want Jeanie to worry (or get any angrier at me than she already was), so I left her a note telling her I'd gone for a walk to clear my head.

The park was a little farther than I'd remembered, but it was actually a pretty nice night. Some part of me was hoping Gavon might show up again, either because the park was on his evening walk, or maybe because he took pity on me. How had he known I was magical? Was it just fate that he was walking around and came across me? Were there more magical people I didn't know about in this town?

The park was empty, so I plopped down inside the gazebo and put the book out in front of me. There was a voice in my head reminding me that Jeanie had expressly forbidden me to do magic unsupervised and in the open like this, but, then again, no one was around.

"Okay, Lexie," I said, gearing myself up. "Bring my sunglasses to me." I held out my hand. When they didn't appear, I frowned and said, "*Come to me, sunglasses—*"

To my delight, they appeared in a puff of dark purple smoke. But somehow, I knew it wasn't my magic that had summoned them. I looked up and saw Gavon behind me, a pleasant smile on his face.

"Seems a bit late for those, don't you think?" he asked,

glancing at the dark sky.

"Well, I was..." I sighed. "I think I broke my magic."

He made a sound between a cough and a laugh. "What?"

I flexed my hand in front of my face. "It's broken. I can't spark. I can't even... I think I wished it away or something."

He looked as if I'd said something ridiculous, but was trying not to make me feel bad about it. He cleared his throat and smiled. "I think you've still got plenty of magic. Otherwise, you wouldn't be sitting here."

"What do you mean?"

"If you lost all your magic, you'd die."

"*What?*" I said, heart pounding.

"Relax." Gavon smiled. "You're a far way from that, I promise you."

"*You can die?*"

"If you use too much of your magic, yes. But, like I said, you look perfectly healthy to me."

"But I can't...I can't *do* anything. At least, not like this morning. This morning, I was..." I waved my hands around. "Yeah."

"Sounds like you've had an eventful first day as a magical," Gavon said with a small chuckle.

"Eventful? Setting my room on fire then transporting myself back to my bedroom isn't what I'd call...*eventful.*" I slumped and pressed my cheek into my hand. "And now I can't even...I can't even bring a pair of sunglasses to myself."

"Well, I can assure you that your magic is perfectly fine. Maybe there's something else bothering you?" He blinked, then said, "I'm sorry, did you say you transported yourself to your bedroom today?"

I nodded. "I magicked this book to me—"

"Summoned."

"Summoned, yeah. At lunch. Then I tried to send it back home, and I ended up sending myself back with it." I frowned. "And when I called Nicole, she acted like...like I meant to do it! Like it was my fault and asking her to come get me was..." I blew air out between my lips. "And my aunt isn't helping either. She came home and *yelled* at me for using magic."

"Why'd she do that?"

I blushed. "Because...because she told me I wasn't allowed to use it at school, which I *didn't*—"

"But you summoned a book to you?" Gavon asked, although his query was much less accusatory and more amused.

"Yeah, but...I don't know." I picked at the table. "I just feel like this big gift got dumped into my lap and I'm trying to figure out what to do with it. And everyone's busy telling me I shouldn't use it, and I can't use it, and every time I *do* use it, something horrible happens. And..." I sighed and glanced up at him. "I'm sorry for venting."

"Sounds like you needed to." He tapped the table. "Might I offer a suggestion or two?"

I shrugged.

"First, I do want to assure you that your magic is perfectly fine. It's a little overzealous at the moment, perhaps due to fifteen years of disuse, but it's there." He pulled the primer closer to him. "Second, I think you'll find magic a little easier to wield once you understand the basic theories—"

"*How*?"

"Did you read the primer?" he asked.

My cheeks warmed. "I mean...I got through the first few pages..."

"Look here." He flipped through to the first chapter. "Read what this says."

I peered at the pages. "*A Magical's best tool for spell work is a well-crafted mind.*"

"Now, what do you think that means?"

"It means that...you have to control your mind to control your magic," I said. "But I don't know what that *means*. Keep in mind, I have zero frame of reference for this."

He nodded, scratching his chin in thought. "Magic is like...another sense. Like breathing or hearing. Just as you learned how to process the words you hear without thinking about it, you'll learn how to process magic."

"One problem: I've been hearing since I was a baby, I've just learned about magic. And..." I shook my head. "It's starting to piss me off that everyone assumes because I'm 'so smart' I'll just...figure it out. I don't have the room to figure it out because I have Jeanie breathing down my neck and..." I closed my mouth when I realized I'd started ranting again.

Gavon, however, seemed unfazed by it. "I think you are suffering from the common affliction of the brilliant mind."

"Oh yeah?"

"Overthinking. You're trying too hard."

I shook my head. "So I don't try at all, and I blow up my nightstand. Now I'm trying too hard and I can't even summon my sunglasses?"

He seemed to consider for a moment. "To wield magic, you must focus on what you want and have the mental strength to do it. If you're too emotional and unable to focus, you can't perform magic." He pointed out another passage in the primer.

"*Magic is but an extension of the Human Will, and it is as powerful as the mind it inhibits,*" I said, reading from the book. "So what do I do about it? How do I *not* overthink this?"

"Well, let's first start by taking a deep breath," Gavon said, placing his hand on top of mine. It was warm.

I took a short breath.

"Deep breath."

I inhaled deeply then let the breath out slowly. Some of the anxiety I'd been nursing in the pit of my stomach went with it.

"Good. Now." He placed a fallen leaf on the center of the picnic table. "Use your magic and pick it up."

I looked at the leaf and willed it to rise, scrunching up my face.

"Don't try so hard. Magic should be natural."

"Easy for you to say."

"Just relax."

I looked at him then looked at the leaf. I tried to relax, but kept thinking about all of the reasons why I couldn't make this leaf levitate.

"It's no use," I said finally.

"With that attitude."

I glared at him then set my chin on my arms, looking at the leaf. It continued to sit there, mocking me.

"Close your eyes and clear your mind."

I closed my eyes and, although it took me a few breaths, I was able to quiet the noise in my head. That's when I felt it—a hum of energy. It had always been there, but I'd been too distracted to see it.

"Now, tell your magic to levitate the leaf."

Feeling like an idiot, I released my hold on the energy. I felt the rough texture of the wooden picnic table, the delicate crunchiness of the leaf, the cool air as I lifted the leaf into the air.

"Alexis."

I ignored him, focusing intently on the image in my head.

"Alexis..."

"What?" I didn't open my eyes.

"You—"

"I'm trying to concentrate!" I snapped, finally looking. To my shock, the leaf was steadily floating in the air, just as I'd imagined.

"Wow," I said, reaching out to touch it.

"See, you have plenty of magic," Gavon said. "You just need to find the balance. Don't overthink it."

"What else can I do?" I asked, as the leaf twirled in the air.

"Why don't you read chapter two?" Gavon said. "You should probably start with the basics or else—"

The leaf spun faster and faster until finally bursting into flames.

I nearly fell off the picnic bench.

"Okay," I said, watching the smoking ash drift to the table. "I'll read chapter two."

Six

Bolstered a little by Gavon's confidence in me, I was able to stomach returning to the house. He'd pointed out a few chapters I should work on—summoning and such—but I was just glad that *someone* was listening to me. Now that I wasn't on the verge of freaking out, I might be able to communicate with Jeanie better. I just needed to catch her in a good mood so I could explain my feelings to her.

The lights were on in the house and I hurried up the steps. The time on my phone said nearly eight and I'd left a note, but I couldn't help feeling like I was walking into a trap.

"Hello?" I called.

"In here, Alexis."

Crap. *Alexis* wasn't a good sign. I left my primer on the staircase and walked into the living room, where Jeanie was sitting with Nicole and a gray-haired woman who was facing away from me.

Jeanie cleared her throat. "Lexie, come in here and say hello to Gram."

"Gram?" I blinked, not moving into the room.

I'd never met my maternal grandmother. She'd call on birthdays and other important holidays, and it was always the same. How were grades (top of my class), was I playing any sports (no), was I otherwise doing well (yes).

"Well, girl, put your tongue back in your mouth and come in here," she barked, and my legs moved of their own accord—out of fear or magic, I wasn't sure.

I stood in the center of the living room and pressed my hands into my sides, so I wouldn't offend her any more than I already had.

Gram studied me like I was hopelessly underwhelming her. She was maybe mid-fifties, but she carried herself like a woman who was used to having others do as she said. Her sweater didn't have a yarn out of place, her black shoes even intimidating as they shone back at me.

"Hullo, Gram," I said after a moment of silence.

"Sit."

I sank into a nearby chair.

"Jean tells me you've been having some trouble with your magic," she said, placing her wrinkled hands on her knees. "Seems to be pouring out of you, isn't it?"

I glanced down at my hands, grateful they weren't purple. "What do you mean?"

"Jean, I'd say that you should have Nicole whip up a calming potion for the girl. She's obviously distraught from learning about her magic."

"I already did, Gram," Nicole replied softly.

"And?"

"It worked last night, but—"

"I don't think calming draughts are what she needs," Jeanie said, perched on the edge of her seat. It was the first time I'd ever seen my aunt look so eager. I compared the two women, and could see where Jeanie got her short temper.

"And what do you think she needs, Jean?"

"I think she needs to come up to the compound for a few days. Be around her own kind and learn—"

"No," Gram replied, a lot harsher than I'd have expected. "That won't be necessary."

Jeanie made a noise then seemed to consider her words carefully. "Mom, it would be *very helpful* if you'd let Lexie have some one-on-one time with someone up there."

"Up where?" I asked, glancing at Nicole.

"The Carrigan Clan has a compound in the northeast," Gram replied, her hawklike eyes focused on me. "It's where the rest of your family lives."

"There's more of us?" I asked, now looking at Jeanie. Growing up, all I'd known was her, my sisters, and the telephonic voice of Gram. But if there was a bigger family out there...

"I will consider your request to come up for Thanksgiving, but you will take care of the girl's magical surplus in the meantime. She seems relatively fine to me."

I found it rather off-putting that this woman was making assumptions about me when she'd known me for all of a minute. Nicole must've read the look on my face because she silenced me with a shake of her head. That turned my annoyance to curiosity. Why was everyone bowing to Gram like she was some sort of god?

Her Royal Stuck-up-her-buttness stood and smoothed the lines of her black skirt. "Happy birthday, dear." She waved her hand, and a crisp fifty dollar bill appeared in my hand. Then she was gone in a puff of dark gray smoke.

Jeanie let out a loud breath and offered me a smile. "Sorry about all that. I would've told you Gram was coming, but I didn't know where you were."

"Just out for a walk," I said, pocketing the cash. "So who wants to explain what the hell *that* was? How come she's so...demanding?"

"Gram's the matriarch of all the Carrigans—including the extended family. She's used to barking an order and getting her way."

"Magically?"

I'd said it in jest, but Jeanie nodded. "Any group of magicals is powerful. They harness the power of their members to enforce their rules. So because Gram is our Clanmaster, we're all bound by what she says."

"Sounds like the old bag needs to retire already."

"*Alexis!*" Jeanie bellowed.

I jumped at her ferocity and expected Gram to return at any

moment to flay me or something. Then I remembered that I was talking about her mother. "Sorry, Jeanie."

"Mom's...special in her own way. She does love us, but she's never really been the touchy-feely kind."

That probably explained why Jeanie wasn't that way either. "So why did she come all the way down here? Just to give me fifty bucks? She could've mailed it."

"I asked her to come down and check on you."

My eyebrows shot upward. "You did? Why?"

"Because I was worried about you!"

"Uh, so why did you let me go to school then?"

"You seemed fine this morning. I thought you'd just gotten a little overexcited," Jeanie said. "But then Nicole tells me you're transporting yourself and..." She shook her head. "Look, Lexie, I'm a bit out of my depth here. When I got my magic, it wasn't nearly as explosive as yours."

"And neither was Marie's," Nicole added. "But it looks like everything's settled down anyway, right? You haven't had any more episodes."

I furrowed my brow, but said nothing to contradict her. I wasn't eager to bring up my lunchtime mishap, which might've been parlayed into another lecture about doing magic at school. And as many questions as I still had about magic, I wanted my answers to come from someone a bit more patient. All Jeanie seemed to do was lecture about what I wasn't supposed to do, and Gavon at least let me finish my sentences before responding.

Besides, it seemed like Jeanie and *Gram* had still been keeping some secrets from me, so I felt justified in keeping a few from them.

"So exactly how big is our family? And what is this compound thing?"

"Our clan's pretty big," Jeanie said. "It's one of the largest in the US. Most of our closer family lives in Salem."

"So...do I have other aunts and uncles?"

Jeanie shook her head. "But you have some great aunts and uncles, close cousins."

"Why did we move down here if everyone else is in Massachusetts?"

Jeanie shrugged. "Too cold up there. I like the Florida winters."

"But—"

"And besides, I can get to Gram's house in the blink of an eye," Jeanie said, but she didn't quite meet my gaze. "I'm starving. How about we try at that birthday dinner again?"

I didn't buy for one second that Jeanie had voluntarily uprooted us from a mystical compound of magical family members to some Podunk town in Florida, but it was clear that any discussion was over. Jeanie either ignored or deflected all my questions during dinner, and when I asked her if she'd show me how to use magic, she straight-up told me she wasn't the best person for the job and she'd keep pressing Gram to find someone to tutor me.

Later, when I asked Nicole the same questions, I got about the same response, except at least Nicole had a good excuse.

"Lexie, I would if I could but, I really...can't." She glanced out the door. "Jeanie, or even Marie would be better—"

"Marie?" I said, blankly. "Little Miss Let's-Give-Lexie-A-Heart-Attack? Like she'd teach me anything. Why can't you help?"

"Because like I said, I don't have the same kind of magic as you do," Nicole said. "I'm physically incapable of summoning, charming, whathaveyou. So as much as I'd like to help you...I truly, honestly *can't.*" She blew air out between her lips. "Jeanie's working on Gram. I'm sure she'll change her mind soon."

That night, I lay in bed and let all my questions circle my head. My life was like a giant, magical puzzle, and Jeanie and Gram were keeping a few key pieces to themselves. Which, of course, led to more questions about *why* they felt it more prudent to keep me in the dark.

Even more frustrating was that I felt unsettled. Everything I knew to be right was on its head, and no one, save Gavon, was empathetic to it. Jeanie had always been short, but for her not to help *at all* was hurtful. Nicole seemed to *want* to help, but since she didn't have magic or whatever-it-was, she was handcuffed. And forget Marie.

The only person giving real, honest answers was Gavon, but I was limited to hoping he'd show up to deal with my neurotic whining. And the questions currently taking up the most real estate in my brain—those about Gram and the clan—he probably wouldn't be able to answer.

The glow of my magical spell book caught my eye and I

wondered if, perhaps, I'd find something of value inside. It wouldn't tell me why Gram had been lying to me, but it might help in some way.

I flipped through the book until I saw a section that looked promising.

A DISCUSSION ON CLANS AND GUILDS

A CLAN is a group of Magicals bound by blood. It is inherently less powerful than a Guild, as a Clanmaster generally may not choose who will and won't be inducted.

A GUILD is a group of Magicals assembled through INTRODUCTION and then INDUCTION.

INTRODUCTION to a Guild may happen when a Magical has learned to toddle, or a Guildmaster may set an older age. If the Magical has shown a preponderance for a magical specialty, he may be tested in a formal INDUCTION ceremony. Once a Young Magical's Master has determined the Magical is of age to be a useful member of the community, they will be formally introduced based on the laws set down by the Guildmaster.

The collective power of the CLAN or GUILD is sourced by the powers inherent in its membership to enforce its governance. A member of the Guild or Clan will be Magically compelled to adhere to these rules.

Well, I thought, *that explains the butt-kissing.* A magical compulsion, I read a little further, meant the person was physically restricted from doing whatever was against the rules. So even if Jeanie and Nicole had wanted to tell me the truth, they couldn't.

That still didn't mean I wasn't irked that Gram had made such a stupid rule.

I found a blank page in one of my discarded notebooks and began to jot down all the inaccuracies and questions I had. I was under no illusion that anyone would actually answer any of them, but perhaps if I knew what I didn't know, I could construct a line of discussion.

Why did my magic go haywire?

Why did it take me fifteen years to meet Gram?

Why am I not allowed at the compound yet?

And the biggest question of all: *If I didn't have magic for the first fifteen years of my life, why not tell me sooner?*

I stared at the paper for a while before I realized how late it was. If I wanted to be halfway awake for school tomorrow, I needed to go to sleep. So I folded up the paper and used it as a bookmark in the primer before crawling into bed.

If I'd thought I'd have more clarity on my magical life puzzle the next morning, I was sorely mistaken. I'd tossed and turned most of the night, dreaming about a rocky beach in Massachusetts and Gram pointing at me and telling me I was evil and would bring ruination to our entire clan. The dream had been so vivid that I'd actually asked Nicole if Gram hated me, which she'd assured me wasn't the case.

Making matter worse, Marie kept talking with Charity about how weird I was the whole way to school. There was an uneasy feeling in my gut. My mind kept replaying the dream and splicing it with meeting Gram and the questions I had about myself.

"Miss Carrigan," Mills said, snapping me from my reverie.

I bolted upright and tried to look interested. "Yes?"

"What are the benefits of the Acts of Trade and Navigation?"

I swallowed, glancing at the chalk on the board and wishing that he wasn't standing in front of the answer. Then I looked down at my paper.

I had transcribed the entire chalkboard.

And magically highlighted the answer.

Score one for magic.

"Er..." I swallowed and hoped my magic was right. "The colonies could only trade with the English, and all goods and services had to go to England, versus any other trade."

"Good, and how was that a positive?"

I glanced down again, "It was a positive because...it meant more shipbuilding for New England. Chesapeake tobacco had a monopoly in England?"

"Very good." He beamed at me, and I tried to feel guilty for using magic, but I didn't care. Sure, I wasn't supposed to at school, but...being able to magically transcribe everything? That was a game changer.

Mills had moved on to pepper another student with questions about mercantilism, and I flipped through my notebook happily. No more hand cramps, no more racing with myself to write down everything that was on the board before class started. There wasn't any puffing or poofing. There was no way that I could screw—

My thoughts ended abruptly when I realized that the chalkboard was completely blank.

I'd *erased* it.

"Crap," I whispered.

My first thought was to remain calm, or else I would start shooting magical laser beams out of my fingers.

My second thought was to observe the room and make sure all the students were stuck in their usual early morning stupor. It was a good thing we had history in first period, or else I might really be in trouble. And Mills' back was to the chalkboard, so he hadn't noticed his hour's worth of work had been completely erased.

I took a long breath and remembered what the book and Gavon had said about controlling magic. *Think about what you want and it'll happen,* I told myself. I envisioned the words on the page and an invisible piece of chalk writing on the board.

I opened an eye and saw one sentence written.

"*Crap*!"

My time was running out, my anxiety was getting worse (and my fingers growing a little purple), so I knew I had to do something fast. I envisioned my magic "selecting all," like I would on my laptop, then "control+c" to copy and "control+v" to paste onto the chalkboard.

I cracked open an eye—the writing had returned, exactly as it had been, just as Mills turned around to reference it again. I slumped in my seat and exhaled silently. That had been a little *too* close. I supposed that I wasn't quite ready to do magic at school, or at least, transcribe my notes. I opened my notebook and searched for the first blank page.

The only problem was the entire notebook was blank. All the notes I'd taken since the beginning of the year were *gone.*

I closed my eyes and wished for the undo button.

Seven

The rest of my day was similarly terrible. Thanks to Gram and questions and my birthday, I hadn't completed any of my assignments, earning another glare from Ms. Benoit and a talking-to by my English teacher. For a student who was consistently in the top ten of her class, my behavior had changed enough for my teachers to notice.

Then, as if she knew I was already having a rough day, Marie left me at school. The sun broiled the back of my neck and I was a sweaty, miserable mess. I powered through my homework, the voice in the back of my head reminding me that colleges didn't consider "magical prowess" in admissions or scholarship criteria. But every time I went to start my history homework, the sight of my blank notebook just reminded me how much I'd royally screwed up.

By the time Jeanie got home, I was desperate. "Jeanie, I need your help."

She put down her purse slowly. "Is everything all right?"

"No, I accidentally erased my history notebook," I said, showing it to her. "Can you help me reverse it?"

"How'd you do that?"

"I was..." Technically, I'd broken her rule about using magic at school unsupervised, and I didn't want another lecture about it. Jeanie was still waiting for my answer, so I said, "I don't know. It just happened."

She flipped through the blank pages and shrugged. "I don't know how to reverse it. Guess you'll have to copy from a friend."

"Jeanie, *I'm* the only one who takes notes in history," I said. "And we're talking about eight weeks' worth of notes here!"

She shrugged. "Get to copying then."

I glared at her retreating back and slammed my notebook shut. "I'm going for a walk."

I was hoping, perhaps, Gavon might show up for a third time. I stormed the entire way to the park, clutching the primer to my chest. I was tired of everything blowing up in my face and Jeanie simply shrugging and telling me to figure it out. "Figure it out" was sound advice when I struggled through chemistry formulas, but not with this. I wasn't smart enough to figure out magic on my own.

I plopped down at the picnic table and opened the primer to where I'd left off the day before. Stuck between the pages was the list of questions I'd written about Gram from Jeanie. After unfolding the questions and re-reading them, I balled the paper up and threw it in a nearby trashcan.

Screw them and their non-answers. I didn't want to know anyway.

I huffed as I sat back down and began to read spitefully.

TO SUMMON

One of the Magical's most oft used spells is to SUMMON, that is, to use Magic to retrieve an Object. This does not extend to Persons, whether Magical or Non-magical, that is known as TRANSPORT.

It is often the case with Young Magicals that they can summon items without considering a full Summon spell. True, often babies will Summon their favorite toy, even and especially when in trouble. But just as a talented artist improves with classical training, a Magical with training over their gift will be much more successful.

A SUMMON spell consists of three specific acts;

ONE, to identify the object to summon;

TWO, to use one's Magic to locate said object;

THREE, to use one's Magic to retrieve said object.

It is imperative that a Young

Magical without training perform each step as a separate thought, else the Magic might retrieve the incorrect object, or more than anticipated. A Master might recommend to Summon an object within the Young Magical's view.

Once control over Magic has been established, and the comfort of understanding each step by the Young Magical, the three acts will occur without thought.

I glanced around the park, looking for something I could practice with. There was a small plastic shovel and pail a kid had left in the sandbox. Squinting, I concentrated on the objects and willed them—

"You're trying too hard again," came the pleasing baritone behind me.

I released my focus and smiled as Gavon took a seat across from me. "How can you tell?"

He mimicked my focused face, scrunching his nose and squinting.

"Funny."

"What does the primer say?" he asked, glancing at the open book in front of me.

"Identify the object, use my magic to locate it and retrieve it," I said, looking at the pail again. "But how do I do that?"

"Your magic isn't confined to your physical body. It can grow, shift, travel faster than light. You can send it out to another location—a known location, of course—and it will act as your eyes and ears in that location. Let's try it, hm? Close your eyes."

I did so and waited.

"Now, can you feel your magic?"

I furrowed my brow. The hum of electricity had become familiar over the past forty-eight hours, but it became more pronounced the more I focused on it. "Yes."

"I want you to send it back to your bedroom. It's the most familiar place, I'm guessing?"

I nodded, keeping my eyes closed. "How...how do I do that?"

"Your magic knows. Stop trying to control it so much."

At his words, I felt the control and released it. My magic, or what I assumed was my magic, shotgunned away from me and in my mind's eye, I saw my bedroom and the object I was seeking. Before I could complete a thought, the book materialized in my hand.

"*That was so cool!*" I grinned at Gavon, who had something of a proud look on his face. Remembering my notebook, I released my magic again, and it retrieved the blank notebook.

"What's this?"

"I was," I swallowed, "practicing in history today. Accidentally erased the chalkboard, then when I went to put it back, I ended up erasing my whole book."

"What exactly were you thinking?" At my confused look, he added, "I mean, what was your thought process?"

"I was thinking of my book like a computer, control-c,

control-v...that sort of thing." His brow quirked, and I flushed. "I was trying not to panic. It was the only thing I could think of. And I've been trying all afternoon to restore the words on the page, but so far...nothing."

Gavon pulled the notebook to himself and stared at it for a moment. Then, to my *intense* relief, my handwriting reappeared on the page.

"*Thank you*," I said. "How'd you do that?"

"There was a magical signature left on the pages. I simply reversed it," he said, almost a little too quickly. "So, you're summoning fairly well, and despite erasing your notebook, you seem to have a handle on magic now."

"Yeah, but...I still have a ton of questions. I'm trying hard to...well, *not* try hard, but it just feels like I'm trying to carve an ice sculpture with a machete."

He smiled and chuckled. "If I were to guess, I might say that your magic has been pent up for too long and it's overflowing."

"Is that...normal?"

He shrugged, but didn't meet my gaze. "Not usually, but fairly easily dealt with. The more you use your magic, the more it will even out until your...what did you say, *machete* becomes a regular ice pick."

"Well, it would be a lot easier if I had someone around who actually *listened* to me instead of lecturing me all the time."

"Parents aren't perfect, you know."

"If I had any," I said with a small snort. "I just have my aunt and maybe Nicole, my oldest sister. But they've been...unhelpful too. Nicole would help, except she doesn't have magic."

His face flashed in anger for a moment. "That's not true."

"Well, she's a...potion-maker?" I said, still not sure about the phrasing. "She can't summon or anything like that."

"Oh, she has magic, I assure you, just not the typical kind. For example, *you* could mix dragon's blood and worm root together and nothing would happen but a globby mess."

"D-dragon's blood?" So they *were* real! "Is there a cure for potion-makers? I mean, to get their magic back?"

Gavon looked taken aback. "Potion-making is not a disease. It's a specific brand of magic that deals with the complexities of chemical reactions in potions."

"Yeah, but...she can't summon, or even...I don't know, summoning is as far as I got in the primer."

Gavon tilted his head. "Thomas Edison couldn't summon. Did that stop him from inventing the lightbulb?"

I paused, realizing how I must have sounded.

"I know having magic is a big change for you, but don't let it go to your head," Gavon said gently. "Many, many great potion-makers have existed in history. Just because they don't have the same kind of magic as you and me doesn't mean they aren't powerful."

An awfully impassioned speech, I thought. "Do you know any potion-makers then?"

"A few," Gavon said. "But in the magical communities, there's a lot of prejudice against them."

"Magical communities," I breathed to myself. Gram and that

mysterious compound that I wasn't allowed to go to came to the forefront of my mind. But Gavon wouldn't know the intricacies of my family drama. "My other sister is a healer. What about her? I think...I think she was able to conjure herself a car. But she won't tell me *how*."

"Healing magic comes from the same wellspring as the others," Gavon said. "But you can't just make things out of thin air. What's the Law of Conservation of Mass?"

I blinked at him and twisted my brain to recall my chemistry. "Uh...I know this..."

"Matter cannot be created nor destroyed. That rule's still in effect here. Magic can't create matter, it can only use what already exists. Your magic comes from the energy created in the cells of your body, just like everything else."

I appreciated this scientific analysis, especially as it answered some basic questions. "So how does a Healer's magic work, then?"

"Depends on what she's trying to heal. Most healing magic is a transfer—she'll give you energy when yours is depleted. But just as you don't have unlimited magic, neither does a healer."

"But the more you practice, the more you'll have, right?" I asked, recalling a line from the book.

"Exactly. It's like training for a marathon. You couldn't just walk out the front door and run twenty-six miles. You'd have to train for it. And even then, there are some who are just better at it than others."

I nodded. "So if Marie's a healer and Nicole's a potion-maker, what other kinds of magic are there?"

"None, really," Gavon said after a moment. "Back before the Separation, there used to be more but—"

"What Separation?"

He sat back and stared off into the distance, as if collecting his thoughts. "I suppose you could say that the Separation happened in 1692 but...it had really been festering since magicals and nonmagicals had been living together. But it really got going once European magicals finally made it over to America in the seventeenth century. Because there was so much space here, some of the magicals thought that, perhaps, there was an opportunity to start fresh. To have a community of *just* magicals. So, when Plymouth was founded in Massachusetts, a group of settlers did just that."

Massachusetts, where the compound was. "Are they still there?"

"Kind of," Gavon said. "After a few years, it became clear that a magical village could not sustain itself without trading with the nonmagicals. As we've discussed, matter can't be created or destroyed, and the magicals only had what they'd brought with them to settle the village. They needed nails and cooking pots and those kinds of things, and the trading ships only came to the nonmagical cities. In order to survive, the magicals had to either steal from the nonmagicals or announce their presence."

I considered those options for a moment. "I'd just steal."

He chuckled. "Trust me, many of them wanted to do just that. There had been a generation that had never had to hide their magic, and to be told that they had to revert to the old ways...they didn't take too well to that suggestion."

"But why the secrecy?" I asked. "Not to sound...callous, but if we're more powerful than they are, why are *we* the ones to hide?"

Gavon smiled. "And that is exactly what they thought as well. But think on that a little more, Alexis. Why would that be a bad idea?"

I tapped my finger against my chin. He sounded an awful lot like Mills asking us to consider the implications of historical events. "Well, based on the witch burnings, they might not take so well to the idea of magic existing. And...maybe there were more of them than us?"

"Exactly." Gavon beamed. "Nothing good would've come from that—only bloodshed. Which is why the magical council decided to go forward with the original plan, despite the protests." He sighed. "But that's the thing about magicals, especially powerful ones. They don't like to be ordered around. So, a very bloody war broke out between the two main factions—one comprised of Warriors who wanted things to remain, well, separate. These were the Separatists, and James Riley was their leader. They declared war against the others and the nonmagicals."

"He didn't win, obviously."

Gavon shook his head. "Magicals from all over the world, including the natives already living here, came to the aid of the leader of the other side—John Chase—and they defeated the Separatists after two years of bloody war. But Chase wasn't a murderer, and too much magical blood had already been spilled. So the collective came up with an idea to create another world—"

My hands thudded on the wooden table. "Wait, there are *other worlds too*?"

"Kind of," Gavon said. "Think of it like a little pocket of reality torn from this one. It's a place where Chase could imprison the separatists and they could live as they pleased."

"So he was really doing them a favor?"

"I wouldn't want to live there," Gavon said with a smile. "The texts say there was no sun, no warmth. A cold wind blows the stench of death and decay, and nothing grows except by magic. And even then..." He closed his mouth. "It's meant to be a punishment. The amount of magic it took for Chase and others to create the tear killed him and ten others."

I swallowed.

"But it was done. Afterward, the remaining magicals came together in what was known as the Council of Danvers. They set forth magical law for this country, and it was soon adopted globally. First and foremost, traditional guilds were outlawed—"

"But I thought clans still existed? I'm kind of in one, I think?"

"Clans are different, remember? They're formed by a blood bond. Family. A guild is more selective in their membership. A prospective inductee has to be introduced through a duel then trained by a Master—"

"*Master*!" I said, remembering a question I had. "The primer talks a lot about Masters. What are they?"

"You have to remember, this primer was written and used before the Separation, so it still contains some of the old language that's not in use anymore," Gavon said. "Before the magical age was set at fifteen, magic appeared at birth. So, in a guild, a Master was chosen once a young magical was introduced to the guild. They would train the magical until they came of age, then the magical would fight in *another* duel, and they'd be formally inducted."

Gavon paused and held out his hand. In a puff of purple smoke, another old, weathered book appeared. He flipped through the rotting pages like a man looking for the answers to life. Halfway to the end, he stopped and turned the book around to me.

"Here's the full decree of Magical Law that was set down. No magic until fifteen, nonmagicals not bound by marriage or birth are not to be told, and the removal of specialties, like Warriors, among more details."

"'No one shall use dragon blood for anything other than healing?'" I pursed my lips. "I don't think I want to know."

"It's actually a fascinating account of the history of that time," Gavon said, admiring his book. "Would you like it?"

I glanced down at the pages, yellowed with age, and I salivated, just a little. "I couldn't. I'm not even finished with the first book you gave me."

"I insist," he said, sliding it over. "The primer is a little dry. This, at least, has some excitement."

I placed my hand on the book and glanced up at him. "You aren't dying, are you?"

"I'm sorry?" he said, taken aback.

"You've given me some expensive, rare books. This one looks

like it was written *during* the seventeenth century..." I gauged his skin tone, his thick hair. Didn't look like he had cancer.

"I assure you, I'm perfectly fine," he said. "But I've read both this book and the other many times. The knowledge in them is useless to me. Books are meant to be read, are they not?"

They were, but I also knew that reading this book wasn't going to get me very far. I needed someone like Gavon to show me what the hell I was doing.

"Hey, so..." I shifted. "Can we talk again tomorrow?"

His face shifted for a moment, and I was afraid he would say no. Instead, he forced a smile and said, "Absolutely."

Eight

Gavon was obviously telling me the abridged, G-rated version of the Separation.

The book had been written by one of John Chase's seven sons, and he'd gone into painstaking detail—from the lives lost at each battle and skirmish to the minutes from each of the Council meetings. One event that stuck out in gory, graphic detail was the account of the great potion-maker massacre in May 1692. Riley and his faction had obtained a list of all the potion-makers in the village and marked them for death. They took out almost two hundred people in one night, including fifty children. Knowing that Nicole would've been one of his targets, I was very glad that Riley and his idiots had been banished to the other world.

But, in my opinion, the Council of Danvers went a little overboard in preventing the recurrence of such a traumatic event. Some of the rules didn't really apply to me, especially as they related to potion-making, but there was a really big one that confused the hell out of me: No more specialties. All the Warriors, Healers, Empaths, Potion-makers, Charmers, Enchanters—they lost their unique magic and became the mishmash of powers that I had. The Council said it was to prevent another Guild of Warriors from rising, one which could wreak havoc like Riley's did.

So then why were my sisters a healer and a potion-maker? The only thing I could think of was that perhaps, over the four hundred years since it was first enacted, the council's decrees had become less potent.

"Whatcha doing in here?" Nicole asked, walking into the kitchen. As usual, her eyes danced everywhere except the spelled book on the table.

I opened my mouth to ask about the Separation, but that might invite more questions about how I'd suddenly become so knowledgeable about magical stuff. Nicole was usually on my side, but she also wasn't above telling on me. And somehow, I didn't think Jeanie would approve of me meeting with a strange guy in a park to practice magic out in the open.

"Just thinking about stuff," I said, after a few minutes of working my jaw.

"Uh-huh. What kind of stuff?" Nicole asked with a genuine smile.

"Like...do you have a job?"

Nicole quirked a brow. "What kind of a question is that?"

"I mean, you say you do, but with magic—"

"Yes, I have a job," Nicole said with a laugh. "As do Jeanie and Marie. And if you want to save for college, you might want to think about getting one soon, too."

She pulled one of the three barstools from the middle island over to the fridge with a loud scrape. I winced and asked, "What are you doing?"

"Getting the big pot down."

My heart leaped to my throat. "Are you gonna make another potion?"

Another quirked brow. "I was going to make dinner. Feeling like some beef stew tonight."

I closed my eyes and released my magic, finding the pot in the cabinet and retrieving it. It was heavier than I anticipated, and fell out of my hands, clanging loudly on the floor.

"Lexie, really," Nicole said, climbing off the stool and taking the pot I sheepishly offered to her. "You can't just...use magic whenever you feel like it."

I frowned and sat back down on the stool.

"I'm sorry," she said after a moment. "That was really great, what you did. Just *be more careful*. I don't want you to hurt yourself."

"How is summoning a pot out of the cabinet going to hurt me?" I asked, pointedly. "And how am I supposed to know what to do if no one will help me?"

"Jeanie's working on Gram," Nicole said, as if that were a real answer. "And in the meantime...just do *little* things."

I was about to remark that summoning was about as basic as it got, per the primer, but neither she nor Jeanie knew about it. Instead, I asked, "Who taught you how to make potions?"

She flushed a little, then turned to retrieve the carrots from the fridge. "No one did. I don't make them, really. The calming draught was just a fluke." She placed the bag of carrots on the counter and half-smiled. "Want to help me peel?"

"Can I try to use magic?"

She sighed. "Be *very* careful."

I closed my eyes and released my magic. The carrots sat in the plastic bag, their skins connected to the flesh of the vegetable. I could almost *see* the molecular connections, and severed them at the same time.

"*Shit, Lexie!*" Nicole screamed, dropping the bag that had burst into purple flames.

"Sorry! Sorry!" I cried. "Let me try to—"

"*Don't do anything else!*" Nicole screamed, throwing the bag into the pot and tossing the lid on top of it. After a moment, she lifted the pot and the flames had disappeared.

For a few moments, we stared at each other as the air increasingly smelled of burnt plastic.

"I'm sorry..." I said quietly.

"Just...go to your room," Nicole said. "And don't use any magic until Jeanie or Marie get home."

Unsurprisingly, Jeanie came to give me a long lecture about the dangers of using magic unsupervised.

"Well, I *was* supervised," I said. "Nicole was—"

"Nicole is a potion-maker," Jeanie said, although she lowered her voice to a whisper. "If you decide to blow up the house—"

"I thought you said she has magic." Memories of the Separation and James Riley came bubbling to the surface, as did Gavon's mention of prejudices.

"She does," Jeanie said, sitting down on my desk chair. "But it's different from yours. So you can't practice magic unless Marie or I am here."

I stared at her. "You *can't* be serious. You're barely home as it is, and Marie would think it was *funny* if I ended up killing myself."

"I'm barely home because I'm trying to convince Gram to let you come up to the compound," Jeanie said. "And it's taking a lot more convincing than I thought it would."

"Yeah, so." I folded my arms over my chest. "What's *that* all about, hm?"

"Gram's got her reasons, and she's the boss, so we have to do what she says."

There was one thing I was definitely sure of: the more I heard about Gram, the less eager I was to see the woman again. Especially since it was obvious she wasn't eager to see me.

I went to school the next day in a funk, annoyed by my still machete-like magic and the lack of understanding from Jeanie and Nicole. My locker took three tries to open, thanks to Callista and Joel fighting right in front of it. Ms. Benoit assigned a mind-numbing set of exercises in French and chemistry literally made zero sense to me. Then I got to English and realized I hadn't prepared anything for class, and Ms. Grace kept calling on me, as if she *enjoyed* seeing my deer-in-the-headlights look. I had to eat lunch inside thanks to a downpour that ended just as my lunch period did.

Then, in graphic design, I spent half an hour working on a texture on a font, only to have the program crash and realize I hadn't saved jack. That was when I noticed my nail beds glowing purple, and when I went to grab the mouse to salvage my project, I shorted out the computer.

So when I stormed out to Marie's car, I just knew she'd do something to piss me off because it was that kind of day. The only thing that kept me from blowing up her car was knowing I was going to have another chat with Gavon. Maybe he'd teach me those transport spells I was reading about so I'd never have to ride with Marie again.

A twittering of laughter drew my attention. Marie and Charity were walking arm-in-arm, bright-eyed and excited. I groaned; Charity was the last person I wanted to be stuck in an enclosed space with. If I were being honest, I wanted to ask Marie why Gram hated me so much. Marie might just tell me the truth, out of spite.

Neither noticed me, so I climbed into the backseat and listened to their inane conversation. Marie'd bombed another test, but so had Charity. They talked about their favorite TV show that had aired the night before, squealing and gasping as they recounted every second of the show. I was sure Marie would watch it twice more before the next one aired. She was such an idiot.

"Lexie." Marie's sharp tone made me jump and I stared at her reflection in the rearview mirror. Her eyes were a warning. But why?

Then I heard it—the cracking and popping sounds coming from my hands. My magic was gathering in the center of my palms, swirling into an orb—

"*Lexie*!"

I glanced up at Marie and remembered that Charity was in the car with us. I inhaled and exhaled, closing my eyes and willing the magic to disappear.

The car lurched to a stop, and I opened my eyes. To my horror, my magic hadn't disappeared, but was now spinning rapidly in the palms of my hands. I glanced at Marie, terrified, but she was talking to Charity.

"Sorry, you gotta get out here," Marie said. "I forgot I have to take the idiot to the doctor today."

"But I thought—?"

"Bye, Charity."

"Marie, this isn't my house—"

"*Bye, Charity.*"

Charity made a disgusted noise, but grabbed her things and got out. Before I could say anything to Marie, she stomped on the gas and we zoomed away from Charity, peeling around the corner toward the house.

"Put your damned magic away!" Marie snarled at me.

"I can't!" I cried.

The car screeched to a halt in our driveway and she stormed around the other side of the car, ripping open the door and pulling me, and my purple, swirling hands, out by the scruff of the neck.

We were inside the house in two seconds, and Marie tossed me onto the couch.

"*What the hell is wrong with you?*"

"W-wrong with me?" I cried, looking at my hands. "Wrong with me? *I have no idea what I'm doing*!"

"Then just *stop* using your magic!"

"*I can't*!"

She let out a groan of frustration. "Yes, you can, just *stop* thinking about it and do it! This isn't rocket science."

"Obviously not, if *you* can do it."

That was the wrong thing to say, as Marie's face grew red and blotchy under her makeup. I knew I'd crossed the line, but I didn't care.

"I thought magic just existed in the movies! I didn't know I could summon stuff or conjure things or that there were things like healers and potion-makers and—" I almost said 'the Separation,' but I stopped myself. "And if I do or don't do something, I have no control over it."

"Well, *get* control over it."

Something snapped in the back of my mind and the strangest feeling of déjà vu came over me. I'd been arguing with someone about magic at some point, or maybe I'd just been arguing, but I'd been angry like this. My magic was begging to be released, to act on its own, so I released it and the feeling multiplied. I was hyper-aware of everything around me, from the way my magic crackled around me to the sound of Marie's heartbeat to the white magic that surrounded her.

White? I remember a different color...

"Lexie, I mean it. Put your magic away."

She sounded afraid, and it made my power grow more frenzied beneath my skin. I heard crunching of gravel, I smelled the sea, I saw a flash of lightning. The way he'd sounded as he taunted me, expecting me to lie down and die. The delicious knowledge that I would end him, even if it ended me too. The guilt of knowing I'd be leaving them behind.

The purple light glowed so bright I was nearly blinded. The recoil of the blast sent me back a few steps, before the world tilted and I fell to my knees, dizzy and lightheaded. I swooned on my hands and knees for a moment, waiting for the sickness to pass. When the world stopped spinning, I realized I no longer heard my sister yelling at me. Slowly, I lifted my head, and my heart stopped.

The whole living room wall was destroyed, the drywall broken and crumbled, the insulation hanging from the splintered studs. I could see straight into the kitchen, which was black and burning.

What I didn't see was Marie.

"M-Marie?" I whispered, inching closer to the pile of rubble that used to comprise our living room wall. "M-Marie? A-are you okay? Marie, I'm so..."

I saw her pale hand hanging limply from beneath the rubble. A scream left my mouth and I furiously pulled off the pieces of wall until I found her. She was bleeding from the head, her face black with soot and ash.

"Marie?" I whispered, brushing the dust off of her perfect face. "Marie, I'm so...Marie..." I began to cry.

I'd killed my sister.

I stood up, looking around frantically.

Then I ran out the door, headed straight for the park.

Nine

"Oh my God, oh my God, oh my God."

I'd never run faster in my entire life. I was fairly sure that my magic was pushing my legs to move faster than was actually possible, because I made it to the park in record time. I began to wonder how I'd even contact Gavon, I didn't have his phone number or email address—

"Alexis, what's wrong?"

I turned around, knowing my face was red and tear-streaked, and heaved a sigh of relief. "Thank *God*."

"Are you all right?" he asked, rushing forward to grip my shoulders. "Is everything—"

"*I killed my sister.*"

He stared at me. "What?"

"*I sent her through a wall and I think I killed her!*" I broke into ferocious tears, my wails echoing into the park.

"Take a deep breath," he said calmly. "And start from the

beginning."

I snorted back a glob of snot and wiped my face. "I was having a bad day and Marie was being mean and this *spell* just happened and—"

"What kind of a spell?"

I shrugged. "I don't know. It was all purple and..." I swallowed and stared into nothing. "And it came out of me and it sent her flying through a wall and *Gavon, I killed my sister*!"

"Deep breaths," Gavon cooed. "I'm sure you didn't kill her. She's probably just hurt. Nothing a quick healing potion won't fix."

"H-healing potion?"

"Do you want me to go check on her?"

I nodded. "T-thank you."

"Let's go then."

The walk back from the park went a lot slower, or perhaps I was noticing every step because I dreaded what I'd find when I got back to the house. Even more concerning was how much a little voice inside me wanted to use that spell again.

"What did I do?" I asked quietly.

"Hm?"

"That...spell," I said, remembering how it had felt, how expertly I'd wielded it. Nothing—magical or otherwise—had ever felt so *right*. "It just...it came out."

"Magic does that sometimes, especially when you're emotional. A calm magical is—"

"A useful magical," I recited.

Gavon didn't say any more, and I kept silent. I didn't want him to think I was insane, though he'd never given me any evidence that he'd react that way. There was also another fear—I had enjoyed doing that spell, and that spell hurt people...so what did that make me?

We rounded the corner to my street and I stopped dead in my tracks.

Both Nicole and Jeanie's cars were in the driveway.

"Uh-oh," I said. They were home three hours early. Had they felt my explosive power? Had they felt Marie's life end?

"I'd offer my help, but between your aunt and your sister, I think they have it covered," he said, taking a few steps forward. "I'm sure she's fine, Lexie."

But it was no longer the fear of killing my sister that spiked my pulse. I'd broken Jeanie's first rule of using magic. I was pretty sure I was about to walk into World War III.

"Coming?" Gavon asked.

"Jeanie's gonna *kill* me," I whispered.

"It was an accident, yes?"

"I..." *Was* it an accident? I'd never felt so in control before. I'd wanted to see where it would go. But I certainly didn't want Marie dead. "Yeah, it was an accident."

"Then I'm sure they'll understand."

I shook my head. Jeanie was already on edge with me, and after my mishap the night before, Nicole was too. When they came home and saw the house destroyed and Marie... I hiccuped and wiped my face.

Gavon put his hands in his pocket and we stood there for a moment. "Would you like to do another stroll round the block?" he offered. "Delay the inevitable."

I nodded and we turned to walk the other way.

After a moment, my thoughts became too much and I blurted, "Ifeelsobadbutitfeltsogood."

"What was that?" he asked, looking down.

"I said," I sighed, ashamed of myself, "I feel so bad, but...it felt so good."

"What, to get the best of your sister?"

"No, to do whatever it was," I said, squinting up at the afternoon sky. "It felt like I'd done it before." I chewed on the inside of my lip. "*Have* I done it before?"

"Not to my knowledge."

"So why did it feel so good?"

"I would guess it had something to do with how you felt towards your sister," he said. "And you've had so much magic bottled up for so long that it needed a release." That part sounded more convincing, but it didn't answer how natural it felt to let that sort of spell come out. It felt like breathing.

"What kind of spell was it?"

He was quiet for a moment and I feared I'd said the wrong thing. Maybe I was some kind of deranged person like James Riley. Maybe I took—

"It was an attack spell," he said, finally.

That seemed obvious, but something about the way he said it gave me chills.

"Unfortunately, or I suppose, fortunately," he winked at me, easing some of my worry, "the only real use for an attack spell outside of a magical duel is in a sparring match. So there's no reason to teach you about them."

I recalled a brief line about a magical duel in the book, but couldn't recall the specifics. Still, knowing that Gavon wasn't going to teach me how to wield attack spells left me inexplicably sad.

Worse still, we'd finished our walk and were back at the precipice of peace and the fury I'd encounter when I got home.

"I find, with things that I'm concerned about, that just marching forward and doing the thing tends to make it less scary," he said. "'Fear makes the wolf bigger than he is' says an old German proverb."

There was certainly a big wolf growling in my head at the moment—or maybe it was a dragon.

I didn't move, and neither did Gavon. We stood on the sidewalk for several minutes without saying a word to each other. I kept telling myself to move, but I wasn't listening.

"Tell you what," Gavon said after a long stretch, "why don't you go home and accept your punishment, whatever it happens to be. Then, if you keep your head down and complete your homework, behave yourself and don't use magic at school, and definitely don't hurt your sister anymore..." He paused and stared at my house for a moment. "This weekend, I will show you a few sparring moves."

A gasp escaped my lips, and suddenly facing Jeanie didn't seem so terrible. "You will?"

He nodded then wagged his finger in my face. "But you have to behave until then, understand?"

"Yes, sir!"

"You're a good kid, Alexis," he said with a kind smile. "Now go on and get home."

I turned and marched toward my house. After I'd gotten two steps, I turned back to Gavon, but he'd already disappeared. As did most of my gumption.

There were seven houses between me and my home, and the walk was the longest of my life. I felt like a condemned prisoner being led to my own execution. I tried to focus on the fact that I'd get to perform that spell again—in a safe space, where I couldn't hurt anyone—but the closer I got to the house, the less it seemed to boost my confidence.

Before I knew it, I stood in front of my door, staring at the knocker and the numbers and wishing I had more bravery. With a deep breath, I put my hand on the knob and twisted it, ready for the horror.

"Thank God!" Nicole's shrill voice echoed before she crushed me to her in a fierce embrace.

"W-what's going on?" I stammered.

"Did he hurt you? Are you hurt?" Nicole said, holding my face.

"Who?" I blinked.

"Nicole, let her breathe," Jeanie said, sounding much more calm than I would've thought. "Lexie, what happened here?"

The wall had been repaired, the dust cleaned. In fact, it looked like nothing had even happened. Then my gaze fell to Marie, lying on the couch, still unconscious.

"Marie! Is she—"

"She's fine, just recovering," Jeanie said. "Tell us what happened."

"I..." I glanced at Jeanie, then to Nicole. Neither seemed angry with me, so perhaps this wasn't going to be as bad as I'd thought. "It was an accident. I didn't mean to. I didn't know what I was doing, and it just happened and—"

The tone in the room changed abruptly. "*You* did this?" Jeanie asked.

"Who else would have?"

"*You* did this?" Jeanie repeated, glancing down at Marie on the couch. "You hurt her like this?"

I took one step back. "It...it was an accident, I swear. She was...she was being mean and..." A foul stench reached my nose and I gagged. "What is that smell?"

"I am making a healing potion," Nicole said, sounding much less relieved at my safety than before.

"I didn't mean to—"

"Right, because you would never use magic against your sister, who teases you all day?" Jeanie said as Nicole left for the kitchen. "Who makes your life miserable? I find that hard to believe, Alexis."

"I swear, I didn't mean to!"

"Magic happens because you will it to, Alexis," Jeanie said.

"Consciously or subconsciously."

I swallowed and looked at the floor. "I didn't know...I didn't mean to hurt her."

"You *do not* use magic to hurt anyone, do you understand me?"

"Yes, ma'am," I whispered.

"You have to learn to control your magic. You cannot just let your emotions get the best of you."

The urge to remind her that she hadn't done anything except tell me what *not* to do bubbled up, but the reminder of a weekend training session with Gavon kept me quiet.

"I really didn't mean to," I said after a few moments.

Nicole emerged from the kitchen holding a steaming mug that smelled like the inside of a diaper. "Help me get her to drink this."

Jeanie used her magic to elevate Marie, and Nicole gently tipped the mug into Marie's open mouth. Marie's cheeks turned from pasty to rosy, and she murmured as she woke.

"There we are," Nicole said, standing back up. "Marie?"

"Wha..." Marie said, looking around. "What...happened?"

"You took a little fall," Jeanie said. "But you're all right now."

Marie took another sip of the potion and her eyes grew more focused, searching the room before landing squarely on me.

"You little bitch!" She flew off the couch, but only made it two steps before falling to the floor, moaning and clutching her head. "What the hell?"

Nicole winced and chewed her thumb. "It's supposed to completely heal her. Maybe I didn't add enough aloe? The book said three palmfuls, but it seemed off to me..."

"Don't worry about it, Nicole," Jeanie said. "Marie probably deserves to heal a little bit slowly."

Marie took the mug of potion from the table and sniffed it, retching loudly. "I'm not drinking this crap. I can heal myself." She placed her hands on her upper arms and closed her eyes, but nothing happened.

"Healers can't heal themselves," Jeanie said with a knowing smirk. "Drink up or you'll have to sport that bruise at school tomorrow. I don't think your boyfriends will like it."

Her steely gaze then turned to me.

"As for you, Alexis—"

I swallowed.

"Go to your room. I don't want to hear a peep out of you for the rest of the night."

"That's *it*?" Marie bellowed. "She nearly *killed* me and gets a slap on the wrist?"

"She's got a lot of credit for good behavior, unlike some people." Jeanie paused and put her hands on her hips. "Speaking of, we need to talk about you not coming home last night."

I took that as my cue to hurry up the stairs, though I could hear the strains of their screaming long into the night.

The next morning, things seemed to have returned to somewhat normal. Jeanie was only slightly annoyed with me as we ate breakfast, and Nicole even offered to wash my dishes so I could get out the door.

The only evidence that I'd done anything amiss was Marie. Fully healed, thanks to Nicole's potion, she breezed into the kitchen looking as perfect as ever. But when I asked her how she was feeling, she walked right by me.

"Hey, Marie, I asked you a question."

Her gaze darted to me for a second before she turned her nose up. "I'm sorry, did anyone hear that? Sounds like the ghost of a dead-to-me sister."

"Grow up, Marie," Jeanie said before checking the time on her watch. With one puff of smoke, she was dressed in a suit, and then another, and she was gone.

"How often does that happen?" I asked Nicole, who shrugged as she put our bowls in the dish rack.

"Daily," she said then furrowed her brow. "Where'd Marie go?"

Outside, I heard a car start and rolled my eyes. "She's *not* leaving without me, is she?"

"Better hurry up then, because I'm not taking you," Nicole said with a wink.

"*Crap.*"

Ten

The only thing that kept me from losing my mind for the rest of the week was the promise of a sparring lesson with Gavon. Every free moment I had, I was scouring the primer, looking for something that could help me be ready for whatever he had planned. But the primer was, for once, unhelpful. There was one line in the preface about attack spells, but the only thing I could find about a duel was one section:

AS TO THE MATTER OF A DUEL

In the Magical communities, it is oft the nature of Man to have disagreements. While most Magicals may settle disputes of business or trade through mediation by the Clan- or Guildmaster, on the occasion of accounts that may not be settled with words, Magic may be used in the form

of a Duel. The rules of the Match will be set by the participants, or, in such cases where it is merited, by the respective Clan- or Guildmasters.

It is recommended, however, that words be used before magic.

I couldn't argue with that logic, but at the same time, I couldn't stop thinking about how the spell had *felt* and how much I wanted to feel it again. Sometimes, I wanted it so bad that my hands began to spark, and I had to quickly divert my thoughts to something less magical.

I wasn't surprised that Marie left me at school, but the ominous black clouds in the sky were a different story. And I hadn't gotten two steps before the deluge began.

I cursed and ran back to the school, standing under the awning and wiping rain out of my eyes. Carefully, I tested a bit of a magic to dry my clothes, and to my delight, the wetness disappeared without any adverse effects.

I looked at my hands, considering how...well, un-eventful the past few days had been. The magical hum was there, but I didn't feel like my magic was bursting at the seams to get out. Only when I was thinking about sparring did things get a bit purple.

I wondered if it had anything to do with the spell I'd used on Marie, but I couldn't ask anyone about it. Not when I was almost back on Jeanie's good side.

So, instead, I sat down on a bench and found the notebook that I'd been using to jot down questions for Gavon. I squinted out at the parking lot, barely visible in the rain, and wondered how long the storm was going to take and if it meant a cancellation on our sparring plans. A quick check on my phone told me it would pass within the hour.

But that still meant I was stuck here until it passed.

Unless...

I summoned my primer from the space under my bed where I'd hidden it and flipped the pages until I found what I was looking for.

TO TRANSPORT

One of the most helpful aspects of Magic is the ability to transport oneself from one place to another. The effort is very similar to the Summoning Spell, but care must be taken, as physical harm or death can come to the untrained Magical.

A Magical must take great care to Transport to an unknown place, and the longer the distance of the Transport, the more magic is required. This is why Transport across the Atlantic is ill-advised.

The TRANSPORT spell occurs in three acts;

ONE, the identification of the Magical to be transported;

TWO, the discovery of the location

to which the Magical shall be transported;

THREE, the use of Magic to transport the Magical to the location.

It is recommended that a Magical first practice their Transport with the help of a Master until a comprehensive understanding is achieved.

I chewed my lip. I knew the distance between my school and my house like the back of my hand, but something about the warning in the book made me nervous to try it without help. And the rain had stopped, as was the case in the weird weather capital of the world, so it was time for another three-mile walk back to my house.

I wasn't sure what time Gavon would be meeting me, but I made sure that every single piece of my homework was finished before I came downstairs.

Jeanie was in the living room, staring at her phone. She hadn't said two words to me since the mishap with Marie, which was better than her yelling at me. But I still wasn't sure if I was in trouble or not.

"H-hey, Jeanie," I said slowly.

She glanced up from her phone then back down. "Yes?"

"Can I go take a walk?"

Another glance. "Why?"

"Um..." I shrugged. "Clear my head?"

She stared at her phone for almost too long then heaved out a loud sigh. "Fine. Take your phone."

I pulled the device from my back pocket and waved it. "Got it."

She didn't say anything else, so I inched toward the door, scurrying out before she changed her mind. The storms of the afternoon were a long-gone memory, and the sunset cast a pretty orange glow over the houses. Gavon was already waiting for me at the park, his face lighting up when he saw me approach.

"How's your sister?" he asked.

"My s... Oh, she's fine," I said with a wave of my hand. "Nicole made her a healing potion."

Something like amusement crossed his face. "How bad was it?"

"What? The potion? It *smelled* for days."

He laughed. "No, your punishment."

"Oh, it actually wasn't that bad," I said, rubbing my hands along my arms. "Weirdly."

"So maybe you should give your aunt a *little* more credit, hm?" His eyes twinkled.

I pursed my lips at him. "Aren't you supposed to be on my side?" He laughed, a genuine sound that dissolved whatever annoyance I'd had. "I've done my homework and I've been a good girl, so...sparring lesson?"

"I suppose you won't stop asking until we have one, hm?"

"Nope."

Another smile from him. "We can't spar here, though. Too many people, and I'm not quite sure that we should be throwing attack spells around where the nonmagicals can see us. So we'll practice a transport spell."

"A transport spell?" I asked, excited. "I read about them today, but I didn't want to attempt one—"

"As well you shouldn't without supervision." He held out his arm to me. "Hold on, and I'll walk you through it."

I placed my hands on his forearm and waited.

"Now, do you remember the three steps?"

"Figure out where you want to go, use your magic to find it, then go."

"Good girl. But since you don't know where we're going, we're going to do things a little differently. Close your eyes." I did so. "Now, can you find my magic?"

I released the grip on my magic and it smashed into his. He chuckled. "Bit excessive."

"You could feel that?"

"Indeed. You've still got a lot of pent-up energy, it seems." As he spoke, I felt his magic grab hold of mine as if he were taking my hand. Then his magic and mine zoomed through time and space to a dark spot where there was sand, and water, and the smell of the ocean and—

And I opened my eyes and I was standing on the white sands next to a rolling ocean.

"Holy crap!" I said, releasing him and spinning around. "How did we do that? What just happened? Where are we? What—"

He held up his hands. "One question at a time, Alexis."

"Where are we?" I asked. "I mean, I know this is the beach, but

—"

"This is a training ground for a local Air Force base about fifty miles east of you. There are no people, no roads. Plenty of space to practice. Any...mess we make can be attributed to their munitions testing."

"Mess?"

"Mess." A purple glow surrounded his hand, illuminating his face. "Are you absolutely sure you want to do this, Alexis?"

"Yes," I said. "I—"

The magical orb hurled toward me with the rushing sound of a freight train. I squealed and dove out of the way faster than I'd thought possible.

"*What the hell?*" I screamed at him. "You could have *killed* me!"

"You would've gotten a bad sting, but I wouldn't have killed you," Gavon said, with another deep purple spell ready in his hand. "Besides, as I said, sparring is based on instinct, not thought. The best way is to just react when you're being attacked."

I stood and brushed the sand off of my pants. "Yeah, but a little —*Gack*!" I fell backward, the purple spell landing square in my solar plexus and my butt landing hard on the white sand.

"Warnings mean you think about it. Instinct is acting."

"But I don't even know what to do?"

His eyebrow quirked. "Is that true? What about what happened with your sister?"

"That was...an accident."

"That was instinct. You know what to do, you're just overthinking things."

I pushed myself off the ground just in time for another spell to knock me back down. I cried out in frustration and glared at him. "*Stop doing that*!"

"Make me."

I would've laughed, except he was serious.

I was able to get to my feet again before another spell zoomed toward me, but I ducked out of the way. It exploded into the sand behind me, showering me with fine grit. I swerved left then right then another hit me square in the chest and I found myself face up, staring at the darkening sky.

I looked over at Gavon. The son of a bitch was smiling.

"Ready to quit?" he asked.

"Not on your life," I grunted, coming to stand. "Let's—"

Another attack spell had me scrambling, but this time I felt the growing power in my own hand. It was the same calmness, the same knowing that I was in control. That this spell would do what I wanted it to do. And when he struck again, I would be ready.

He didn't keep me waiting long, and once I'd dodged his spell, I released the power from my hand, the release washing over me and filling me with excitement and something else I couldn't place. I readied another spell in my hand, taking in the swirling, pulsing purple that cracked and sparked. It looked dangerous, and yet, it was part of me. I didn't fear it—I reveled in it.

"What is it?" Gavon asked.

"Just...I've never looked at my magic like *this* before," I said, mesmerized by the power I held in my hand. "It's beautiful."

Gavon had a strange look on his face, one I couldn't pinpoint in the fading light. My magic whispered to take advantage of his distraction, and I released a purple orb of my own toward him. He sidestepped it with ease, and I earned a small chuckle.

Then the world tilted and I fell to my knees, feeling very much like I was going to empty my stomach on the ground.

"Yes, I forgot to mention that," Gavon said, sounding like he hadn't forgotten it at all. "Attack spells use a lot of magic. So when your magic is very quickly depleted, you will feel pretty awful."

"I'm..." I swallowed through my dizziness. "I'm low on magic?"

"Not dangerously so," Gavon said, kneeling in front of me. "And it will replenish with rest."

"How come you aren't...aren't on the ground?"

"I've been doing this a very long time," he said. "With practice, you'll be able to build your tolerance and stamina. But I think that's it for tonight, hm?"

All of that, for just one minute of sparring? "No," I said, struggling to my feet. "I'm fine. We can continue."

"Are you sure?" Gavon asked. "You shouldn't push yourself if —"

"I'm *fine*." I pushed myself out of the sand, only to topple back over. "I promise. Just need a second. One second."

His face filled my vision. "I think that's enough for tonight, Alexis."

I blew air out between my lips. "Can we try again tomorrow?"

"That's inadvisable. May take you a few days to fully recover."

"But if it feels so...why?" I apparently also lacked the ability to form coherent sentences.

"Because you've had your magic for less than a week, if you'll recall." He held out his hand and I took it, carefully rising to stand. "Now I'll send you back home. Go get some rest, all right?"

Before I could respond, his magic surrounded me and I found myself standing in my bedroom. A thousand questions circled in my head, but my body fell back into bed and I was asleep in seconds.

The man before me was menacing, his eyes borderline insane. He stood in the threshold of my house, as if drinking in this moment and this night. Behind him a bolt of lightning split the sky, and thunder echoed.

"He's not coming, you know."

My voice answered, "He'll come. But I don't need him."

But that wasn't my voice.

"Oh? You've been practicing?"

My magic gathered in my hands, almost by instinct. I had been practicing. We'd been practicing for months. But not for this, never for this. Not with my girls sleeping upstairs.

Where was he?

Eleven

"Alexis, I know you're a teenager, but it is *one in the afternoon! Get your ass out of bed!*"

I opened my eyes slowly, blinded by the brightness of the room, then lifted my too-heavy head to look at Jeanie who stood in my doorway.

"Get up."

"Why?" I moaned, rolling over slowly and pressing my head back into the pillow.

"Because...because I said so," Jeanie said. "You can't spend your life in bed."

Oh, but that sounded so nice. "I wanna."

"Are you sick or something? Or are you...*Lexie, did you go out drinking last night?*"

"Wha?" I lifted my head to look at her. "No?"

"I didn't hear you come home," Jeanie said, running her hand over her face as I face-planted back into my soft and wonderful pillow. "Lexie, *please* don't do this to me. I already have enough trouble with Marie. Please don't turn into her."

"I didn't drink. I'm just tired," I said, my words muffled by my pillow. I lifted my head to look at her. "I swear, Jeanie."

"Then get your ass out of bed and go...do something," Jeanie said.

"*Why?*" It came out more a whine.

"Because...because..." A pause. "Because I said so. Now get up!"

Her thundering footsteps echoed down the hall and I pushed myself away from the most comfortable pillow ever invented and stared at the open door. The aches that seemed to settle in my bones were more pronounced when I sat up, especially in my chest and butt. I sat up all the way and checked under my shirt for bruises, but there were none. Perhaps Gavon was taking it easy on me, but I was going to need a few more rounds of this sort of thing before I wasn't sore the next day.

Releasing my shirt, I looked at my hands, remembering how beautiful my magic had been. I closed my eyes and tried to gather the power again, but even the hum was muted. Gavon had said using too much magic would make me weak. But this was worse than just feeling depleted—I felt like I'd been hit by a truck. There was no way *this* was normal.

I debated asking Jeanie, but something told me she wouldn't know, and, besides that, she'd probably ask what I was doing to lose so much magic. But since the answers thus far had been in the primer, I climbed off of my bed and retrieved it from the dust-covered floor. Yawning loudly, I began flipping through the book.

ON THE HEALING ARTS

With daily use, a Magical may wield his power without consequence. A well-practiced Magical may indeed exert a large amount as part of their daily regimen.

However, if an extraordinary amount of Magic is wielded, or a Magical is untrained, then it will happen that the Magical shall become faint, even to the point where they lose conscious thought. In very rare cases, a Magical may release all of their Magic, and they will perish.

When a Magical is first learning to wield magic, a Master may find their Apprentice to require the use of a Healer;

Take note that an untrained Healer may also suffer the consequences of more than a daily usage of Magic;

In the absence of a Healer, a healing potion may be used instead.

Well, as Marie wasn't talking to me, a healing potion was going to be my only option. But where was I going to get one of those?

"Alexis, you have five minutes to get out of your room or else!" Jeanie called.

I slammed the book shut and slid out of bed, grumbling about why I had to get up when there was really nothing for me to do. My body creaked and moaned as I walked across the hall to the bathroom to take a shower. I moved like a sloth, staring at the pink tile for five minutes as the warm water washed over me. It soothed my aches and pains, but it didn't do much to clear the fog from my brain.

After dressing ridiculously slowly in a pair of pajama shorts and an old shirt, I finally made my way downstairs. It was a pretty day, the sun was shining, and Nicole was the only one in the kitchen.

"You look like death warmed over," Nicole said, eyeing me. "What's wrong?"

"I dunno," I lied, shuffling over to the coffee pot and starting the process of making a fresh pot.

"Did you go out drinking last night?"

The glass carafe almost fell out of my hand. "Why does everyone think that's what I've been doing? Do you guys even *know* me?"

"I don't know, you've been...strange lately," Nicole said, flipping the page of the magazine she was reading.

"Speak for yourselves," I grumbled, pouring the water into the pot. "You and Jeanie have done nothing but yell at me since I got magic."

"I haven't yelled at you, except when you hurt Marie," Nicole said, glancing up at me. "Not that she didn't probably deserve it, but... And Jeanie's well, she's just Jeanie."

I frowned and watched the coffee drip into the carafe.

"You know how she is," Nicole said after a moment. "She's just...never gotten the hang of this whole parent thing. I mean...she was *my* age when we came to live with her."

I looked at my sister and tried to imagine my aunt as her age taking in a seven- and three-year-old and a newborn. Jeanie seemed like the last person in the world who'd want to raise kids, and now, knowing that there was an entire family available, it made even less sense to me. Especially as my earliest memories were of Jeanie struggling to finish her education.

"Just cut her some slack, okay?" Nicole said. "She's trying her best. And I'm no help." She looked down at the magazine, a small blush creeping up her neck. "I really wish Gram would've..."

"Would've what?"

"Sent someone down here. Someone better equipped to answer your questions. Jeanie's just...I mean, I know she's pretty good with magic, but she's not great at it. You need someone who's been practicing—really practicing—for years."

"And why can't I go up to the compound or whatever it's called?"

Nicole stared out the window for a second. "That is a question Gram will have to answer."

I wondered if that response was genuine or magically compelled. I also began to wonder how much of the lies I'd been fed my whole life were because of Gram.

I thought of Gavon and smiled. "Are there any other people with magic in this town?"

"Not for a few hundred miles at least," Nicole said.

That was interesting; Nicole didn't know about Gavon. Did Jeanie know about him?

"I'm surprised you haven't had more questions about magic," Nicole said, before adding, "Not that I could answer any of them but, still..."

This was my chance! "You could teach me how to brew a potion. A healing potion."

Nicole's eyebrow lifted. "Why? Hangover cure?"

My face soured as I sucked down coffee, and Nicole laughed.

"Fine, fine, you haven't been drinking. But a healing potion isn't what you think it is. They're usually for magical ailments, that kind of thing."

"So? Maybe I'll get a magical flu and need it."

Nicole sighed loudly. "Also, I'm not...I don't really *make* potions."

"That thing you gave me the first night—"

"The first potion I'd made in probably ten years," Nicole said with a half-smile. "And I screwed it up by putting too much valerian root and knocking you out. And that healing potion for Marie was...well, it wasn't very good either. It should've perked her right up."

"No, they were great potions. You should make more. Make me a healing potion. Or at least teach me how to make one."

"Even if I wanted to, I don't know how I'd teach you. While I don't have a *lot* of magic, the magic I do have is...unique. You and I can mix the same ingredients and come out with vastly different potions."

I remembered Gavon telling me the same thing, but I wasn't deterred. "But there must be some potions that don't require potion-maker magic, right?"

"Oh sure," Nicole said. "But I don't want you brewing any."

I frowned. "Why not?"

"Because potion-making is dangerous, smelly, and messy. And there's no point to it, not with modern medicines. And to my eyes, you look completely healthy, except for staying up too late." She paused then continued, "That's what Jeanie's been trying to tell you all this time. Magic's not something you can use to get ahead in life."

"So why does Marie have a red convertible?"

"Because Marie's a horrible person," Nicole said with a laugh. "And I don't want you to turn into her. She's going to get a rude awakening when she graduates and has to make it on her own. You can't just wave your hand and make things happen."

To my eyes, that was *exactly* what magic was, but I didn't argue. "So you won't teach me how to make a potion?"

"No, but how about we go out for the day? Spend the day together?"

"Why?"

She snorted. "Because you're my sister and it was your birthday this week? Also, Jeanie told me I had to get you out of the house because you've been sleeping too much."

Going back to sleep sounded like a better plan, but I didn't say it.

I couldn't remember the last time I'd spent the day with Nicole, and I kind of wished I was a little more awake to enjoy it. She and I piled into her neat little compact car and hit the highway, when Nicole announced we'd be going to the mall.

I groaned. "Why?"

"Why not?"

"Because...there are people there."

"You're sure in a mood today, Lexie."

"I'm *tired,*" I said, yawning to prove a point. "And you're dragging me to the *mall*. Which I *hate*. Because *people*."

"Duly noted." Nicole shook her head. "Where would you like to go instead?"

"Mmdunno."

"How about the bookstore?"

I sat up. "Yes, please."

Nicole reached across to jab her thumb into my thigh. "Brat." But she exited off the highway, driving toward our small city center.

We passed by the exit to Nicole's university, so I asked, "How's school?"

"Could do without the forty-five minute drive every morning, but other than that, it's great." Nicole flashed me a smile, and I pressed my head against the glass.

"Why don't you just have Jeanie magic you there?"

She sighed. "Lexie, magic isn't—"

"I know, but it almost seems like if you're not gonna use it, why have it?" I yawned again. "It's not like your appendix or anything. It's useful."

"I suppose it would be if I had it."

My eyes opened. I'd hurt her feelings. "Nicole, I'm sorry, I didn't mean to—"

"It's fine."

I slouched in my seat and picked at my hands the rest of the awkward car ride. Nicole was soon distracted by hunting down a parking lot, and I did my best to help her find one. We parked a few blocks away from the center, and I was more than happy to get out of the car into the pleasant October air.

While my town had the big box stores, we also had one small independent bookstore in our city center. Even better was the small coffee shop next door, which usually satisfied Nicole while I perused the overly crammed shop.

"Do you want anything?" Nicole asked.

"Coffee, please," I said, hoping that she still wasn't angry about my insensitive comment. "And...could you spot me fifty bucks? Gram gave me birthday cash, but I left it at home...Or wait, couldn't I just—"

"Lexie, this is how you get into trouble," Nicole warned me. "I'll pay for whatever you want. *No magic.*"

I wasn't sure I had the energy to summon the bill from the other side of town anyway, so I accepted the offer. While Nicole went to get us some coffees, I entered the store, breathing in the scent of old books and the almost-magical hum inside the shop.

I nodded to the old clerk and ducked between two rows of books. I ran my fingers along the spines, wondering if there were any magical books tucked between the spaces of financial management and investment books. Then again, if my family were the only magical ones in the area, why would our local bookstore have them?

"Reading something good?"

A smile grew on my face at the voice behind me. "Gavon! What are you doing here?"

"Was in the area and I saw you in here. Thought I'd check up on you after our match last night."

So does he live here or not? I dismissed the question and offered him a smile. "I'm sore as hell and exhausted."

His eyes twinkled. "Sparring's not so great after all, is it?"

"Are you kidding me? *I love it!* When can we do it again?"

He surveyed me like he was gauging my magic. "You've got a few days of healing left to do. I'd say we should hold off on any more matches until Friday at the earliest."

"*Friday?*" I said a little too loudly, catching the attention of the clerk at the front of the store.

"Oh, it's not that bad," Gavon said, plucking a book off the shelf over my head. I turned my head to read the title, *eCommerce and You: Making Your Fortune in the Modern Age*, then looked back at him with a frown.

"I can't wait until Friday," I said. "Why not...tomorrow?"

"Trust me when I say you won't be feeling back to normal until the end of the week." He finished flipping through the book and tucked it under his arm. "Look at you."

I looked down at myself, wondering what he saw. "I'm fine. Been caffeinating."

"Caffeine does many things, but it doesn't replenish magic, I'm afraid."

"Isn't there something that you can do? The primer said something about a healing potion. Or a healer—"

The stern look on his face cracked a bit. "Don't you happen to have one of those in your house?"

"Yeah, but she's not speaking to me after I...you know...the whole wall thing."

"Might be a good chance to kiss and make up then."

I groaned. "Come *on*, Gavon! Help me make a healing potion! I want to keep sparring."

"I'm sure you do, but taking shortcuts is never the way to accomplish anything—especially in magic. You'll just need to heal on your own. Or ask your sister for help."

"You know, I'm starting to think magic is one big cop-out."

"That's the spirit," Gavon said, sliding another thick book into my hand. "A consolation prize, to keep you busy for the next few days."

The Warrior's Guide to Dueling

"Sweet!" I cheered. "The primer is really lacking in this department."

Gavon laughed. "George Fisher, the man who wrote that primer, was a bit of a pacifist."

"He's a bit wordy too," I said, turning over the old book. I smiled at Gavon. "Thanks for this."

"Get some rest. I'll see you on Friday." And just like that, he was gone in a puff of purple.

"Lexie?" Nicole's voice echoed through the store.

I gripped the old book as she turned the corner, but yet again, Gavon seemed to have bewitched the book so she couldn't see it. And while I was grateful neither she nor the clerk asked me about it, I was starting to question why he felt the need to keep things from my aunt and sisters too.

Twelve

By Monday morning, I was still feeling the aftereffects of sparring, mostly because Jeanie came into my room and kicked me out every time she caught me sleeping during the day. I couldn't tell if she was punishing me for some unknown slight, or if she really thought I was that lazy. Either way, she never asked me why I was feeling so depleted, which saved me from coming up with a believable excuse.

I'd also spent most of Sunday trying to read my new dueling book, but would only get through a few pages before dozing off and incurring Jeanie's wrath. Still, what little I had read left me intrigued and desperate to read more.

As I was packing my bag for school on Monday, I deliberated if I should take it with me. I hadn't chanced bringing spell books with me, mostly because I could barely fit my own books in my bag. But the dueling book was only a few hundred pages, instead of seven hundred, so it fit neatly between my chemistry and math books.

"*Lexie*!"

I pulled my backpack on and walked down the stairs to meet Nicole at the landing. "What's up?"

"I'm taking you to school," Nicole said, her keys jangling in her hand.

"What about Marie?"

"She's...being a pill this morning," Nicole said with a tight expression. That was when I heard the raised voices coming from the kitchen. "Let's get out of here before they start throwing knives at each other."

All things considered, driving to school with Nicole was much more pleasant.

"Hey, so...can I magic myself home?" I asked as she parked in front of the school.

Nicole's eyes narrowed. "No magic at school, Lexie."

"Yeah, but—"

"And transport spells are complex—from what I hear. You shouldn't practice them without supervision."

"Can Jeanie show me?"

"How about this: when we go up to the compound, I'll make sure to get someone to show you how. If Gram says you can magically transport without help...*then* you can."

I stared at her. "Gram *still* doesn't want me to come up?"

"It's not that she doesn't want you to—"

"And meanwhile, I'm down here..." I was going to say on my own, but I really wasn't. I had Gavon, who, although for *some* reason thought it better to let me heal slowly, was pretty damned awesome.

"I know it's frustrating, but you just have to be patient. I'm sure it'll all get sorted eventually." She glanced behind me. "Get going and don't be late for class. And *no magic!*"

But Nicole's worries were unfounded, as my magic was still in no shape to be any trouble. I wondered how long it would take for me to be like Gavon, able to fire off attack spells like it was nothing. I was also secretly hoping the dueling book would give me some insight into how I could heal a little faster.

My first period was English, so I prepared myself to ignore whatever discussion we were having and dive into my book. I doubted I'd ever been so excited to read. I was careful to watch the reactions of my classmates as I pulled out the dueling primer, but not even Ms. Grace's attention drifted my way as she called the class to calm down for the morning announcements.

I chuckled to myself and opened my beautiful, big, magical, hidden book on dueling and dove in.

DUELING,
AN INTRODUCTION

Dueling is a time-honored tradition of the Warrior Magicals to settle disputes of land, honor, and leadership.

WHILE the specifics of the exchange of attack spells may vary from duel to duel, there are generally

three types of engagements;

inter Dominus, a duel between Guild- or Clanmasters. These duels may end when one party relents or perishes. In the event of a death, the successor to the Clanmaster may choose to continue the duel. This can result in days or even weeks-long duels. In 1412, the masters of clans McDonald and Campbell entered into a duel lasting seven months and killing twenty-seven Clanmasters on each side.

inter Hominus, a duel between two Magicals to settle personal disputes, is less commonly used, as it is often outlawed amongst clans and guilds. However, many a determined Magical has found loopholes in lax laws. Therefore, a comprehensive list of laws that Clan and Guildmasters may utilize is located in Appendix D to prevent such subterfuge.

Praecursio and Inductio are duels associated with memberships of a Guild. While an Enchanter Magical or a Healer Magical will have an effort commensurate with their specialty, Warrior Magicals will almost always duel. Depending on the age of the Magical, a Praecursio duel may test the strength of an untrained Magical against a trained magical his own age. Once the strength has been established, the Young Magical will be given to a Master to continue their training.

Inductio matches are almost always between the inductee and an established member of the Guild. The Guildmaster will select the inductor, or, if allowed, the inductee may choose.

Duels begin with the agreement between duelers and the shaking of the hands to seal the magical pact between them. A spelled circle will be constructed by the Bound Magic to keep the Attack Spells from causing any ill effects to the surrounding village.

All duels may end in one of two ways—ad deditionem, to the surrender, or ad mortem, to the death. Once the end of a duel has been set, the magic of the duelers bound them to the outcome.

There was an ink drawing of two men standing in the center of a large shaded dome. The attack spells in their hands was drawn eerily similar to how my magic looked. A crowd of people stood just outside, excited looks on their faces.

But I didn't recall a dome when I'd sparred with Gavon, and we hadn't shaken hands or anything like that. Then again, we hadn't done much of anything before I'd fallen ill.

The bell rang and I glanced up. I hadn't paid one bit of attention to anything in the class. Quickly, I jotted down a few notes from what I saw on the board, but they were nothing but mismatched phrases that made little sense. Frustrated, I tossed my notebook into my bag and hurried off to chemistry.

Promising myself I'd do better in my worst subject, I put the dueling book away. And I was good. For a few minutes. But the longer class droned on, the more my mind began to drift back to the book. I knew I shouldn't take it out—chemistry was my weakest subject and it would be easier to learn it now than try to play catch up later.

Five minutes into class, I pulled the dueling book out and kept reading.

THE ART OF SPARRING

SPARRING should be required as part of any Warrior Magical's daily regiment. A sparring match should be conducted by the same rules as a duel, except for the outcome-bounding by magic.

Because an agreement is not enacted, sparring should only occur with a Master or a Magical of equal power.

I'd gotten another three chapters about strategies and theories around attack spells in when the bell rang. Yet again, another class had passed me by and I couldn't recall a single thing other than what I'd read in the dueling book. Shouldering my bag, I trudged to history, hoping it would be a quiet class, and promising myself that I'd at least pay attention there.

But when I opened the history classroom door, I stopped short. The chalkboards were clear. I glanced around the room, looking for a possible substitute, but Mills was at his desk.

An empty chalkboard with the teacher in attendance meant only one thing.

Essay test.

I had no idea what it was on, and I sure didn't prepare anything. In fact, I couldn't even remember what we'd been studying up until this point. Something about colonialism?

A growing feeling of dread swam in my stomach as I took my seat. The rest of the class seemed unconcerned, so this must've been a planned test I'd forgotten about. Mills began passing out the test and I grimaced when I saw the topic—Mercantilism.

I tapped my pencil on my desk and glanced up at the chalkboard. Even though my magic was low, I was desperate. I couldn't fail a test, that would be... I couldn't even think about the consequences of it.

But I wasn't completely lost, I still had my magic. Maybe if I released a little bit down into my bag...

The room swam in front of me and I gripped the edge of my desk to keep from toppling over.

Mills glanced over to me. "Everything all right, Lexie?"

I nodded as I righted myself and released a nervous breath. The blank piece of paper stared back at me, all empty and...well, empty. So with a small prayer, I gripped my pen and began to write.

I was pretty damned sure I'd failed my history test. Then, as predicted, Marie left me in the parking lot. Already frustrated and cranky, I spent the long walk arguing with myself for being so irresponsible and reckless. My homework was a non-starter, too, because I'd no context for the haphazard notes I'd taken during the day.

Still, when seven rolled around, all I wanted to do was throw some spells around. Saying a quick goodbye to Jeanie and promising her I had my phone, I slipped out the back door and headed to the park.

Gavon was already waiting for me with the kindest smile I'd seen all day. "You look upset. What's wrong?"

"I just...can we spar again?" I asked, even though I really wasn't feeling up to it.

"That's not a good idea with your magic so low."

I slumped onto the picnic table and pressed my chin into my hand. "How can you...well, how can you tell?"

"Besides the fact that you look like a dead girl walking?" He joined me at the table. "I can sense your aura—all magical users can. Can you sense mine?"

I squinted at him for a moment. He looked the same as always. "What am I looking for exactly?"

"Can you feel my magic when I transport you to the beach?"

I nodded.

"You should be able to reach out with your magic, then," he said.

I closed my eyes and released my magic from the tight coil in the pit of my stomach. The world spun, and I retracted it quickly.

"See?" Gavon said, as if he could read my magic like a gas tank. "You're in no position to even use your magic, let alone spar with it."

I groaned loudly. "Is there nothing you can do to speed this process up? I'm just...I had a really crappy day and I want to blow some things up."

"What happened?"

"I think...I think I failed a history test," I said, picking at the wood.

"Failed?"

"*Failed.* Like, I don't even remember the topic," I said. "I couldn't even use my magic to help me. I was done."

"Alexis, I don't want this to interfere with your schoolwork. If you can't handle sparring at the same time, then we'll put it aside for a while—"

"No!" I wailed, taking him, and me, by surprise with the

ferocity. But for some reason I couldn't quite explain, I needed to spar with him. "No, I just...there's just so much to learn, and I'm trying to learn it all at once. But..." I sighed loudly. "I know that I screwed up today, and I promise I'll do better."

He considered me for a long time, then nodded. "Then we'll continue. But not tonight." He held out his hand and his magic flashed. When my eyes readjusted to the light, there were two large ice cream sundaes in his hand.

"W-what's that for?" I asked, taking one.

"You said you had a bad day, and I've had a trying one myself," he said, dipping his spoon into his and taking a bite. "I figured we could both enjoy a little treat."

I grinned and dug into my own. "So why was your day crappy?"

"Difficulties in the political sphere," he said, staring off into the distance.

"So you're in politics?" I asked, mouth full of ice cream.

"Not in the traditional sense. But any grouping of individuals tends to result in some political strategy to get them to agree on anything."

"Can't you just hocus pocus them?" I asked, waving my spoon around like a wand.

"If it were only that easy," Gavon said with a wry smile. "No, magic is of little help in my case. As is true with most things in life. A shortcut is rarely the easiest way to get something done."

"Poetic." I bit down on my spoon in thought. "That's kind of what Jeanie told me when I got magic. She said nothing would change, or that nothing should change. But everything has, you know? I can make light shoot out of my fingers and move from place to place without needing a car." I considered Marie's beautiful red convertible. Marie had magic, but she still chose to drive that thing around. "Then again, I guess we still have to live with the nonmagicals, huh?"

"What do you mean?"

"I'm just thinking about my sister. She can get to school every day using magic, but she chooses to drive that car, which I'm sure she used her magic to fix up," I said with a small scowl. "But it's like...even though we *can* do things, we still want to be seen by the nonmagicals as normal."

"Mm."

"So maybe outwardly, nothing's changed," I finished, realizing I'd eaten the last of my sundae. "I don't know. I'm still trying to make sense of everything."

"I think you're thinking too hard about it," Gavon said, placing his similarly empty bowl next to mine. They both disappeared in another flash of magic. "I've always considered magic to be simply another facet of my being."

"One you can't tell anyone about."

He smiled again. "Speaking of, I believe someone needs to get home and study their history so they don't fail another test."

I frowned; I'd almost forgotten about that. "How soon until we can spar again?"

"When your magic is back to full strength."

"And how long's that going to take?"

He smiled knowingly. "How long until you and Marie bury the hatchet?"

I glared at him. "Like *that'll* ever happen."

"I think you should give your sister a little more credit."

"I think you should *meet* her and then tell me I'm overreacting."

He shook his head. "One day, I think you two might be the best of friends. In the meantime, I think it's time you headed back home to study."

"Do you think I can hocus-pocus my teacher so I can retake the test?" I asked, a little hopefully.

"That, my dear, is called an Enchantment spell, and no, you won't be able to do them unless you have Enchanting magic," Gavon said as I opened my mouth to ask. "So you're going to have to figure your way back up to a passing grade the good old fashioned way."

Another night of rest, and I was feeling a little bit better. At least, I only pressed snooze four times on my alarm clock instead of seven. I left all my magical books at home and ignored the growing hum of magic under my skin, promising my magic that we would get all the sparring in at the end of the week. The bargaining worked, for the hum withdrew low enough for me to forget it was there.

There was still the giant problem of the failed history test, which weighed heavily on my shoulders when I walked into the history classroom. Mills caught my eye immediately and motioned for me to come see him. I swallowed and put my bag down, dreading what was coming.

"So about that test yesterday," he began quietly.

"Yeah," I said, unable to meet his eyes.

"Is everything all right with you?" he asked. "It's not like you to do so poorly."

"I just..." The truth was preferable, as best as I could tell it. "I have a lot going on at home right now, and it's been a little distracting."

"Anything I can help with?"

I shook my head. "I'm just...we got some news, and I'm trying to process it all. I'll do better on the next test, I promise."

"I don't normally do this, but I'm going to let you retake the test," Mills said with a look at the rest of the class. "It'll be different questions, but on the same topic."

A relieved sigh rumbled out of me. Some part of me wondered if Gavon *had* hocus-pocused him. But that would've been too good to be true. "Thank you."

The next day, I retook the test and, predictably, aced it. It was amazing what studying and paying attention could do.

Thirteen

By the end of the week, I was feeling like myself again. I could summon without even thinking about it, and my fingers sparked when I thought about sparring. On Thursday night, I even attempted a Transport spell from one end of my room to another, although I ended up banging my knee on the edge of my desk. For a brief moment, I'd thought I'd spliced myself open, so I decided against attempting any more solo trips until I was better at them.

I rushed through all of my assignments on Friday night, even completing a few that weren't due until later in the week. And based on how I felt after half a minute of sparring, it was a good thing I'd gotten ahead.

"*This is ridiculous*," I cried, lying face up in the sand.

Like last time, Gavon wasted no time in firing off attack spells at me, and, also like last time, after just a few seconds, I became incredibly lightheaded and couldn't continue.

Gavon offered his hand to help me up. "Rome wasn't built in a day, Alexis. All things considered, you're doing very well for having magic for less than two weeks."

"Yeah but, *seriously*," I said, ignoring his hand in favor of laying on the ground. After all, the world was spinning, so the more of me that connected with the earth the better. "*Three spells*, and I'm done."

"And last week, you could only wield two," Gavon said, finally retracting his hand. He sat down next to me, facing the moon shining on the gulf waters. "Progress is progress. And you are releasing *all* your energy in those three blasts."

"I can't help it," I said, chancing my ability to sit up. "You said it's all instinct, and my instinct is to fire off...well...*all of it*. And to go one week between spells? That's just...I'll be ninety before we can really get a good sparring match in."

It might've been a trick of the night, but I thought I saw him smile. But he was merely pensive. "Going slowly is preferable when you're learning how to spar. As you can see, you're talking about a lot of power. Wielded incorrectly, you might cause significant damage."

I snorted. "The only one I'm damaging is myself. You *swear* there's no way to speed up this process?"

"I'll see you next Friday."

I was *not* going to wait all week just to throw three spells, especially if sparring made me feel like I'd run a marathon the next morning. Gavon probably had his reasons for wanting me to heal slowly, but by midday Saturday, I was pretty sure his reasons were stupid. I knew he had healing potions, and it irked me that he wasn't handing them over. Especially considering my only other options weren't helping me either. Nicole point-blank told me to stop asking her how to brew potions and the primer had nothing except a long list of ways to maintain a magical herb garden and the best schedule for planting.

Sunday afternoon, I sat in the kitchen, flipping through my primer for the billionth time with a cup of coffee and a frown on my face. Jeanie and Nicole came and went, and neither mentioned the book I was looking at, but Jeanie stopped and asked why I was pouting.

"Just frustrated," I said, sitting up and tapping my fingers on the coffee mug. "Do we have any magic books?"

"Not here. Gram has a couple," Jeanie said. "Next time I go up there, I can grab you one."

"You're going up there?" I asked, sitting up. "Can I go?"

Something unreadable crossed her face. "Not yet, Lexie. I'm still working on it."

"Why does Gram hate me?"

Jeanie sighed loudly. "Gram doesn't hate you."

"So why aren't I allowed to go up to the compound?"

"Because that's what she wants right now."

"And we're magically-bound to that, huh?" I said, picking at my coffee mug.

"Where on earth did you hear that phrase?" Jeanie asked.

"Um..." I swallowed and scrambled through my foggy brain to come up with an excuse. "I made it up? I mean, you said that whatever she says goes, and it's bound by the clan."

"S-sure," Jeanie said, still eyeing me warily. "What kind of book do you want?"

"Potions."

Jeanie barked a laugh. "And have you blow up another room in this house? No way. Try again, kid."

I glared at her. "Jeanie, *come on*."

"If you want a potion, talk to Nicole."

"I already tried that. She said no."

"Then perhaps it's not such a good idea, hm?" Jeanie said, walking out of the kitchen.

"*Then perhaps it's not such a good idea,*" I said, mimicking her. A force smacked me upside the head, and I winced.

"I heard that," Jeanie's voice called.

By Monday, I was getting desperate. There was one thing I hadn't tried, one which had such a low likelihood of actually working that I hadn't actually considered it a viable option. But desperate times and all that.

I turned the corner to the senior lockers and kept my head down. As usual, everyone was too interested in their conversations to notice me, so I was able to thread my way through until I saw the object of my quest.

Approaching slowly, I considered all the things I could use as a bargaining chip. If it were Nicole, I might be able to offer some magic-type favors. But since Marie had just as much ability as I did, that wouldn't work.

I found my sister surrounded by her friends, a veiled smile on her face. She always looked calculating to me, like she was determining which person was of value to her at any given time. Her smile turned into a glower when she saw me standing at the other end of the hall, and she purposefully ignored me.

"M-Marie?" I asked quietly. "Can I talk to you?"

"I'm sorry, do you guys hear that?" Marie said loudly to her friends. "Sounds like the world's most obnoxious wind."

A twitter of laughter erupted around them, but Marie's friends took the hint and left her alone with me. She wore all the contempt of fifteen years' worth of hatred on her face.

"What?"

"I need your help with something."

She snorted. "Really? *Little Miss Perfect* needs my help? After what you did to me?"

"I am *really sorry* I lost control," I said, making sure to pump the sincerity into my voice. "*Really.* But I've been practicing a lot lately and I think I need you to heal me."

Marie studied me for a second and I thought I saw the ghost of concern on her face. "Your magic *is* really low."

"You can tell?"

"Of course I can, idiot. The question is...why?"

"Why is it so low?" I shrugged. "I've been practicing a lot—"

"No, why would I help you?"

I groaned. "Come on, Marie, don't do this. I need your help."

"Well, maybe you shouldn't do whatever it is you're doing if you can't handle it."

"Marie, please. You're my big sister, and I need you."

She laughed, but there was no love in it. "After the stunt you pulled? No way. Figure it out yourself." She slammed her locker shut and glared at me. "And, for the record, you *aren't* my sister."

Marie had been throwing that insult in my face for as long as I'd been alive, and except for a few months when I was six, I'd never actually believed it. But what had truly hurt was that Marie had been my last option for healing quicker, and now that I'd used it up, I had nothing left to try but patience. And even though it was severely diminished, that magical hum tingled under my skin, begging to be used.

Gavon wasn't at the park that night either, which felt appropriate for the disappointing day I was having. I'd gotten accustomed to him showing up whenever I was down or upset, being an ear to talk to.

My face must've betrayed my mood, because Nicole asked me what was wrong when I walked by her open door.

I stopped and leaned against the doorframe. "Had a bad day."

"Wanna talk about it?"

I shrugged and crossed the room to climb into her bed, like I had when I was younger. Nicole moved her thick chemistry books out of the way and patted her pillow for me to lie down on.

"What's wrong? Did you fail another test?" she asked.

I winced. "How'd you find out?"

"Mills called Jeanie and asked if everything was okay with you," Nicole said with a smile. "Granted, she's used to fielding phone calls about Marie, but this was your first."

"I retook the test and passed it," I said, sitting up. "I was just having a bad day."

"You seem to be having a lot of those recently. So what did you want to talk about?"

How can I heal faster after sparring? Why does Gram hate me? Why didn't you tell me about magic sooner? Why do I get the feeling everyone's keeping secrets from me?

"Why does Marie hate me?"

"Currently? You tossed her through the wall."

I frowned. "That was an accident."

Nicole chuckled and leaned back on her pillows. "Yeah, but...it wouldn't have happened if you didn't want to on some level."

"I mean." I picked at her comforter. "The spell was...I mean, it was really easy to do. I felt like I was..." I wasn't sure I wanted to tell Nicole how great attack spells were, in case she told Jeanie and I got in trouble. "I didn't know what would happen. I didn't want to *hurt* her."

"I know, Lexie," Nicole said. "And Marie's just...well, she's Marie. She's always been Marie and we just have to love her."

"Do we though?"

"Try to understand. Marie's under a lot of pressure right now. She's graduating high school in May. And to be perfectly honest, she's not really doing so hot." Nicole glanced out of her open door. "She hasn't even applied for college. I don't think she has the grades to get in. And her ego's too big to consider community college."

"So what does that have to do with being awful to me?"

"Lexie, can't you see she's jealous of you? School's always come easily to you, and it's never been for Marie. And now she's realizing that you can't just float your way through life and expect everything to work out. Magic and good looks can only do so much for you."

I'd never considered that perfect Marie would ever be jealous of me, but that didn't excuse her crappy behavior. "I think she blames me for what happened to Mom."

"That's ridiculous," Nicole said with a harshness that surprised me. "You had *nothing* to do with Mom's death."

Something tickled in the back of my mind, a memory of a man that disappeared before I could grasp it.

"I think part of the problem is that Jeanie lets her get away with too much," Nicole said, again, glancing out the door. "The thing about magic is that you have what you're born with, and Jeanie never had much to begin with. Marie's more powerful than she is, and Jeanie knows it. But Jeanie can also take away Marie's magic, which she does *all the time.*"

"Take away her magic?" I asked.

"Do you remember your Magic's Eve, when Jeanie stopped all that destruction?" I nodded. "That was a grounding spell. As your guardian, she can take away your magic to punish you."

I gulped, thankful that Jeanie hadn't grounded me yet.

"So when Jeanie does that, Marie gets in that convertible and disappears for a few nights," Nicole said. "And round and round they go. I think Jeanie's secretly counting down the hours until Marie moves out. Marie's never adjusted to living here and as much as I hate it, I think we'll all be happier when we're living in separate spaces."

"Are you going to move out?" I asked quietly. I didn't like the idea of living alone with Jeanie. Something told me I'd suddenly become responsible for all the meal planning.

"Not for a while," Nicole said. "Someday, maybe. After you graduate."

I opened my mouth to respond when my gaze landed on her open closet—or more specifically, the potion book that sat discarded on the floor. And suddenly, an idea took root in the back of my mind. Perhaps I wasn't completely out of options yet.

"Well, I should probably get started on my homework," I said, pushing myself to stand.

"Let me know if you need any help with chemistry," Nicole said, pulling her own books back to her. I glanced at the chemistry book, then the potions book on the floor, and then hurried out of the room.

Fourteen

The next afternoon, I made use of the hours before Nicole and Jeanie returned from school and work. I retrieved the potion book from Nicole's closet and locked myself in my room to read.

POTIONS FOR POTION-MAKERS

The Magic of potion-making is one of the oldest known magical specialties in existence.

The potions in this book should only be used by a practiced potion-maker.

"Yeah, yeah, yeah," I said, flipping past the preface and through the old pages until I found the section I was looking for.

HEALING POTIONS

One of the Potion-maker's most oft-requested concoctions is the Healing Potion. Hundreds of variations exist and each Potion-maker may find their own peculiarities and tastes when making the draught.

Most Healing Potions contain some variation of calming herbs such as lavender and rosemary or echinacea and peppermint combined with a magical conductive object such as unicorn hair or goblin toenails.

"Unicorn hair? Goblin—bleh—toenails?"

A truly gifted Potion-maker will be able to convert the herbs without the use of a conduit. Indeed, the more powerful the Potion-making magic imbued within the draught, the more potent the potion.

PREPARATION OF THE HERBS

The most effective healing potions must be kept in a cauldron for up to a fortnight. But in the case of an emergency, additional magical objects

may be added to a draught and the potion may be available in as little as two sunrises.

"A fortnight? Two days?" I grunted to myself. I couldn't wait that long. I flipped through the section until I found something that looked helpful.

HEALING POTION #35

Ingredients:

One Quart of Apple Vinegar;

One bundle of Lavender, grown on the left corner of a south-facing garden;

One quarter pound of Echinacea root, harvested on the Third Saturday in October;

One spider web, found in the seventh Tuesday of an odd year;

Boil exactly thirteen minutes;

Then add,

Seven mushroom caps, added with the caps facing down;

Set aside for one hour in good sun, stir three times clockwise, then four

counter-clockwise.

Drink in good health.

"Gross," I said, shaking my head.

Unfortunately, it was the only spell in the book that had ingredients I could get at the grocery store—minus that spider's web. All the other potions included parts and pieces from animals that I hadn't known existed.

Some part of me began to question whether making and drinking this potion was a good idea. But the other, louder part that wanted very much to start sparring every day told the other part to stuff it.

The next day, I walked to the grocery store with my list of ingredients in hand. The mushrooms and apple cider vinegar were easy enough to find; I decided on the big, beefy portobellos instead of the tiny button mushrooms. But after looking in the hippie foods section, all I came up with for lavender and echinacea were teas.

"Well, it'll have to do."

After the long walk home, the next object I needed was a cauldron. I scoured Nicole's closet, finding a lot of shoes and old textbooks, but no big tubs where I could brew a potion. I'd even spent a few minutes up in the attic nosing around, but found nothing except some old boxes of baby clothes. My time was running short, I decided to use one of Jeanie's cheap pots instead, and hoped that whatever I made, some dish soap would clean it out.

I emptied the bottle of apple cider vinegar and tossed in three bags each of the lavender and echinacea teas. Then, glancing at the potion book again, I tossed in another three echinacea bags, hoping that it would equate to a full pound of root.

Then the last thing I needed was a spider web.

I wasn't particularly squeamish, but the idea of hunting around the house for a spider's web was...unappetizing. Luckily, my magic had returned enough that I could stomach a small summoning spell. I hadn't properly practiced in some time, having been too depleted by sparring, and my magic seemed much more willing to do what I said.

I found a spider web in the corner of the attic, and when I opened my eyes, it floated delicately in front of me. With a nod, my magic dropped it into the simmering pot.

A puff of gray smoke released from the concoction, and the whole kitchen began to smell of rotten eggs. I gagged and covered my mouth, but I was secretly relieved. I'd thought that I was doing a whole bunch of nothing.

I glanced at the clock and counted down the time. Then, holding my breath, I dropped in the seven mushrooms, caps up as instructed.

The mixture, now the texture of thick gravy, bubbled and gurgled then began smoking. I cried out and yanked the pot off the stove, sticking it out the open window and letting it cool down. But when I peered inside, there was a dark silvery mixture, not unlike the one that Nicole had given me to calm me down on my

Magic's Eve.

The kitchen smelled something awful, so I left the pot on the brick windowsill and turned on all the fans and opened all the windows. I even hunted down the air freshener and sprayed it around, which only made the kitchen smell like hot ass and Febreze.

The hour ticked down and the mixture grew more and more gel-like. When enough time had passed, I dipped a spoon into the mixture and jumped back; it was a lot more liquid than I'd expected. I scooped out a small bit and brought it to my face.

"This is probably a really, *really* bad idea," I said, staring at the liquid. But I didn't have time or materials to try again.

Then, I heard tires roll up the driveway outside. So I shoved the concoction into my mouth.

It tasted like toenails.

Trying not to spit it back up, I ran to the fridge and pulled out a cola, cracking it open and sucking it down quickly. The mixture sat horribly in my stomach, but I was more concerned about Jeanie or Nicole finding me with a potion brewed in the kitchen.

Praying that I had more control over my magic, I made all the contraband, including the pot of goopy mixture, disappear and end up...somewhere else. I wasn't quite sure where I'd put it, but I forgot all about it when Jeanie walked into the kitchen.

She sniffed. "The hell is going on in here?"

"Science project," I said, clenching my jaw together to keep the contents of my stomach from coming back up.

"Uh-huh. Where is it?"

"My group just left with it," I said, amazed at how quickly the lies were coming to me. In fact, I felt more energetic than I had in days—weeks, almost. My feet could've lifted off and flown me to the sparring beach.

Jeanie flicked her wrists, and the smell disappeared. "That's better. But hey, I'm glad you're making friends. You're entirely too solitary, Lexie."

"Mmm-hm." I flashed a grin. "I've actually got to go to the library for a bit."

"Want a ride?"

"Nah, I can walk. I've been doing it a lot lately. Might as well keep doing it!" I laughed a little too loudly, and chalked it up to the fact that I was back to full strength.

"Are you okay?"

"*Never better!*"

Jeanie left me in the kitchen, muttering something about teenagers. Giggling to myself, I closed my eyes and sent my magic to the beach then enjoyed the rush as my body followed.

I landed with an *oomph* on the white sand. Looking up, I'd landed *exactly* where I'd wanted to. My first real transport spell and I was already kicking ass at it.

"Alexis, what are you doing here?" Gavon stood behind me, a curious look on his face.

"I transported myself!" I barked.

"I can see that, You didn't answer my question. Your magic's not yet replenished. You should go back home."

"Nah, I took a thing. It's fine." My cheeks were starting to hurt from the smile on my face. His eyes narrowed at my excitement—was I that transparent? Or perhaps I shouldn't have said anything. I bounced from one foot to the other. "My sister, she healed me."

"She did?" He sounded surprised.

"Yup!" Boy, I couldn't believe how easy it was to lie just then.

"Alexis, are you all right?"

"Perfect. Let's go, go, go!" I said with a laugh that was too high-pitched and loud to be mine. Without waiting for him to respond, I formed an attack spell and let it fly.

He dodged it with ease and waved his hands at me. "Lexie, you need to take a second—"

I shook my head and formed three more. The potion, I figured, must be kicking in, for I'd never felt so alive. Spell after spell came flying from my hands without rhyme or reason.

That was, until one came flying back at me, knocking me to the sand with a loud *thump*. I jumped to my feet, ready to return the folly when the world tilted, and with it, came the contents of my stomach.

Gavon called my name, but I could barely hear him over the sound of my retching. When it ended, he rested a hand on my shoulder as he magicked away the mess I'd just made.

"Alexis, at the risk of stating the obvious, are you sick? And why are your hands turning purple?"

My gaze flew to my hands, and my mouth opened in a soundless scream. Thick, dark purple splotches had appeared on my hands and up my arms and, if I were to wager a guess, all over my face.

"Alexis..." Gavon said, sounding more stern than worried now. "What did you do?"

"I...I..." Would dying result in less trouble than telling the truth?

"Alexis."

"I...tried to make a healing potion," I whispered.

Gavon's voice was steady. "And why were you making a healing potion?"

"Because I'm not healing fast enough on my own," I said, shame flooding my cheeks. "And I wanted to keep sparring."

"Why is sparring so important to you?"

I didn't have an answer I was comfortable voicing just yet.

Gavon cleared his throat after a few moments. "Do you want to tell me what kind of potion you made?"

"It was the one...it had..." Another wave of nausea threatened to empty my stomach again. "Oh man... Lavender?"

Gavon cut me off with a loud sigh. "Where did you find this potion? In one of your sister's books?"

I nodded.

"Did you not read the warning on the first page that said these potions were specifically for potion-makers?"

I flinched.

"The first rule of making potions is that you never drink something unless you know exactly what you're doing. If you'd mixed the wrong ingredients together, you could have died. Do you understand how..." He trailed off and considered me for a second. "Please don't do anything like that again."

I looked at my hands, still splotched purple. "Do you think this is permanent?"

He chuckled softly. "I think you got most of it out of your system. They'll probably fade by morning."

"What am I supposed to do about sparring?" I said, on the verge of tears. "Gavon, it just isn't *fair*. I shouldn't have to wait a week and feel so damned *awful* afterward." When he opened his mouth, I growled, "And *don't* say I shouldn't spar because we both know that's not an option."

"I was going to say that you need to be patient. Your progress has been extraordinary so far. You must realize that."

I looked at the gulf again. "It's just frustrating. Especially because..." I swallowed and rubbed my splotchy hands. "Because Marie won't help. I read in the book that Healers can replenish magic. But when I asked her she said...she told me she wouldn't help."

"I'm sure that's not true."

"She told me that I'm not really her sister," I said flatly.

A flash of concern crossed Gavon's face. "She said *what*?"

"When I asked her to heal me, she said that I wasn't her sister. I mean, I know that's not really true, but...Gavon, she *hates* me. I mean, even before the whole attack spell incident, she's always hated me. She's always said that I'm the reason Mom died."

Gavon stared at me, and I couldn't tell if he was pitying me or getting angry. When he finally spoke, his voice was firm. "Alexis, there is no way you should be blamed for what happened to your mother. Even Marie can't honestly think otherwise."

I shrugged. "I mean, if there's such thing as healing magic, why'd she die?"

His mouth opened and closed, and he ran a hand down his face. "I don't have a good answer for that, Lexie."

I wasn't sure which surprised me more, the defeated sound of his voice or the way he called me Lexie.

"Why don't you go home and get some rest. In the morning, ask your sister if she'll help you again. I have a feeling she'll have a different response."

"What, are you going to hocus-pocus her?" I snorted.

Gavon looked at the sky innocently.

"What if she stills says no? I don't think there's enough magic in the universe to make Marie like me right now."

He was silent for a long time. "If she doesn't oblige, I'll bring you a healing potion myself."

I *knew* he'd been holding out on me. "You can brew potions?"

"There are potions that non-potion-makers can make, but you won't find them in a potion-maker's book. And no, you can't have that book," he said when I opened my mouth. "Maybe in a few years, when you've become a little more advanced and a little less...reckless."

"Trust me, my potion making days are over," I said, looking at my palm, still tinged purple.

"Do you want me to get you back home?"

I nodded. "I think I overdid it a bit."

"I'll see you next week." And just like that, I was back in my bedroom.

Fifteen

It took all my cunning to avoid being seen by Jeanie or Nicole for the rest of the night, especially as I had to vomit three more times and my bathroom was down the hall. Twice, Nicole knocked on the door to ask if I was all right, and I told her I'd eaten some bad fish at school.

When I awoke the next morning, my skin was only faintly purple, and only when I looked really closely in the mirror. But even worse, the potion seemed to have worn off, and I was back to the exhaustion levels that had become the norm for me since I'd started sparring.

I crossed the room and cracked open my door, staring at the closed one across the hall. I had a long, silent argument with myself about whether or not I should attempt to talk to Marie, and if Gavon was right about her.

I groaned and banged my head against the frame. Then I crossed the hall and rapped on Marie's door. I heard a grunt then three loud footsteps before the door cracked.

Marie opened her mouth to scream at me, but confusion and surprise crossed her face. "What the hell happened to you? Why are you...*purple*?"

"Ssh!" I said, pushing her inside her room and closing the door. "Is it that noticeable?"

Marie cackled loudly. "You look *ridiculous!* What did you do?"

"I took a bad potion," I said, waving her off. "Because *somebody* wouldn't heal me."

"So you, who's never made a potion in her *life*, decided to brew a healing potion." Her eyes widened and she giggled again. "You didn't use one of Nicole's, did you?"

I glared at her, and she howled in laughter. "*Keep quiet!*"

"Oh, my *God*, this is classic, Lexie. *Classic!*"

"Look, can you just...*please* heal me?" I asked.

I was ninety percent sure she was about to kick me out of her room, but to my surprise, she shrugged. "Fine, since you *obviously* can't do anything right. I don't want people at school thinking I have a purple cow for a sister."

Without waiting for me to respond, she pressed one hand against my chest, and another to my back.

"What are you—"

"Shut *up*. I haven't done this in forever."

The feeling was subtle at first, indistinguishable from the pressure of her hands against my t-shirt. But it grew into a tingling warmth that spread from my core all the way down to my toes. Closing my eyes, I reveled in the sensation, which filled me with the kind of joy that comes with spending all day in the sun.

Just as abruptly, she released me, but the warm feeling remained, energizing me. I glanced down at my hands; the purple was almost gone.

"I... Marie?"

She'd gone pale, bracing herself against her vanity and looking like she was going to hurl. "Scram. We're done here. And don't you dare breathe a word of this to Jeanie or Nicole."

I nodded, but didn't move. "Are you sure you're okay?"

"I said, *get lost*!"

"Lexie, quit bothering your sister!" Jeanie called from up the stairs.

I scrambled out of the room, concerned that Jeanie would ask why Marie and I were suddenly talking to each other and blow whatever secret I was trying to keep from her. I came down the stairs to the kitchen, where Nicole was already waiting.

"Feeling better?" she asked.

"Much," I replied, sitting down. Every few minutes, I glanced at the stairway visible from the living room, hoping I'd see Marie walking down the stairs. When she finally came down, the bags were still visible under her eyes, but her signature scowl was on point.

"Marie, I got another call from school yesterday," Jeanie said.

A huge roll of the eyes. "*And?*"

"You failed another English test."

She flipped a lock of hair over her shoulder. "So? I'm not going to college."

"Oh?" Jeanie asked hotly. "And what, pray tell, are you going to do with your life? Move to Hollywood?"

Marie's eyes narrowed. "For your information, I don't *need* to worry about that anymore. When I move out—"

"Yeah, when you move out, you're in for a rude awakening. I'll be sure to visit at the burger place where you're dipping chicken nuggets."

Marie glared at Jeanie, then stood up. "Let's go."

I ducked my head and followed her out of the kitchen, not wanting to get in the middle of their fight. It took Marie almost the whole ride to school to finally say something.

"I won't be flipping burgers, I know that much. Gonna be moving out a whole lot sooner now."

I didn't know how to respond to that, so I just kept quiet.

Thanks to Marie's magic, I felt more awake than I had in weeks. Even more surprising, my magic felt, well, balanced. I was a little hesitant to ruin this nice feeling by using all my magic sparring with Gavon. But that new voice, the one I attributed to my magic, was ecstatic at the thought of increasing our lessons to more than half an hour every week.

Though I was a little concerned about Marie. When I got home (my very first transport spell from school), her car was already in the driveway and she was passed out on her bed. I asked if she needed anything and she called me a long list of hurtful names, so I left her alone.

I finished my homework just as Jeanie and Nicole got home,

and made an excuse for Marie ("she said she was going out with her friends") so that Jeanie wouldn't bother her.

"That girl, I swear," Jeanie said. "She's in for a real surprise when she moves out."

"Yeah, so...I'm going for another walk," I said.

"You've been walking a lot lately," Jeanie said. "Training for a marathon?"

"Helps me clear my head, control my magic," I replied, hoping it was a good enough excuse.

"Fine, whatever. Take your phone."

I showed her the phone from my back pocket then walked out the door. It was growing darker earlier, but I still didn't want to chance my neighbors seeing me disappear from the front step. So I crept around to the back of Marie's car and released my magic.

Having practiced a few times, I was finally able to land softly on my feet, instead of head-first into the sand. The sun was nearly set, but I kind of hoped that Gavon would—

He appeared before I could finish my thought, a proud smile on his face. "Look who's back to full strength."

"Why are you always here when I get here?" I asked, putting my hand on my hip.

"I have a charm on this area," Gavon said. "Lets me know when someone magical is arriving."

I quirked my brow. "Why?"

"Which of your sisters healed you?" It didn't escape my notice that he didn't answer my question, but I had several others that were more important.

"Marie," I said. "Shockingly."

"I don't find that surprising at all, Alexis."

"You don't know Marie. She's...well, she's really selfish. And up until this morning, she's basically been acting like I don't exist so..." I eyed him. "You didn't hocus-pocus her, did you?"

"As I've explained, the only way to sway a human mind is to use an Enchantment Spell, and only Enchanters can do that."

"Yeah, you say that but..." I stared at him.

After a moment, he sighed. "I swear I didn't...'hocus-pocus' your sister. I simply had a feeling that she would feel compelled to help you when she saw how drained you were. She is a healer, after all. They're hardwired to care about others."

I couldn't help but bark laughter at that. "They must've left out a wire in Marie's brain."

"Be nice."

"Still though, she was kind of sick after she did it," I said thoughtfully. "Why?"

"The same reason you become ill after you spar," Gavon said. "Just like you, the more your sister heals, the quicker she'll be able to replenish her own supply." A large glass container filled with a dark liquid appeared in his hands. "Until then, we'll use this. I brewed it this morning."

I grinned. "What happened to being patient?"

"It seems that you don't listen to me, so we might as well," he said with a tight expression. I had the good grace to blush, but was thankful he was finally letting up a bit. "Are you ready to begin?"

I nodded excitedly.

"Remember," he said, forming an attack spell in his hand. It glowed purple, beautiful with power. "This is all instinct. You'll want to overthink it, but resist that urge." And with that, he released the spell toward me.

I released one of my own, visualizing two pool balls knocking into each other. The spells spiraled out across the water, cutting a line in the waves.

"Excellent work, Alexis," Gavon said, and he actually sounded impressed. "How are you feeling?"

I nodded. "Good."

"Then let's continue."

He let loose two more spells, a little faster than before. I used my magic to deflect the first, but I scrambled out of the way of the second, as it left a smoking mark on the sand behind me.

"Can your spells... Can they kill me?" I asked, looking at the black splotch might've been me.

He smiled. "These will sting a little, but no more."

"What if I hit you?" I asked, flexing my hand. "I'm using a lot of magic, what if—"

"Alexis, you can't hurt me. Not yet, anyway," Gavon said. "Remember what I said about overthinking?"

"Right. Don't," I said, lowering my hand.

"Why don't you try an attack spell on me?" he said. "See if you can find an opening."

Three attack spells came at me in quick succession. I moved faster than I'd thought possible, twisting around them, but I couldn't find the right moment to fight back. Gavon repeated the same three spells, and again, I couldn't figure out how to fight back.

The third time, I saw it—the split second between the first and second spells, and I released a spell before I could stop myself. It hit Gavon and sent him back a few steps, but he remained upright.

"Excellent work!" he said, after coughing a bit.

"Did I hurt you?" I asked, rushing forward.

"Not at all, my dear," Gavon said, waving me off. "Because you don't want to."

"I—What?"

He rubbed the spot on his chest then motioned for me to follow him over to the healing potion. He ladled some in a cup for himself and handed me a glass. It didn't taste much better than the brew I'd made, but I instantly felt better.

"You won't hurt me because you don't want to," Gavon said. "When you attacked your sister, you wanted to hurt her, and so you did."

I blushed and drank more of the potion. I didn't want to think about what kind of a person that made me.

"That's why it's very important for you to control your emotions," Gavon said. "You've got the makings of a very powerful spell maker, but only if you can maintain control over your emotions. That is what separates a true Warrior from—"

"So I do have Warrior magic then?" I said, looking at him.

Gavon was silent, and a flash of annoyance crossed his face. Then he said, "You wouldn't be able to use attack spells if you didn't."

"But didn't specialties die out with the Separation?" I asked quietly. If Warriors used attack spells, that meant Gavon was a Warrior too. My heart beat a little faster for reasons I wasn't quite ready to think about yet.

"Anomalies happen." He placed his now-empty potion cup on the ground. "Ready to continue?"

Gavon's healing potion allowed me to fight for a grand total of fifteen minutes more before I gave up.

"Here," he said, handing me some more potion.

I drank it dutifully, but it didn't seem to pack as much punch as it had before. "I still feel weak."

"You're still strengthening your magic," Gavon said, helping me to stand. "Potions will help, but they aren't a cure-all. It'll still take some time to grow into it."

"How long until I don't need a potion at all?"

"Patience, Alexis."

I blew air out between my lips.

"*Patience.*"

I didn't even remember transporting back to my room, but when I awoke, the familiar aches and pains wracked my body. Sure, I had patience, and at least I was somewhat awake, but I also had a cure-all across the hall from me.

I rolled out of bed and padded across the carpet, knocking softly on Marie's closed door.

A muffled cry and three stomps later, she opened the door, ready to bark at me for waking her up too early. Her eyes narrowed then widened, and she slumped against the door. "Crap Lexie, again?"

"Please?"

"Yesterday really kicked my ass." She opened her door wider and let me walk inside. "I don't have enough juice to give you a full recharge."

"I'm not an iPhone," I said, taking a seat on her bed while she placed her hands over my heart and back. She only gave me a small fraction of her power, but it was enough to clear the fog out of my mind.

"That's all. And I'm not doing this tomorrow, so you have to figure something else out." She sank to her bed and crawled under the covers.

"Thanks," I said, standing but not leaving. A question had been nagging at me since my conversation with Gavon. And if there was one thing I knew, it was that Marie would give it to me straight.

"So what really happened with Dad?" I asked.

"Found out we had magic and left," Marie snapped. "Now get the hell out of my room."

Sixteen

Even a fraction of Marie's magic was enough to jumpstart my own healing, so by the end of the day, I was awake and eager to spar again. But Gavon wasn't having any of it, so we practiced summoning and transporting instead, and he sent me home early with a mug of healing potion. The next night was the same, a few hours of magical tutelage and a cup of healing potion. By the third night, I was back to sparking at the fingertips, so we sparred for half an hour before I threw in the towel.

To my complete surprise, Marie had been willing to heal me the next morning. Whatever had changed with her, she didn't tell me about it. But she'd taken to walking around the house with a smug superiority that even made Jeanie curious. Besides our five-minute healing sessions, Marie treated me exactly the same, and wasn't above leaving me stranded in the parking lot. But the joke was on her, as I was able to transport myself back home.

Gavon and I continued in this pattern, two or three days of

non-sparring tutelage and one night of sparring. I didn't quite miss it, as long as I could spend a few hours picking Gavon's brain. He was so knowledgeable and patient, and on the odd chance he *didn't* know an answer to my question, he was able to summon a book from some unknown magical library. Usually, he gave the book to me afterwards, so I had begun to assemble my own collection. When the pile grew too large to fit under my bed, he showed me how to create a pocket to stick the books into, and then how to grow the size of my backpack so I could carry more books. When I complained that my backpack was too heavy, he showed me how to change its weight.

Unfortunately, I had to keep my magical progress a secret from Jeanie, and, by extension, Nicole. One time, I'd slipped up and summoned a jug of milk from the store in front of Nicole, and she'd lectured me about why I shouldn't just take things that weren't mine. Then I got *another* lecture from Jeanie about when and how to use magic. Ever since, I just didn't do any magic around them period.

So imagine my surprise when Jeanie dropped a bomb the Wednesday before Thanksgiving at breakfast.

"Gram's letting you come up tomorrow," she said with a satisfied smile.

If she'd thought this was welcome news, she was mistaken. It had been over a month since I'd grown into my magic, and not one of the mysterious magicals in Salem had come down to visit. As far as I was concerned, it was too little, too late.

"How generous of her."

"Lexie, don't start," Jeanie said. "You have to be on your best behavior up there. Please. For me."

I opened my mouth to argue that I didn't want to go, that Gram and her stupid magical people could stay up there, but then I noticed the dark circles under Jeanie's eyes. If it had taken her a whole six weeks to convince Gram that I was...whatever, *good enough* to come up to the compound, she must've really worked hard at it. It was the least I could do to just go up there and be a good kid.

But I wasn't doing it for Gram.

"Okay," I said. "I will."

Jeanie smiled and patted my hand. "And I promise you I'll find someone to help explain magic better than I can."

"Right, because I don't know anything about magic," I said slowly. That might be a problem. I *wasn't* a novice anymore; I could summon, conjure, and transport myself, although I was pretty sure Jeanie hadn't noticed any of that. She was definitely unaware that I could spar for almost a full hour, and had gone from simply flinging whatever came out of my hands to making split-second decisions on the type and ferocity of my magic.

"If everything goes well, you might be up there every weekend," Jeanie said excitedly, taking my plate. "Play your cards right, Lexie, and you'll get instruction from Gram herself."

"Hooray..."

Although I'd made a lot of progress in the past few weeks, I was still lightyears behind Gavon. Sparring with him was like trying to tap dance with Fred Astaire, although he had the good grace to be humble in his now almost daily ass-kicking.

"Excellent work, Alexis!" Gavon said as he deflected one of my attack spells and sent back two powerful ones of his own.

I held up my hands and envisioned a forcefield around myself. The spells bounced harmlessly off the edge of it.

"What is that?" Gavon asked, cocking his head to the side.

"I saw it in Star Trek," I said with a small shrug. "I wasn't sure it'd work but—" His spell tore clean through the forcefield and sent me flying back into the sand. I landed with an *oomph*, more pained by my butt than the spell.

"I'd stick with the classical defensive measures we've been working on," Gavon said, reaching a hand out to help me up. "They've worked for thousands of years."

"Fine," I snapped, taking his hand. I sent a spell through my hand to his. Sadly, it didn't as much as leave a mark on him.

"Nice try," Gavon said.

I glared at him, brushing myself off. Then, quickly, fired an attack spell, then another, and with a flourish, once more.

"Very good," Gavon said, deflecting them with ease. "Next time, try getting in two spells before you turn around."

"Wha?" I said, stopping for a moment. That was costly as I nearly missed a fast moving spell. "Time out. What?

"Your technique," Gavon said. "It's a tad showy for my taste, and doing all the spinning slows you down."

I frowned at him. "I thought you said it was all instinct?"

"It is," Gavon said. "And I'm improving your instincts."

"Ah hah—*gack*!" My body moved of its own accord, twisting out of the way of one of his spells. I stopped, gasping at myself and the feeling of having *something else* move me. "What just happened?"

"Ah, magical memory," Gavon said with a smile.

"What's that?"

"When you cast a spell, it leaves an imprint, the same way an experience leaves a memory in your mind. Quick and easy spells fade quickly while larger, more complex spells, such as fighting spells, leave a longer impression. When you spar," he cast a spell, "you are building your magical memory so you can rely on it in a match, versus thinking about it."

"Huh," I said, absorbing the concept in the split second between his magical parries. "So if I keep practicing, you're saying I'll get more of these memories, and it'll start taking over?"

"That's the idea."

"And what about healers? Do they have magical memories too?"

He shook his head. "Not to my knowledge."

"What kind of limits are there to healing?" I asked. "Marie's not getting as woozy as she used to, either. Can she grow stronger as a healer? Could she bring someone back from the dead? Could she cure cancer?"

"She can grow stronger, but her magic will mostly cure magical maladies," Gavon said, continuing to spar with me and not even breaking a sweat. "And, just like you, a healer with no practice can't do much of anything."

"But mostly, they're good for replenishing magic?"

"That, and I've read about healers who become skilled in wound repairs as well," Gavon said. "Mostly, healers were there to heal the warriors."

"It's almost like the yin and yang," I said. "A warrior loses magic, and a healer replenishes."

"You see," Gavon said. "You and your sister have no choice but to get along."

"Someone might want to tell her that." The familiar dizzy sensation washed over me, and I swayed on my feet but remained standing. "I think I need a minute. How long did we spar for?"

"Almost a full hour," he said, surveying me. "Are you all right?"

I considered my power. It was low, but not dangerously so. "I don't want to push it tonight. I've got a big day tomorrow, apparently."

"Oh?"

"We're headed up to my Gram's for Thanksgiving," I said, stretching my arms and rubbing my shoulder. "First time seeing the family since...well, since ever."

"You haven't seen them? That's surprising."

"You're telling me," I said. "First I find out I have magic then I find out I apparently have this *huge* family up in Massachusetts that I've never met. Cousins and aunts and uncles."

He made a noise that sounded like annoyance.

"Hey, how would I transport myself there? Like, how do I get somewhere I've never been?" I was stalling, but I didn't like the idea of not seeing Gavon for a few days.

"You might not be able to transport into the compound. My guess is that it has some magical protections around it that prevent anyone from just showing up."

That made sense, I supposed.

"But the general technique is similar to summoning an object in an unknown location. The farther away the location is, the more magic is required. Let's practice step-by-step. I want you to transport yourself to the waterline."

I pursed my lips at him; I'd been transporting easily for weeks now.

"Just trust me on this," he said. "Do it."

I popped to the waterline then popped back to the seated position.

"And how did you do that?"

I sighed. "I sent my magic to the location I wanted to go then followed it."

"Very good. Now, I want you to send your magic to the oyster restaurant twenty miles from here."

"Where's that?"

"Ah-hah, not so smart now, are we?" Gavon said with a knowing smile. "Go find it."

I closed my eyes and released my magic, but it had nowhere to go. "I don't know how."

"So perhaps you should lay off the attitude, hm?" he said with a small chuckle. "Your magic is quite intelligent. Ask it to find the restaurant for you."

I breathed the query to the power humming in my veins then released it. I gasped as it shot away from me, disappearing into the darkness of my mind's eye. For a few breaths, I heard nothing...then a faint whisper of "Come to me." I let go of the grip on my physical body and the scent of seafood and fried potatoes filled my nose.

I stood in front of an oyster house I'd never seen before. My jaw dropped at my own talent; this opened so many doors for me.

Beaming, I transported myself back to Gavon.

"Well?"

"Found it!"

"You went all the way over there and didn't bring me anything back?"

I laughed and concentrated, sending my magic back to the restaurant to bring back a plate of raw oysters in rock salt.

Gavon's face lit up. "That's more like it," he said, taking the platter from my hands and placing it on the sand in front of us. "I haven't had oysters in years."

"Any reason?" I asked, slurping one down.

He smiled a little sadly. "Not since I lost my wife. She was a big fan."

I swallowed the first oyster in one gulp, and felt guilty that I knew absolutely nothing about the man who had been teaching me magic, other than his affinity for history and science. But then again, I had become quite nervous to ask him, afraid of what I would—or wouldn't—find out.

"So do you have a family?" I asked quietly. "Somewhere to go for Thanksgiving?"

His face warmed, and he chuckled. "I'll be fine. Why don't you hurry on home? I'll see you next week."

"You just want to eat all the oysters..."

He shrugged and slurped down another one. "Guilty?"

Seventeen

There was a nervous, excited energy in the house when I walked down to the kitchen the next morning. Even Jeanie looked happy for once, or perhaps it was because she wore her best dress and earrings. Nicole, too, wafted into the kitchen wearing her nicest clothes, pausing to press a kiss onto my forehead. The only other person who was lukewarm about the whole "Thanksgiving" thing was Marie, who sulked and rolled her eyes about having to be gone from her friends for a week.

"You can just transport back?" I asked her, but she glowered at me and told me I knew nothing about anything.

"Marie, take Nicole. Lexie and I will transport together. The location of the compound is Salem, Massachusetts," Jeanie said. Another trademark eye roll from Marie then she and Nicole were gone in a poof of white.

Crap. Jeanie didn't know that I knew how to transport. I offered a weak smile and wondered how I'd play this off.

"So there are a few steps to learning how to transport," Jeanie said. "First and foremost, the location—"

"Salem."

"Right, so now that you know the location, what I want you to do is to put your magic there."

"...Put my magic there?" All I could think of right then was how grateful I was that Gavon had been teaching me the finer points of magic, and not Jeanie.

"Yeah, just..."

"I think I got it," I said, saving her from having to struggle anymore. I closed my eyes and grabbed onto her magic as I used to do with Gavon's.

"W-what are you doing?" Jeanie replied, taking a step back.

"Following you?" I replied.

This was stupid. Jeanie might hurt herself teaching me how to do something I already knew. Besides, she'd find out soon enough.

"You know what? I'll just see you there."

With that, I released my magic and it flew faster than light across the plains and mountains and rivers until it landed on what it knew to be the front lawn of my grandmother's house, and then the rest of me followed it. I landed on brown, dead grass and a shot of extraordinarily cold air blew at me.

Obviously, I'd left my coat in Florida.

"*Geez,*" I said, wrapping my arms around me and summoning my coat.

"Alexis Renee, how the hell did you know how to do that?" Jeanie said, appearing next to me.

"Do what?"

"Transport spell."

"I taught her," Marie said, standing on the front porch.

"*You what?*" Jeanie and I said at the same time.

Marie shrugged. "I got tired of having to drive her ass everywhere."

"Oh, is that Jeanie and the girls?" a voice called to my right. Out of the neighboring house, an old woman who looked similar to my grandmother poked her head out. Unlike Gram, who wore a mask of indifference, this woman was warm and inviting and put me at ease.

"Nina, these are the girls," Jeanie said, also growing a bit warmer with this new woman's presence.

"Nicole, you're all grown up, aren't you? And Marie! Spitting image of Mora, look at you. And—" When her eyes landed on me, they filled with tears and she covered her mouth. "Little Alexis. The last time I saw you, you were just a few hours old."

I stood awkwardly, glad that at least Marie was looking as nervous at the familiarity as I was. If this woman had been so worried about us, how come this was the first time I was ever seeing her face?

"Er..."

"Lexie, this is your great aunt, Nina," Jeanie said, saving me from asking the question. "She's Gram's sister."

"Jeanie, my love!" Nina said, moving from me to my aunt, who flustered and grimaced at the attention she'd been getting since she was probably my age. "What a fine job you've done with these girls. I just can't believe...and so *powerful.*"

Nicole shifted nervously, but Nina was quick to tut.

"Even you, dear. That potion-making magic is pretty potent!" She laughed. "Look at me, alliterating like a fool."

I shared a glance with Marie, but she just looked bored. "This is so stupid. I'm going back to bed." And with that, she disappeared.

"Marie—" Jeanie began, but Nina cut her off.

"Oh, Jeanie, you know you were just as bad when you were eighteen. You and Mora, fighting like cats and dogs all the time!"

"Well, girl, you've grown into your magic, hm?"

Gram's voice echoed through the yard and pierced me. I straightened and nodded, unsure of why I felt like I needed to bow to her. She had appeared on her porch and was evaluating us against some yardstick we weren't aware of.

"Gram?" Nicole asked. "Is everything okay?"

"She's powerful," Gram said, looking me up and down. "Much more in control of her magic than the last time I saw her."

"I've been practicing," I murmured.

"Indeed."

"Marie said she's been teaching her," Nicole interjected, taking Gram's attention away from me.

"And you?" Gram asked her. "Your potion-making skills improved any?"

Nicole's face turned bright red and she looked at the ground. "I haven't really...there's no need to..."

"She made a good healing potion!" I interjected, wanting to

protect my sister as much as she protected me.

"Why did you need a healing potion?" Gram asked.

Nicole shot me a look that very plainly told me to keep my mouth shut. "Lexie was having some problems controlling her magic at first. But she's got a handle on it now."

I nodded.

"Mm." Suddenly I felt like I'd be safer in Florida. "And where is Marie?"

"She's...decided to go back to the house," Jeanie said. "I was going to go get her and bring her back—"

"I shall send for your niece," Gram said. Her fingernails glowed a pale green and the hairs on my arms stood up.

A second later, Marie appeared, surrounded by a green glow. She'd obviously been halfway to putting her pajamas back on, as she stood in a lacy white bra and short, bright green shorts.

"W...*Gram!*" she screamed, struggling against the magic holding her in place.

"When I call you, girl, you answer," Gram said to Marie. "I may not be your mother, but parental magic has strong bonds. You understand?"

Marie whimpered and glared at me as if I'd had something to do with her being plucked out of her bedroom half-dressed.

"Girl, I won't ask you again," Gram said. "You'll be without your magic for a month."

"Yes, ma'am," Marie murmured. Apparently, the threat of being magicless was the only thing to cow Marie's super-sized ego.

"Very well, hurry up and get clothed. You are needed here."

To my surprise, Marie nodded meekly then disappeared. A few moments later, she reappeared fully dressed with a bag in her hand, unable to look at anything but the ground.

"...Why don't we get settled and then we can catch up," Jeanie offered to Nina, who was watching the entire event unfold with pursed lips. I half-expected her to say something in our defense, but she remained silent and followed us as we entered Gram's house.

A roar of excitement greeted us before we were even past the threshold. My magic swirled and bumped against my skin, as if it knew that it was finally amongst a crowd of its peers. The faces were as familiar as their magic, although I'd never met a single one of them.

"Alexis, as I live and breathe!"

"Nicole, you certainly have grown into a remarkable young woman."

"Marie, you're just Mora all over again. Rest her soul."

"Alexis—"

"Marie—"

"Nicole—"

Around and around, my sisters and I were manhandled by people who seemed extraordinarily excited to see us. They introduced themselves as cousins and second-cousins and great aunts and uncles once removed as if they expected me to remember some great family tree I'd never known existed until now.

"I'd like to speak with Alexis alone." Gram's voice cut through the din of conversation. I felt the sweep of gazes fall on me, and I marched forward, not knowing what to expect.

"Lord, don't scare the poor girl," Nina said with a dry look at her sister. "She hasn't done anything wrong."

"Nina, I'll thank you to keep your opinions to yourself," Gram replied, beckoning me forward.

I followed her down a long hallway. There had obviously been a *ton* of magic saturated into this house, making it much larger on the inside. In between the doors were oil paintings of men and women and each painting showed a different decade of dress, all the way to—

"John Chase!" I exclaimed before I could stop myself.

"Oh, so you're familiar with our ancestor?" Gram asked, lifting an eyebrow at me.

"I...Marie told me about it. But I didn't know he was our ancestor?"

"Then I'm sure she didn't tell you the whole story. Come in."

We had arrived at a large office with windows overlooking the Atlantic Ocean. The drab November day seemed fitting as the gray waters crashed against the rocky shore. It was as far from my sparring beach as I could get.

"Sit, girl," Gram ordered, herself taking a seat behind a desk.

I crossed the room in three steps and plopped down on an antique chair in front of her.

She watched me for a moment, and I got the feeling she was reading my magic, especially as something foreign poked at the energy under my skin. After a moment, the probing stopped and she sat back, looking neither pleased nor upset.

"I am the leader of Clan Carrigan," she began. "This clan has roots that go back to John Chase, the man who stopped the Two Year Magical War and created the Separation."

I nodded, hoping she wouldn't ask me what I knew about the Separation.

"I am the Clanmaster. Do you know what that means?"

Again, I nodded.

"That demonstration with your sister was just a fraction of what I can do. Understand?"

Another nod.

"Above all else, the safety of this clan is my utmost priority. And I will do whatever it takes to keep its members safe."

I swallowed and nodded. I wasn't quite sure what she was getting at, but I felt it best to keep quiet regardless.

"This compound is sealed by magic, and only those I deem safe are allowed in this space. You will not be able to tell others about its location unless I allow you to. Do you understand?"

My head was getting tired of nodding my understanding, but I did so again.

"Within the compound, which comprises all the houses on this street and the four adjoining ones, you may practice magic at your discretion, but you will not use it to bring harm to others. Do you understand?"

"Yes, ma'am," I said, hoping that speaking would, perhaps, get her to stop asking if I understood.

"Good. Dismissed."

I blinked at her, having never been ordered around in such a way.

"Are you deaf, girl? I said *dismissed.*"

I popped to stand, spun on my heel, and scurried out of the room.

I could scarcely believe that all the people walking in and out of Gram's house were related to me in some form or another. They all seemed to know exactly who I was, which left me feeling a bit strange as I had no idea who they were. It was a relief when I finally found Nicole and Jeanie in the kitchen, talking over steaming cups with Nina.

"There she is!" Nina said, spotting me first. "Come in, Lexie. I hope my sister didn't scare you too much."

I shrugged and took the empty seat next to Nicole. With a flick of her wrist, Nina conjured up another mug of tea and teabag. Seeing so much magic in use after all the times Jeanie had barked at me never to use it was startling.

"Jeanie tells me you're into history?" Nina asked, bringing the mug to her mouth.

I glanced at Jeanie. "She does?"

"I'm a bit of a history scholar myself," Nina said. "You know you're welcome at my house any time you need help with homework."

"I am?" I said, glancing at Jeanie, who nodded. But after Gram's threatening welcome, I wasn't so sure that was the case. After all, it had taken her nearly eight weeks to grant me entry in the first place. Had Gavon not shown up, I might've had a much worse time of it.

"What's that face for?" Nicole asked.

I swallowed a comment about being welcome, because my gaze landed on a photo on wall. A blonde woman who heavily resembled Marie stood with two girls in her arms on a beach not unlike the rocky one just beyond this house. I stood from the table, crossing the room to get a closer look. There was something familiar about the house visible in the background. About the beach. The woman.

"That's Irene's favorite photo of your mother," Nina said, standing behind me. "We miss her every day."

But that didn't fit with my grandmother's actions. She'd done everything in her power to make me feel *un*welcome. She'd threatened me, she'd isolated me and my sisters for fifteen years. So why would she have a photo of my mother on the mantle?

"That was taken a few months before she became pregnant with you," Nina said with a sigh. "Your mother loved that house almost as much as she loved this one. She'd been so happy when Uncle Ashley had bequeathed it to her." She chuckled. "And I still remember you, Nicole, coming over to play in my herb garden. I should have you come look at my lavender plants. They haven't done as well as they did when you were around."

My thoughts slowed, as a few pieces fell into place. My mother had inherited a house here in Salem. Nicole had played in Nina's herb garden. That meant they'd been in the clan before I'd been born; they'd *lived* amongst magic. Which also meant that my father had lived here, and had known about magic. Everyone had been happy.

And everything changed when I'd come along.

But why?

I looked at Jeanie, who must've read the question on my face, because she quickly said, "Lexie, why don't you go outside? Don't leave the compound."

"No, I think I'd rather stay."

"Oh, you shouldn't disobey your aunt, darling," Nina said with a pat on my hand. "Jeanie's got Irene's patience. Run along, and we'll talk more later."

Before I could argue, Nina's magic, a yellow-sunshine-y feeling that left me both happy and annoyed, pushed me out the door and locked it behind me.

Eighteen

"What the hell?" I said, marching back up to the kitchen door and tugging on the knob.

I could see Nina, Jeanie, and Nicole talking in the kitchen, ignoring me. When I banged on the glass, the curtains on the door closed. And when I pounded on the door, Nina's magic enveloped me and tossed me onto the rocky beach.

I glared at the house, still visible from where I sat. But then the strangest feeling of déjà vu came over me. The way the waves crashed against the shore, the smell of the ocean (similar, but different from the sparring beach). The feeling like I should be meeting someone here. I walked eastward until I came across a newer house in the midst of all the old ones. Something about it seemed wrong, like it didn't belong there. Like some other structure should've been there instead.

"What the hell are you looking at?" Marie asked, appearing beside me.

I broke from my trance and shook my head to clear it. "Where've you been?"

"Staying out of sight of Gram," Marie said. "She's such a b..."

"Bitch?"

"I think she's magicked my tongue," Marie said, casting furtive glances at the house that loomed above us. "But seriously, what the hell are you looking at?"

"Nothing," I said after a long silence. "Want to go exploring?"

"Better than staying in this dump."

Since neither of us wanted to figure out how to summon Marie's car from Florida, we had to settle for exploring on foot. We didn't really speak to each other, but that also meant Marie wasn't being awful to me, so I didn't mind it.

I wasn't sure what I'd expected in a magical village, but I found myself a little underwhelmed. It looked awfully...normal. I didn't know if I'd expected dragons or wyverns or spells shooting across the street. The only thing half-interesting was that each house boasted what might, in the summer, be a sizable garden, but now was nothing more than a patch of dead leaves and vines.

"Did we live here?" I asked Marie after we'd rounded the block and came onto a main street.

Marie made a noncommittal noise and shrugged.

"Are you magically compelled not to tell me about this stuff?"

"What stuff?"

"About living here, about Gram. Not telling me about magic for fifteen years. All the secrecy—"

Again, she made a noncommittal noise and shrugged.

"I'll take that as a *yes*."

My mood soured considerably as our short journey ended, and we stood on the street, watching Gram's house bustle with activity. People arrived in puffs of different color smoke, grinning and hugging each other as long-lost friends. Others left their houses with casserole dishes in hand, and children chased each other through the brown, dead grass. No one seemed bothered by the cold, chatting with each other with bright, warm expressions.

"This is going to be painful," Marie said, pursing her lips. "I don't know these people and I don't appreciate them acting like we're all close and shit."

"Yeah," I said with a nod, glad that she wasn't magically compelled to not speak ill of Gram.

"And Gram just showing up and ordering us around like she's the queen of England."

"Yeah!"

Marie shrugged. "That's why I'm moving out."

"Are you...really?" I risked a glance at her. She was completely serious. "Really?"

"Yup."

Somehow the thought of Marie leaving made me sadder than I'd expected. Even though she didn't speak to me or act any differently toward me now that she was healing me after sparring lessons, we'd still spent a lot of time together. And despite everything, she *was* my sister.

"And she won't have any control over you?" I asked softly.

"Neither of them will. I'm so tired of Jeanie's bullshit. And

Nicole's just a pushover and does whatever she says." Marie's face grew darker. "When I turn eighteen, they won't have any power over me."

"They won't?"

"Not if I renounce the clan."

I chewed my lip. That didn't sound so terrible.

"Maybe I should do that, too."

Marie shrugged. "Do what you want."

We stood in silence, watching the crowd ebb and flow in front of the house. Twice, Jeanie walked out to greet someone, and they hugged like family.

Nicole appeared on the stoop and spotted us. Wrapping her coat around herself, she hurried over, a frown on her face.

"Where the hell have you two been? I've been stuck making dinner for the past three hours."

"Nina kicked me out of the house, if you'll recall," I said, channeling a bit of Marie's attitude.

"Don't start with me, Alexis," Nicole barked.

"Then why don't you tell me the truth, for once?" I snapped, storming toward the house.

Before I even got through the front door, the smell of Thanksgiving hit me. In Florida, we usually had a small meal together which Nicole had made for the past few years. But I'd never seen such an assortment of food as was in the dining room. Three turkeys, rows and rows of casseroles and vegetables and rolls and cranberry sauce. I lost count of the number of seats crammed around an impossibly large table. Even more tables were stashed wherever there was a place.

"Ah, Lexie," Nina's voice pulled me from my amazement. "This is my seventy-fifth Thanksgiving, and the sight of all these people never ceases to amaze me. We just keep getting bigger and bigger every year."

I half-smiled, the memory of her kicking me out before I could ask more questions about my father fresh in my mind.

"Now, you'll be with the rest of the children," Nina said, pointing to a table already prepped with high chairs and booster seats. "I used to have to sit at the kid's table when I was younger. When Irene took over the clan from your great-great uncle, I got to move to the main table." She sighed, glancing at the nondescript chair at the front of the room. "He was such a fun man. I still remember he always had candy in his office when I came to visit."

"How is that decided?" I asked. "The Clanmaster?"

"Power, prestige, age, wisdom...and, of course, the support of the clan itself. We Carrigans are quite powerful when you get us all rowing the same way. The problem is, of course, the rowing." She tittered to herself. "We're nearly five hundred strong, you know."

That got my attention. "*Five hundred*? I have *five hundred* family members? And they're all coming here?"

"Oh, heavens, no. When you get to fifth and sixth cousins, it tends to dilute the familial bond, don't you think?"

"Do they all live here?"

"Some do, others with more distant limbs on the family tree

have established offshoots out west. But most of the northeastern clan lives here in Salem, except, of course, for you girls."

I glowered at one of the three turkeys. What made us so special that we'd been cut off from the rest of the family? "And does that mean that *everyone else* knew about magic before they turned fifteen?"

"Why, of...oh that's right, Jeanie didn't tell you until your Magic's Eve, did she?"

"No, she did not."

"Well, dear, we have our reasons for doing things."

I turned to face her, straight-on. "Did my parents live here before I was born? And why did we move to Florida, and—"

"Darling, all of those questions would be best answered by your Gram," Nina said, patting me on the head and floating away as if on a cloud.

My anger boiled, and out of the corner of my eye, a boat of gravy rose off the table. I released it gently, and took three deep breaths. It wouldn't be very smart of me to lose control, so I found what I presumed to be the kid's table and sat down in a hidden corner to cool off.

But the longer I sat and watched the room fill with people, the more my anger simmered. They all seemed so close and welcoming, as I caught snippets of conversations about jobs and sports tournaments. Nicole, Marie, and I were the only strangers in this house, which, *again*, made no sense considering that the woman who owned it was *our* grandmother.

I was joined at the table by an eight-year-old named Beth and a ten-year-old named Mark, who apparently belonged to my third cousin. They reminded me a bit of myself and Marie, who'd taken a seat across from me, although their insults were more along the lines of who was going to turn whom into a toad when they got magic. Their arguments only served to turn up my anger, because it reminded me that *I* was the only one in this family who hadn't known about magic until she was fifteen.

"Attention, attention." Gram's voice floated through the enlarged space and all conversation ended as we turned to look at our Clanmaster at the head of the table. She was surrounded by men and women who seemed, if possible, twice as old as her.

I looked around for Jeanie and saw her at the other end, crammed into a corner with Nicole.

"I want to thank you for coming to the Clan Carrigan Thanksgiving feast," she said. "We have several announcements that I'd like to get out of the way before we begin our meal. First, a moment of silence for those in the clan we lost this year. Nan, Hartley, and Milton." The collective group bowed our heads for a brief moment and an older woman dabbed her eyes. "We've welcomed a few new members of our clan by marriage, Ira and his nonmagical wife, Luella." The couple stood, the wife looking like a deer in the headlights. I guessed they hadn't been married for very long. "And Robby and Harvey, who recently got married after a very long waiting period."

Nina clapped loudly for that one.

"We had a boom of children born this year. Erin, Christa, and Don and Leon, the twins. We can't wait to see what sort of trouble they get into, if they're anything like you, Teresa."

The woman sitting in-between two baby carriers blushed and laughed.

"And we've had two come into their magic this year, who we formally welcome into our clan. Rachel and Jonathon." Two teenagers about my age stood and waved nervously as they received loud applause.

Wait a minute...

"Mom, didn't you forget about someone?" Jeanie said.

"Right, of course." The look on Gram's face said she hadn't forgotten about me; she *intentionally* hadn't mentioned me. Which I wouldn't have minded, except for the *mountain* of evidence that said she was doing everything in her power to make me feel *not* welcome.

"Alexis has also grown into her powers."

A ripple of curiosity swept through the room and I didn't understand why until I realized that she hadn't specifically welcomed me into their clan. And based on the way everyone had begun whispering, that was significant.

"Mom—" Jeanie began.

"That's enough, Jean. Now, everyone—"

"Hang on a second." I found myself on my feet and addressing a room full of strangers. "What the hell is your problem with me?"

"*Lexie*," Jeanie hissed.

Gram stared me down from across the room. "Alexis, sit down. We will discuss this—"

"No, we're going to discuss this *right now*. Like why you guys never told me I had magic. Like why my sisters and I—your grandchildren, I might add—have been banished to Florida while the rest of you guys just wander around this stupid magical neighborhood."

"Alexis, *sit down*."

I could feel the magic in the room rising, and I wasn't so sure it wasn't just my own. "I'm not in your clan, apparently, so you can't order me around." I leveled my stare at her. "Why wasn't I told that I was magical?"

She rose from the table. Jeanie and Nicole had turned pale, but no one made a sound.

"It was for your own good," Gram said.

"My good, or yours?" I spat back.

She shot a look at Jeanie, who looked stony-faced and then turned to me, furious. "If you don't sit down—"

The words died on her tongue, and her gaze drew to my hands. I didn't need to look to know that they crackled with unused magic. I'd never been this angry in my entire life, and I was dangerously close to losing control.

"Lexie, sit down," Marie whispered, scared.

Instead, I concentrated on a spot very far away, and let my magic pull me out of the room.

Nineteen

I landed on our beach, the sandy dunes feeling familiar under my feet. I released the pent-up energy across the ocean in a dizzying light show. And I waited.

Waited for Jeanie to come after me.

Waited for Gram's magic to drag me back to New Salem.

But nothing happened.

The sand glowed purple with my magic, and I struggled to take a deep breath. Gavon said that my magic only worked when I was calm, but the way my magic coursed through me, I felt the distinct need to *hit* something.

Hard.

With a roar, I released my magic over the ocean again. The purple ball zoomed across the water, cutting the waves in half until it exploded far out in the distance. Then I released seven more, relishing how it drained me of anger at the same time. When the last one exploded, I fell to my knees and panted for a moment.

"Well, that seems overdramatic." I wasn't even surprised to hear Gavon's voice behind me, or to have him stand next to me. "What's the matter?"

"Nothing."

"Something, obviously, because you just sent half of your magic flying over the Gulf of Mexico," Gavon said, watching me get up gingerly. "What happened at your grandmother's house?"

"Nothing."

"Doesn't appear to be nothing."

I sighed. "Apparently, there's something wrong with me. Because *I'm* the only one who didn't know about magic. For some reason, I'm not actually in the clan and my own grandmother thinks that I'm going to, I don't know...kill them all or something." I looked at the distance, where the remnants of my spell were wafting down into the sea. "Is it because I have Warrior magic?"

"That's a question only—"

"Oh my *God*!" I screamed, taking him by surprise. "I am *so sick* of no one telling me *anything*!"

"Alexis, calm down," Gavon said, holding his hands up. "I can't tell you because I don't know why your grandmother said what she said. I don't know why your aunt decided not to tell you about magic, but what I do know is that you need to calm down before you pass out."

"And now...and *now* she won't even let me in her stupid clan!" I huffed. "I thought you couldn't do that! I thought that you *had* to allow your blood relatives into your clan! That's what makes them different from guilds, right?"

Gavon stared at me for a moment, then shook his head. "There are a thousand different ways to draw up bylaws in clans, so it's *possible* there's a loophole, but—"

I let out a roar of frustration, and an attack spell came out with it. The feeling was delicious, and I wanted more. "I want to spar."

"That is a terrible idea."

I spun on my heel and released an attack spell toward him. He moved out of the way, furious.

"Alexis, I'm not sparring with you—"

"Fine!" I growled, throwing another one his way. "I'll just throw spells until I pass out."

"In—" He moved too fast for me. "—advisable."

Gavon took a step back, and my body began to tingle. Somehow, this was familiar, standing in front of someone, demanding that they quit talking and *fight me*. I released my mind and let the memory take hold. I stood on gravel in front of a burning house, staring at a man I'd never seen before. And I was waiting—waiting for someone to come.

My magic moved of its own accord, remembering how to work as if I'd used it in a former life. Power gathered in my hands as easily as anger burned in my chest. There was a powerful spell, something that throbbed with the beat of my heart.

A spell came toward me, but I deflected it with ease. Someone was screaming my name, but I was too far in my own—or my magic's—memory to remember.

Finally, I could hold onto the spell no longer, and let it loose.

The magic left my body and so did my strength. In slow motion, the spell slammed into Gavon, knocking him backward. My knees gave way beneath me, and I fell to the soft, cold sand. And the last thing I thought before the world faded to black was just how familiar this whole scene really was.

"He won't come, you know."

The ground gave under my feet as I adjusted my stance against the pebbles and coarse sand. But this, this was where we'd practiced for months. Even now, I could feel the power growing within my hands.

"Did you really believe this would end any other way?"

"I'm stronger than you think."

"Oh, I think you have power, but there's only so much that can be taught in a few months. And he's just so gentle and kind, I doubt you even know what it's like to be bruised by him."

"Yeah, well I know you're in for a world of hurt."

The magic left my body, colliding with his in a flash of purple and gray. I knew I needed to act quickly, so I released more and more, praying that I could keep enough in reserves until he came.

He had to come. He had to know.

Why hadn't he come yet?

My body hurt.

I opened my eyes to a dark room and then squeezed them back shut. My head throbbed and even the dim light in the room was painful. My hands closed around soft fur—

Furs?

My eyes opened wide and I sat up, immediately regretting my

decision. My head swum and every inch of me screamed in achy pain. After a moment of heavy breathing, the throbbing subsided and I took stock of the room.

The small amount of light came from a fire burning in an ancient hearth. The floors were old and creaked when I slid off the bed, a four-poster. It was definitely fur that I felt under my fingertips, though I had no idea what kind of creature it had belonged to. The walls were adorned with oil paintings, and I inched closer, hoping to not make a sound on the squeaky floors. In one, a large dragon stood on the edge of a cliff, looming over a girl. Something bright and red glowed around her neck, and the dragon seemed not to be liking that very much.

I swallowed and took a step back, nearly tripping over my own shoes, which had been placed by my bed. My toes were starting to get cold—even with the blazing fire, it seemed this place wasn't heated very well. I slipped on my shoes and crept toward the door.

The hallway was similarly dark, although there were small candles lighting the way. I ran my hands along the wood-paneled walls and stopped at another painting, this one of a group of people wearing puritan outfits. But what struck me more was the magic flowing between the two groups.

I kept walking, finding a set of stairs at the end of the hall. The candles and the paintings continued down the staircase, but I stopped looking at them, more interested in finding someone who could tell me where I was. On the lower story, I saw more closed doors as upstairs, except for one at the end of the hall. Light spilled out from the open door, flickering as if lit by another fire.

Curiosity took hold and I stepped into the light. My jaw dropped.

It was a library. Rows of books lined the walls that seemed taller than I thought possible in such a small space.

"Oh, you're awake."

I snapped from my reverie. Gavon stood behind a table on the other side of the room, an open book before him, and spectacles on his nose. He wore a weird outfit—almost like he'd stepped out of a history book.

"How are you feeling?"

"About normal for a morning after sparring," I said, half-smiling and continuing to look around.

"Here," he said, flicking his wrist, and conjuring an old-looking goblet. With another flick, it gently appeared in my hands. "Healing potion. I just made a fresh batch this morning."

I took a tentative sip and nearly spat it out. It tasted worse than usual. "Ugh."

"You should drink that," Gavon insisted, closing the book and levitating it back to its rightful place. "You've had a rough night."

"So...what happened?" I asked. "The last thing I remember is...sparring?"

"It would appear you lost control and used too much magic," Gavon said simply. "So you collapsed."

"Wait, isn't that...can't I...die from that?" I asked, eyes wide.

"Yes, and that's what was so concerning," Gavon said. "Alexis, I know you were upset last night, but you have to keep your emotions in check. I don't even know *how* you were able to use so much magic, but..."

"It felt like a magical memory."

Something unreadable crossed his face. He wearily plucked his glasses off his face. "Alexis, I was very worried about you. I had no other choice but to bring you here. That's the second round of healing potion you've had."

"Why not ask my sister for help?"

"Well, for one, I don't think she's quite powerful enough for what you needed. Second, I believe they were still up in Boston. And third, your family isn't a big fan of mine." At my quizzical glance, he smiled and said, "A story, perhaps, for later."

"So where is here?"

He furrowed his brow and pinched the bridge between his nose. "My home."

I walked to the window, if it could be called that. It certainly wasn't letting in much light. "What time is it?"

"Ten o'clock in the morning," Gavon said, his voice oddly hesitant. "Unfortunately, it looks that way all the time."

"Dark?" I asked, peering out curiously. Below the window was a tiny village with old houses, and smoke twirling from little chimneys. "We're not in Florida anymore, are we?"

Gavon sighed.

"This is where John Chase banished the Separatists," I said quietly.

"Yes, it is."

"So you're a Separatist?" I asked, more curious than concerned.

"My ancestors were," Gavon said with a wry smile.

"Remember, three hundred years have passed on this side as well."

"But you were banished? How...how did you get back?"

"When I was a much younger man, I was fascinated by the banishment spell. Understanding the mechanics of how it worked, how it was cast, and how it had stayed in place all these years, long after the group who'd cast it had died. So I spent a few years studying it, playing around with counter spells, until one day, I made a tear."

"A tear?" I asked. "Like, tearing a piece of paper?"

"More or less," Gavon said. "Since then, I've been able to pass freely between this world and yours."

I stared at him, mind numb from exhaustion and shock. Gavon was a descendent of James Riley's faction. That didn't make sense with the man I knew him to be. He was kind; he'd *defended* Nicole after I'd tried to tell him she had no magic.

"I promise you, I'm not interested in what Riley was," he said, as if reading my mind. "I doubt many here even remember why we were banished."

"So if you aren't interested in killing the nonmagicals...what *have* you been doing over there?"

"Learning everything I can about the past three hundred years," he said, a wistful look in his eyes. "So much has changed. Magic is almost pointless, now. Nonmagicals can fly, talk to each other instantly, drive cars. The internet was..." His eyes grew wide with excitement. "I had a lot to catch up on."

I brought the potion to my mouth, sipping it gingerly and hoping my mind would switch on so I could process all this new information.

Unfortunately, that wasn't in the cards, as Gavon joined me in the center of the room with a grim smile. "It's time we get you home, though. Finish that potion and we'll—"

"Master Gavon, I—"

I nearly jumped out of my skin. A boy about my age stood in the doorway. He wore a similar style of clothes to Gavon, but his dark hair was long and tied in a ribbon. There was also a growing scowl on his face, and I could feel his hatred from across the room.

"What is *she* doing here?"

"Lexie, this is my apprentice, James," Gavon said, giving a sharp look to the boy. "James, I will return within the hour. Please continue your lesson on Ingmar the Terrible."

"Apprentice?" I asked.

"Yes," Gavon said. "Over here, it's common practice for a Warrior to take on an apprentice to train."

"So, I'm kind of like your apprentice?" I asked cautiously.

"*No, you are not!*" James snarled.

"James," Gavon snapped. "Your lesson, please?"

He gave me one final glare before disappearing through the door.

"He's...well, he's a very powerful young man, but his temperament leaves something to be desired."

"So, does he live with you?" I asked. "Here?"

"He does," Gavon said, helping my off the chair. "Now, let's hurry home before your aunt starts to worry."

"Oh...well...let's not be too hasty," I muttered, remembering how much trouble I was going to be in when I got home.

But Gavon wasn't deterred as his magic gripped mine a little roughly. "Follow me and don't go anywhere other than where I take you." He'd barely finished his sentence and we left the warm library and had arrived at some frigid, dark cliff-side. The wind howled and cut right through me, as if trying to push me off the edge of the cliff.

"W-w-w-where are we?"

"The very end of our land," Gavon said, unfazed by the chill. "The place where I made the tear."

I wrapped my arms around me to keep warm. "Couldn't have picked a warmer place, could you?"

"Oh," Gavon said, looking back at me. "This is warm. For this area, anyway."

He waved his hand in front of the open air and stepped back. A crack of energy echoed across the land, followed by flashes of light. Before my eyes, the air ripped in half, and the crackling, moving tear appeared.

"After you," Gavon said, placing his hand on my shoulder.

"Is it safe?" I asked, looking at him dubiously.

"It's how you got here," Gavon said. "After..." He scanned the distance, and his hand tightened on my shoulder.

"Gavon?"

He forced a smile onto his face. "After you, dear."

With a deep breath, I took one giant step closer, and something hooked around my navel and tugged me forward. I landed with a *thud* on my butt, my hands buried in sand. But not the white, grainy sand of our sparring beach. This was harsher. Coarser.

Massachusetts sand.

Two feet landed beside me, and I glanced up at Gavon.

"Where are we now?"

"Close to your family's compound," Gavon said quietly. "Now, hurry back—"

"I'm not going back there!" I said, jumping to my feet. The healing potion hadn't completely replenished my energy, so I swooned a little.

Gavon held out a hand to steady me. "Alexis," he said. "You can't avoid punishment forever."

I looked up to the moon overhead and whined, "But they're going to *kill* me."

"They won't kill you," Gavon said. "You're a Warrior, aren't you?"

I nodded sadly.

"Warriors do what has to be done," he said. "We don't question. We don't whine. We just do."

I pursed my lips at him, hating him for using my magic against me. But before I could argue further, there was a tingling around my hands, that spread across my body. The magic was yellow, and it felt like—

"See you later," Gavon said as the world dissolved in front of me.

And faded into my living room in Florida and the white, angry face of my aunt.

Twenty

"*Where the hell have you been*?" Jeanie bellowed.

I took a step backward then was frozen in place by yellow magic. Jeanie stood before me, screeching loudly and incoherently, but I couldn't even process what she was saying. Then, she was joined by Nicole, and I wasn't sure who to focus on.

"I couldn't find you." Jeanie's anger had taken on a note of fear. "I...Lexie, I was so scared."

"I'm sorry," I whispered, glad that she was worried about me and not angry that I'd spoken to her precious Gram so rudely.

She sank down onto the couch and buried her head in her hands. I waited for her to ask again, to press me where I'd been and why she hadn't been able to find me.

"And talking to Gram like that...I...Lexie... You *can't* do that!" Jeanie sighed. "I just don't know what's gotten into you. Ever since you've gotten magic—"

"Surprised you noticed," I said, unable to stop myself.

She gave me a sharp look. "What is that supposed to mean?"

Saying more would only dig the hole deeper, so I kept my mouth shut.

"Fine, Lexie, just...fine," Jeanie said, rubbing her face. "You're grounded for two weeks. I don't want to hear about you acting out again, all right?"

"Yes, ma'am," I said, knowing those were the only safe words right now.

"Go to your room," she said, sounding tired and old.

The magical bonds that held me upright disappeared, and I stumbled forward, wavering for a moment before high-tailing it up to my room. I quietly shut the door behind me and flopped onto my bed, staring at the ceiling.

Gavon was a Separatist from that crazy secret world John Chase had created. New Salem, he'd called it. He was a descendent of the Separatists. And he'd figured out how to tear a hole into this world.

The rational part of me knew I should tell Jeanie about him, but...I wasn't sure what would happen then. I needed time to sort through all these new pieces before the adults took them away.

More than anything, there was a middling thought in the back of my mind, a truth that I wasn't quite ready to accept. Because if it weren't true, I might not be able to handle it.

Instead, I sat up right and held my hands out, expecting to see my old book on John Chase and the Separatists appear.

Nothing happened.

I took a deep breath. Perhaps I was simply too emotional. My pulse calm and my mind clear, I summoned my book to me.

Again, nothing happened.

I frowned, trying three times in succession.

Still nothing.

I tried to bring my pencil case to me.

Stubbornly, it remained in place.

The magical hum under my skin was gone, too.

Then I remembered what being "grounded for two weeks" meant in magical terms. And worst of all, my magical books had been hidden away where I couldn't get to them.

"*I hate being grounded!*" I bellowed.

"That's the point!" Nicole called back.

As per the rules of my grounding, I could go exactly two places —school and home. And since we were still on break for Thanksgiving until Monday, that effectively left me chained to the house for the long weekend. Jeanie still couldn't look at me without grinding her teeth, and though Nicole's anger had lessened somewhat, there was still a clip in her voice when she spoke to me.

I hadn't realized how dependent I'd become on my magic to keep me occupied. Marie had gone to the Black Friday sales, and Jeanie disappeared early with a warning that if I left the house, she'd know and extend my grounding to three weeks. I was already aching to get my books back, so I heeded my warning.

First, I attempted to work on my history homework, which took a lot longer when I had to do it by hand. After I finished a terribly written essay, I moved onto science homework but got bored after the second question. I stood and walked to the window, staring out into the distance.

I spotted a figure in my backyard and grinned.

After barreling down the stairs, I nearly flew out the back door when I remembered Jeanie's warning. So I stood there awkwardly and waved to Gavon. "Hey!"

"Hello there, jailbird," Gavon said, turning his head to the side. "I just wanted to check on you and make sure you were okay after your little..."

"Hissy fit?" I asked, with a weak smile. "I'm still headache-y but nothing too bad. Not that I could tell anyway. My magic's gone."

"Grounded, hm?" Gavon said with a smile. "I suppose you should've expected that. Frankly, speaking that way to a Clanmaster should've resulted in worse punishment. In the days of John Chase, you would've been put in the stocks or hung upside-down by your ankles."

"Doesn't make it any less sucky." I chewed on my lip for a moment. "Hey, do you think you could... I magically hid my books under my bed and without magic, I can't—"

"They're sitting under your bed," Gavon said with a small flick of his wrist. "As are a couple new ones to pass the time. How long until you're free?"

"Two weeks, but..." I panicked at the thought of not seeing him for two weeks. "But I still want to...train."

"Going to be awfully difficult for you to defend yourself without any magic, Alexis."

"I mean, maybe not *spar* but..." I glanced up at him. "I have so many questions. About New Salem, about you, about..."

He considered me for a long time before he glanced at the sky and sighed. "All right. But only if your aunt says you can leave the house. No sneaking out."

I nodded and grinned at him. "I think my rule-breaking days are over."

"Good girl."

He disappeared in a puff of purple, and I spun and ran back upstairs. I released a loud sigh of relief when I saw a pile of spell books under the bed. I'd amassed quite a collection already—the original primer, the book on the Separation, and a couple odds and ends that Gavon had given me when I'd asked. Even though there were a few new ones, I picked up the Separation book. The first time I'd read it, I'd thought it a fascinating study of some event that had happened over three centuries before.

But now, I was searching for clues.

April 1st 1692. At the request of Guildmaster Chase, Johanna, his daughter, presented an idea to the Salem Guild to use a Magical Space as a prison and performed a demonstration. She was able to create a habitable space before her magic gave way, and she fainted from exhaustion.

April 10th 1692. Johanna, Abigail, and Hannah Chase demonstrated how a Magical Space could be enlarged to the size of a town until their magic gave way.

April 15th 1692. A second attempt was made with Johanna and sisters, plus three brothers from the McMahon family. John Chase toured the world for ten minutes before the six Magicals gave out.

April 18th 1692. Ulysses Mark suggested the Magical Space could be created permanently by a coven of Thirteen Magicals.

April 29th 1692. A coven of Thirteen Magicals attempted to construct a permanent Magical Space. Their attempt failed.

May 1st 1692. Separatists obtained list of potion-makers and non-magicals living in Salem. Fifty deaths accounted for. Guildmaster Chase determined Magical Space must be created at all costs.

May 13th 1692. One hundred and sixty-nine magicals—a coven squared—gathered in Salem. A Magical Space was created and the world called New Salem.

May 15th 1692. Guildmaster Chase determines the world is habitable by eating from the magical plants and drinking from the well placed in the world. He declares the war between the Guild and the Separatists must end.

June 12th 1692. John Chase and seventy Warriors attacked the Separatists, capturing them with the help of a clever potion-maker by the name of Loren David. He developed a potion using iron dust to trap the Separatists in their camp.

June 13th 1692. Trial of Separatists. All sixty Magicals found guilty and sentenced to life in New Salem. James Riley sentenced to death by potion, and it was done. John Chase sealed the portal between worlds and perished.

I sat back, watching the sun shine outside my window. When I'd first read that passage, I'd been more focused on how James Riley had gotten what he'd deserved (and the juicy poetic irony that he'd been captured and executed by a potion-maker). I'd thought the Separatists had gotten off relatively easy. Having a brand new world created and all of the amenities that they'd ever need included? At first blush, it had sounded to me like Chase had been too lenient.

Having actually *been* over there, it really was a prison. Even more surprising was someone as brilliant as Gavon could've grown up in such a place. Until he'd made that tear, he'd never known what the sun felt like, or the waves of the ocean. He didn't even know that *electricity* existed, or coal-burning machines. His whole world was stuck in 1692, just because his ancestors decided to run amok.

It was no wonder he decided to try to figure a way out.

At least Gavon wasn't three hundred years old. I wasn't sure how long magicals lived, but I knew they weren't immortal.

Still, I had thousands of questions for him, but as the sun set, I didn't even bother to get up. I knew I'd just be making things worse if I even broached the subject of leaving. But I was starving, so I closed my book and carried my questions downstairs.

"...She can't possibly be serious. We haven't seen him in...in years!"

"It's not him she's worried about, it's Lexie. She's powerful."

I stopped mid-step on the staircase, recognizing the hushed voices of Nicole and Jeanie.

"So, what? Gram thinks Lexie could take over as Clanmaster?"

"Of course not. That's silly." But the way Jeanie phrased it, it didn't sound all that silly.

I folded my arms across my chest and pursed my lips. If that woman was pissed off at me because she thought me a threat, she had another thing coming. The *last* thing I ever wanted to do was take over a big group of Magicals—let alone Magicals who had ignored me for the first fifteen years of my life.

I'd thought it was because they hated my Warrior magic. But were they actually *afraid* of me? Did they think I was more powerful than someone as formidable as Gram?

"But we're... None of us are allowed back?" Nicole sounded stunned.

"Just for now. Just until Gram figures out...figures out what we're doing with her."

My excitement evaporated in an instant. They weren't letting *any* of us back? I could understand why they'd ban me, but Jeanie and my sisters?

"She's not... She's a good kid, Jeanie."

"I know that. But she's not acting like it right now."

I chewed my lip and looked at my hands, expecting them to start glowing before I remembered I had no magic. Perhaps the punishment fit the crime after all. Just like Gavon was dealing with the aftermath of decisions his ancestors made, Jeanie and Nicole were having to deal with my mess. It wasn't fair to Gavon, and it wasn't fair to them.

Instead of continuing downstairs, I turned and walked back to my room. Later, when Nicole brought me a sandwich, I made sure I was working on my homework.

Twenty-One

I spent the entire weekend keeping my nose clean and head down. I wanted to prove to Jeanie, and Gram, if she was watching, that I was a good kid. Not that I wanted to be in her stupid clan, but she shouldn't punish my family for my actions.

When Monday morning rolled around, I assembled my books and supplies into my backpack the way I'd done for weeks before my fifteenth birthday.

"How the mighty have fallen," I muttered, hoisting my backpack and grimacing under its weight.

Jeanie, Nicole, and Marie were sitting around the counter eating breakfast when I came into the kitchen. Jeanie's eyes drew to me sharply as I silently joined the trio at the table, but she said nothing. I'd received three variations of the same lecture about the dangers of shooting my mouth off, so I was glad not to get a fourth iteration.

Nicole slid over the cereal, a sign, perhaps, that she was ready to forgive me. I poured the cereal into a bowl and, out of habit, reached out to summon the milk.

Nothing happened.

Marie snorted into her cereal bowl.

Oh, right.

I sighed quietly and stood up to get the milk from the refrigerator. I opened the door but didn't see the carton.

"Where's the—"

"Milk?" Marie taunted, holding it in her hand. When I stormed across the kitchen, it disappeared before I could grab it.

"Marie, for crying out loud," Nicole said.

"What? It's up there." She pointed to the ceiling where the milk levitated above our heads. "You could get it, if you had your magic back."

"That's it," Jeanie grunted. "Marie, you're grounded."

The milk fell to the table and exploded, covering Marie from head to toe.

Nicole and I shared a look of shock and horror and glee. Marie slowly realized that her hair and makeup and perfect outfit were all ruined. The only sound in the kitchen was her loud panting. Then, sloshing in the wetness around her, she turned to Jeanie and asked in a too-calm voice, "For *how long*?"

Jeanie brought her coffee cup to her lips. "Until Lexie gets her magic back."

Marie's angry gaze swept to me, as if I were somehow responsible for her punishment.

"Be good, girls. I'm off to work." With that, Jeanie disappeared in a cloud of yellow magic.

"You...little...*shit*," Marie said, baring her teeth at me.

"Marie, cut it out," Nicole said.

"Yeah, and what are you gonna do?" Marie snapped.

Nicole looked over to me and smacked her in the back of the head. "That. Now get cleaned up or you'll be late for school."

I took the opportunity to grab a paper towel and offer it to Marie, tauntingly. "Towel?"

"Lexie, really..." Nicole sighed, walking past me. "Grow up."

And then it was just Marie, sopping wet, and me.

"No one here to save you now, twerp!" Marie snarled, getting up from the table, murder on her face.

She lunged at me, but I'd been doing a lot of dodging lately and I easily leaped out of the way. Marie ran straight into the fridge.

I made a beeline for the table, grabbed my backpack, and scampered out the door, not slowing down until I was at least four blocks away from the house.

By lunch, I was hurting. My back, my right hand, and my brain were all cramping. I'd forgotten how difficult it was to write and listen at the same time, and not to mention, lugging around books thicker than my arm. It was with no small amount of glee that I forewent the cafeteria again and found a picnic table outside.

I'd been very good and not looked in any magic books all day, but I was eager to start reading one of the new books Gavon had given me. I settled on the picnic table bench and yanked the heavy tome out of my bag, running my hands along the gold-embossed cover.

A Compendium of Great Magicals

I grinned brightly and gently opened the cover. Inside the front flap was a note handwritten on a bit of old parchment.

Something to aspire to.

-G

I ran my fingers over the note, warm and fuzzy at the thought that Gavon would want me to be a "great magical." I tried not to consider the implications of such a sentiment, but—

"That's an excellent book."

I was so caught up in my thoughts that I hadn't noticed someone standing in front of me. I willed the book to become invisible, but, as I was grounded, it didn't move.

The man before me had an odd look about him, something familiar that I just couldn't place. His reddish-brown hair was neatly combed, his black shirt neatly pressed. The way he was watching me made the hair stand up on the back of my neck.

"I said," he gave a smile that I didn't trust, "that's an excellent book."

"You...you've read it?" I asked, looking down at it. "Do you have magic?"

"You can't tell?"

"I can't tell anything right now," I muttered. "Who... Do I know you?"

"I'm a friend of...Gavon's," he said slowly, as if gauging my reaction.

"Oh," I said, relaxing a little. "So are you from New Salem, too?"

His smile widened and I began to wonder if I'd said the wrong thing. "I am. Has Gavon told you much of our hamlet?"

"Not really."

He took a step forward. "Where are my manners? My name is Cyrus."

"I'm L—"

"Alexis, yes. I've heard a lot about you."

His smile was definitely weird and I wished I had a good excuse to get out of this conversation. But in case this was a friend of Gavon's, I didn't want to be rude.

"So how long have you known our friend Gavon?" he asked.

"A few weeks?" I said. "He's been teaching me how to use magic."

"Has he now?" Cyrus nodded. "I hope he hasn't been boring you with magical history."

"No, we've mostly been sparring," I said, being careful not to reveal too much. Being vague was the best option, I decided.

"And are you any good at it?"

I shrugged. "I'm doing okay."

Cyrus smiled, almost a little too much. "I'm sure one day you'll be as good as the magicals in that book."

I looked down at the book, and the note from Gavon. "I—"

But he was gone.

Standing, I shoved the book back in my bag, deciding it was safer to eat lunch indoors today. Something about this Cyrus dude creeped me out—mostly because I had the strangest feeling like I'd met him before.

I was dying to ask Gavon about his friend, but when Jeanie and Nicole got home, I knew immediately that there was absolutely no way I'd be allowed out of the house. Tuesday was pretty much the same story, so I made sure to do the dishes and be extra respectful after dinner.

By Wednesday, Jeanie could be in the same room with me, and Nicole even asked me what I wanted for Christmas, so I was well on my way to mending fences. Marie, of course, still couldn't stand the sight of me, but she'd also earned herself an additional week of grounding by throwing a tantrum when Jeanie told her to do the dishes, as I'd done them three nights in a row.

As Nicole and I excused ourselves, I said, "Boy, maybe I can get out of grounding sooner, you think?"

"Don't push your luck," Nicole replied, shoving me up the stairs.

But I was beginning to really miss my daily chats with Gavon. Without the hours spent on magical study, my regular homework suddenly didn't seem so challenging. Also, I had thousands of questions for him about the Separation, about life in New Salem, and, more importantly, about the weird guy who'd shown up a few days before.

Friday night, I was feeling confident in my good behavior, so I decided to ask Jeanie if I could take another walk after dinner. But Nicole and I ate alone, as we'd done for the past few nights.

"She's been gone a lot," I said, helping Nicole put away the dishes. Marie hadn't even bothered to come home yet, so we didn't save her any food.

Nicole sighed and looked out the dark kitchen window. "She's trying to smooth over the giant shitstorm you caused at the compound."

I winced. This wasn't the way I wanted this conversation to go.

"I can apologize to Gram." I didn't want to, but if it meant I could get off grounding, I would've sold my soul.

"If it were that simple..."

I wondered if I should tell her that I'd heard her and Jeanie talking about me, but I decided against it. Focus on the mission—get out of the house tonight.

"I'm really sorry," I said quietly.

"I know you are, Lexie."

Good! I thought. *Maybe I have a chance here. Gotta play this right...*

I sighed loudly. "I just wish I wasn't grounded so I didn't have to ask this."

Nicole looked at me, unconvinced.

"I have to go to the library."

"Why's that?"

Another loud sigh. "Be-*cause*, I have this research paper due in a few weeks."

"Isn't that what you have a computer for?"

"My history teacher is old school. You know Millsie. He says we have to have four non-internet sources."

There *was* a research paper due (at the end of *next* semester) that required that sort of source-finding, so it wasn't like I was totally lying.

"Can't you go to the library at school?"

I was really milking these sighs. "I *could*, but they won't give me a hall pass because I *asked* and they said *no*. And I can't go between classes because there are only a few minutes and if I'm tardy, they'll mark it and more than ten tardies and they drop me a letter grade, and I can't go after school because the library closes at three and—"

"All right, all right," Nicole lifted her hands in surrender. "I'll take you to the library tomorrow."

Ah-hah...wait, crap. "Oh, you don't need to take me."

"You're grounded, remember? Jeanie'd kill me if I let you leave without knowing where you were."

"I'd be at the library?"

"And I'll have eyes on you to make sure you are."

Under normal circumstances, reading history books at the library would've been a great way to spend a Saturday. But today, all I wanted to do was talk to Gavon. And with Nicole sitting across the table from me, I doubted that was going to happen, unless I devised a way to get her to leave.

One hour and three books later, Nicole was starting to show signs of boredom. She fidgeted and glanced at the clock and grown tired of reading on her phone, but would pick it up every few minutes.

When she muttered something about her phone dying, I knew I had her. I closed the book I was reading, stood, and walked back to the shelf where I'd taken it. Nicole breathed a sigh of relief, until I grabbed another one.

"That's the fifth book," Nicole said. "Didn't you say you needed four?"

"Yeah, but..." I sighed loudly. "I haven't found all the information I need."

Nicole groaned, and I knew I was in. "Okay look. I'm headed *two streets over* to the Starbucks. When I get back, you'd better be right here."

I nodded.

She stood and stared at me for a moment then swiped her keys off the table and walked off. I blew out air from between my lips and sat back. Somehow, I didn't think it would be long until...

"The old boring-library routine?"

I glanced behind me to where Gavon stood, reading another book about investing strategies. Even though I wasn't surprised, I still asked, "How come you always know where I am?"

He had the good grace to look offended by my accusation. "I happen to frequent the library often."

"But you own one?" I said, remembering it with no small amount of envy.

He scoffed and crossed in front of the table to sit. "Magical authors tend to be repetitive and long-winded, I enjoy the variety found here."

"Yeah, but investing strategies?" I asked, picking up the book.

He nodded. "Indeed. It turns out my ancestors had an account with the Bank of England that's been lying fallow for a few centuries. Trying to keep up with the times. Recommended by my investment banker."

I laughed at the idea like Gavon having an investment banker. It seemed so horribly mundane.

"So, you were set free, I see."

"A short reprieve." I glanced around for Nicole. "And *still* no magic."

"It's probably for the best."

I thought about Gram and nodded. "Thanks for the books, though. It's helping me pass the time. That great magicals book has some...intense people."

"Did you get to the story about the Mad Hunstman?" Gavon asked with an uncharacteristic sparkle in his eye.

"I did. What a freakin' nut job!"

He chuckled. "That book was one of my favorites when I was your age."

That pesky, terrifying thought entered into my head again and I banished it. But we didn't have much time before Nicole got back, so I needed to make it count. I didn't feel comfortable bringing my long list of questions, just in case Nicole saw them, so I settled for the most obvious one.

"Tell me about New Salem," I said.

"Oh," Gavon said, thinking for a moment. "What do you want to know?"

"What do you do over there?"

"Not much," he said after a moment. "Remember, the world is intended to be a punishment, so it's just the small village of people."

"And they're stuck in the year 1692, right?" I asked. "Is that why everything looks so old over there?"

"Yes," Gavon said. "Very little progress has been made on that side. Nonmagicals are much more innovative than magicals."

I rested my head on my hand. "But what do you do over there? How do you have that big house?"

"It belonged to my Master," Gavon said. "And his Master before him, and his Master before him. And so on."

"What about your parents?"

"My father was a..." He tapped his finger to his chin. "An Enchanter, I think."

"Enchanter?" I asked. "That's the one where...they can use magic on other people, to bewitch them, right?"

"Right. And my mother was a Warrior."

"Are they still alive?"

"No. I didn't have much of a relationship with them anyway—my Master raised me from the time I was very little." To my questioning look, he replied, "Warriors are a rarer specialty in New Salem. We get perhaps one or two per generation, and they usually become the Guildmaster. So, to ensure we maintain knowledge, older Warriors take the younger ones as apprentices from a very early age."

"Is that why you have an apprentice?"

Gavon nodded then smiled at me curiously. "Why the interest in the New Salem?"

"Just interested," I said, picking at the table. "Is it customary for parents not to have a relationship with their kids?"

Gavon paused for a moment. "For Warriors, it is. There are so few over there that the Guild wants to ensure the children are reared in an environment conducive to creating the strongest Warriors."

"Why? I mean, there's nobody to fight, right?"

Gavon paused again. "Tradition, I suppose." He checked the surprisingly modern watch on his arm and stood. "I guess I should let you get back to research, hm?"

"But..." I frowned, then thought better of it. Nicole would be back soon, anyway. "All right. I guess I'll see you..."

"How about this: when you get your magic back, meet me for a sparring lesson. I have a feeling you'll be eager to blow off some energy."

Next Friday seemed forever away, but I nodded. "I'll see you then."

Just as he was disappearing in a puff of purple, I realized I'd forgotten to ask him about his friend Cyrus.

Twenty-Two

I stared at the clock on the wall, watching the seconds slowly tick by. It was one minute and thirty-seven seconds until I got my magic back. I was in sixth period, English, and I didn't give one crap about who or what we were studying.

All I knew was that I was getting my magic back in one minute and twenty-three seconds.

I tried to distract myself by paying attention, by watching Ms. Grace talk, with counting the seconds myself, but I couldn't overpower my anxiousness. Fifty-three seconds.

Would it be better to get a pass to the bathroom when my magic returned? I wasn't sure if I'd start glowing or shooting sparks or any of that. Forty seconds.

Then again, it would take a few seconds for her to notice me, to go through the whole process of asking to go then taking the pass, and by then, I might already be firing off lightning bolts. Thirty-two seconds.

And it might be better if I just kept to myself. I was in the back corner of the room anyway, and everyone was already in the post-lunch doldrums. Twenty-four seconds.

As long as I kept my hands under my desk, I could probably manage the magic. Eighteen seconds.

My pulse quickened, and I chewed my lip. I closed my eyes and breathed in and out to remain as calm as I could. Ten seconds.

After all, a calm magical was a useful magical. Five seconds.

I didn't even see the second hand hit the number, as the force of my magic returning nearly knocked me off my chair. My heart raced and my thoughts scattered as the rush of power flowed from my core to my fingers, which glowed purple.

"Crap," I whispered, stuffing them between my knees. This was quickly turning into a repeat of my first day of magic. This time, I was more prepared. At least, I hoped I was.

I closed my eyes and took a deep breath. The important thing was to remain calm so I didn't make a scene. The power rushed through my veins and instead of fighting it, I let it ping-pong from my head to my toes. The feeling was euphoric, as if a piece of my soul had returned to me.

Opening my eyes, I checked my hands. They were back to normal—no glowing. I breathed a sigh of relief.

"Lexie, can you tell us what Scout means when she says that telling people that Boo Radley committed the murder would've been like shooting a mocking bird?"

I stared at Ms. Grace for a moment then glanced down at my notebook. My magic had flipped to a page I'd written the night before, where the answer to that very question sat.

I cleared my throat and tried not to look too smug.

When the day was over, I practically skipped to my locker to swap out my things. Not only did I have my magic back, but I was demonstrating a ridiculous amount of control over it. I could feel it pressing against the inside of my skin, begging to be released.

But we'd come to an agreement. We would blow off some steam at the sparring beach tonight—Gavon had promised he'd come as soon as my magic was back. In return, the magic would behave. I'd almost forgotten the half-crazy way I would converse with it. I wasn't sure if that was normal or if I was just weird, but that was low on the list of questions I had for Gavon.

It had been torture not being able to talk to him except for the five minutes at the library. I was kicking myself for not asking him about his friend, but I'd also seen no more of him. I'd also read all the new books he'd given me cover-to-cover. My favorite had been the book on famous magicals in history—although the history had ended around 1650, which left a full three hundred years of magicals left undocumented.

I was sure there was probably a book or two in Gram's library that could've answered that question. But as far as I knew, were still on the pseudo-excommunication or probation or whatever it was.

I knelt in front of my locker and twisted the dial to open it when I heard a loud sniff above. Callista stood beside me, her face red from crying.

"What happened?" I asked.

"Joel's an asshole."

So they'd broken up. Good news for my bottom locker, but I still felt bad. "Sorry to hear that."

She shrugged and closed her locker, marching off to join her friends. I swung open my locker before stopping.

Oh yeah, my magic was back. No need to cram books into my bag.

I craned my neck toward both ends of the hall, but it was empty. Shielding my locker with my body, I magicked all of my books from my locker to my bed. Smiling to myself, I stood and kicked my locker closed.

Marie stood behind me, a glare on her face. "I saw that."

"Oh?" I said, smirking.

"So you have your magic back, huh?" She wasn't even bothering to lower her voice, but the hall was empty anyway.

"Yup. Too bad you don't." I shouldn't have been stirring the pot, but my magic was making me cocky and Marie'd been nothing but awful to me the past few weeks.

Her eyes narrowed. "Yeah, too bad because you're shit out of luck in the morning if you go sparring."

"Oh cr... Wait, how did you know I was sparring?"

It was her turn to look smug.

My heartbeat quickened. "Does Jeanie know? Nicole?"

"They might find out. I don't know." She examined her nails for a moment. "Depends on how the next few minutes go."

I sighed. *Of course.* "What do you want?"

"I want you to do my homework and the dishes tonight," Marie said. "And I want you to tell Jeanie that I'm in my room and charm it so she won't check it."

I blinked. "How the hell am I supposed to do that?"

"You're the *genius*, figure it out. Why don't you ask your sparring partner? He's obviously been teaching you *everything*."

Again, my nerves ticked up a notch. "So you know Gavon?"

She laughed. "Oh yeah."

I chewed my lip, debating if I should ask her more. But I trusted answers from Gavon more than I trusted answers from her —especially when she was being overdramatic.

"Fine, I'll make sure nobody knows you snuck out."

"Pleasure doing business with you." Marie adjusted her backpack on her shoulder then spotted Charity and called for her to wait up.

If Jeanie or Nicole were surprised to see dinner ready for them when they got home, or that I told them my homework was complete, or that I was being extra pleasant, they didn't mention it. Nicole did eye me a little more warily as she tasted the food, but Jeanie seemed to be back to normal, especially when I asked if I could go for a walk.

"Take your phone."

I waved it in front of her then bounded out the door, and transported myself to the sparring beach. It was definitely colder now, though nothing compared to Boston or New Salem. The wind on the beach cut through my hoodie, so I tried an easy warming charm on it.

And promptly set my sleeve on fire.

"*Crap!*" I said, waving my arm around.

I heard a snort of derision and the fire disappeared from my arm.

"Gavon!" I said, although my smile was dampened by the sight of his apprentice. The boy didn't look pleased at all to be there, and he tugged at his t-shirt uncomfortably.

Gavon, however, barely acknowledged his apprentice as he crossed the beach toward me. "How are you feeling?"

"Jittery," I said, looking at my sleeve, which had mended itself. "It's like the first day I had magic. Everything's just...overkill."

"I had a feeling that might happen," Gavon said, nodding back at James, who was staring at the waves and the moon, unimpressed. "Thought you might want to attempt a real sparring match with someone your own age. James was kind enough to volunteer."

The look on his face told me James hadn't volunteered for anything.

"Do you...do you think I'm ready for that?" I peered around Gavon to James. He'd probably been sparring since he could walk, since children over there weren't subject to the Council of Danvers laws.

"I told James to take it easy on you," Gavon said. "But you might do better than you think. Give it a shot."

If Gavon thought I was ready, I'd trust him, but it was with no small amount of trepidation that I crossed the beach to face James.

"Do you even know what you're doing?" he asked, disdain dripping from his words. Up close, he couldn't have been much older than I was.

Before I could answer, Gavon had materialized beside us. "Alexis, as is customary, you two will shake hands to begin the match."

I held out my hand, hoping it wasn't too sweaty. James slapped his palm against mine and energy jolted through our hands. A dome of forest green and purple magic appeared around us, illuminating his face the sand. James released my hand as if it were poisonous, a look of annoyance crossing his face.

"What are you waiting for? *Go* to your *side*."

"What?"

"Alexis, in a duel, you'll need to begin on your side of the circle," Gavon said. At least *he* didn't sound like I was a complete moron.

A memory of the dueling book came back to me, and I marched to the more purple end, which I assumed was my side. I glanced up, amazed at the beauty that was my magic.

"Begin."

I couldn't even look at Gavon before the first spell slammed into me. I flew backward, and then, before I even knew what was happening, another came, then another, and another, and another until I was flat against the back of the dome.

"Let her get up, will you?" Gavon called.

"You never let me get up," I heard him mutter before he turned back to me.

This time, I was ready. I rolled out of the way, and the spell hit the sand, sending it spraying. The diversion was enough for me to attack him, but he deflected and returned the volley, which I blocked.

His eyes narrowed.

I half-smiled at him.

He snarled at me, attacking. I stepped backward, parrying off spell after spell and unable to find an opening to fight back.

Then, in a stroke of genius, I was able to knock one of his spells back toward him, hitting him in the gut and knocking him back a few steps.

"Nice one, Alexis," Gavon called.

I grinned, basking in the compliment.

James pushed himself out of the sand, angrily. "Think you're so special? See how you like this one."

The spell hit, and I went tumbling head over heels back toward the edge of the dome.

"James," Gavon snapped. "That was uncalled for."

"You said I was supposed to spar with her," he said, hopping to his feet.

I slowly got to my knees, the cut on my forehead stinging and my head spinning from low magic. But I kept my face stoic; something told me James wouldn't give a rat's ass if I was feeling icky.

"Don't tell me you're done already? I thought you were supposed to be special?"

I looked at him curiously. "Wh—" His assault came

ferociously, and it was all I could do to block and protect myself. I felt the beginnings of exhaustion set in, but my magic hummed in my veins as powerful as ever. If only I could just find an opening...

Out of the corner of my eye, I saw a cloud of black smoke. The momentary lapse in concentration was costly, and James hit me hard.

I looked up at him from my back, as he held a spell in his hand intended for me.

"You don't look so special to me," he said, before throwing it.

I threw my hands in front of my face, and readied myself for the pain, but it never came. The dome was gone, and James and I were bathed in nothing but moonlight. I coughed and my ribs ached as I pushed myself up.

"What happened?" I asked.

"He *took* my magic," James growled, clenching his open palms into fists.

I searched the beach for Gavon. But he'd been joined by another person, presumably the arrival I'd seen a few minutes before.

"Who's that?" I asked James.

James said nothing, but his smug face glinted in the moonlight.

"Fine, be that way," I grunted, pushing myself up and walking to the other side of the beach.

"...and you know this is an illegal match," the dark figure said. I recognized the voice as the creepy man who'd spoken to me at lunch.

"Frankly, Cyrus, I don't give a damn if it's—" Gavon abruptly stopped talking when I walked up.

Cyrus's gaze drifted over me as it had at lunch, although I was sure I looked a sight, bleeding and covered in sand.

"I just thought I'd come let you know," he said. "I'm sure the rest of the Guild would be as interested as I am."

The look on Gavon's face was response enough.

Cyrus nodded to him, and, giving me one final look, disappeared in the haze of black smoke.

"Who is that?" I asked.

"James, this match is over," Gavon called over my head, ignoring my question. "Go home and wait for me there."

"I'd love to," James said, brushing himself off. "But you took away my magic, remember?"

Gavon waved his hand, and James disappeared in a cloud of purple.

"Who is that?" I repeated.

"Nobody," Gavon said, with a forced smile as he gently touched my forehead. "Are you hurt?"

"He's not nobody," I said. "He told me he was your friend."

Gavon's hand tensed. "You spoke with him?"

"Yeah. He gave me the creeps."

"What did you tell him?" Gavon said, an edge in his voice.

"N-nothing. Just that you'd been sparring with me." I watched his face shift. "W-was that bad?"

After a few moments, he smiled. "No, it wasn't bad."

Somehow, I didn't think he was being entirely truthful with me.

Twenty-Three

Without Gavon giving me a healing potion, and with Marie still grounded and without magic, the next morning was a rough one. Invisible bruises covered every inch of my body, and I needed two extra cups of coffee to get out the door.

Surprisingly, my magic wasn't totally depleted, and by midday, it was back to humming under my skin. The pain was still there, but it only reminded me how much I wanted to get back out there. Something about James' arrogance made me more eager to show him up. With a little practice, I could run circles around him.

But when I arrived at the sparring beach, Gavon wasn't there. I waited almost an hour, releasing some practice spells across the water and hoping there weren't any ships out and about, but finally had to admit that he wasn't coming, and I went home.

I tried to concentrate on school, but my anxiety about Gavon was too distracting. Had Gavon's "friend" done something to him?

Was there a problem back in New Salem? I didn't know what was so illegal about our match, but Cyrus had seemed a little too pleased about it. There was some backstory there, and it had been clear that Gavon did *not* consider Cyrus a friend.

When I arrived at our beach the second night and he *didn't*, my concern went into overdrive. This time, I waited for two hours in the freezing cold, practicing my attacks against an invisible opponent to keep warm. When I finally stopped and checked my phone, it was nearly ten at night.

I slumped down into the white sand and kept frustrated tears at bay. Why he wouldn't come, at least to tell me why he hadn't been there. But there wasn't a note or a message or anything of the sort. It was so unlike him that I began to really worry something bad had happened to him.

Finally, I gave in and transported myself back to my room. When my feet touched down on carpet and the warmth of our heater hit my skin, my ears filled with the sounds of yelling from downstairs.

"Ugh, perfect," I said with a heavy roll of my eyes. Normally, I would've stayed in my room to keep out of the crossfire, but I'd skipped dinner earlier, and after running around the beach for two hours, I was ravenous. So I readied myself for battle and crept down the stairs.

Marie and Jeanie were going at it in the living room, with Nicole in the center trying to play referee. I'd almost made it to the bottom step when I heard what they were arguing about.

"What part of 'grounded' do you not understand? You aren't

allowed to spend the night with your friends!"

Crap.

Marie's gaze swept to me and I knew in an instant what she was going to say.

"Yeah well, Lexie's been talking to Gavon."

The air in the room turned thick as Nicole and Jeanie's faces grew pale and their gazes slowly turned to me. I kept my place on the staircase. Perhaps if I stayed still, they'd think I'd turned into a statue and forget all about me.

No such luck.

"Alexis, is that true?" Jeanie asked, her voice barely above a whisper. "Gavon...has he...have you seen him?"

I dipped my chin once in a nod, and all the air was sucked out of the room.

"Marie, to your room, *now*. Alexis, in the kitchen. *Do not argue with me.*"

I marched down the rest of the stairs, meeting Marie on the last step. The look of triumph on her face was even more nerve-racking than Jeanie's quiet words. If Marie had something to gloat about, I was really in trouble.

The walk through the living room took decades. I passed Nicole and chanced a half-smile at her—if she returned it, maybe things wouldn't be so bad. But she looked right through me, shock and...a little fear on her face.

I gulped and hurried into the kitchen to await my fate.

I waited for almost half an hour, worry gnawing at my empty

stomach. Finally, I got up and made myself a sandwich, chewing silently as I strained to hear the conversation in the living room. But they'd either mastered the art of whispering, or Jeanie had charmed the room to be impervious to eavesdropping.

I finished my sandwich and magicked the plate into the dishwasher, resuming my place at the kitchen counter to await my fate. I supposed it was a good thing I still had my magic. If I was really in trouble, Jeanie would've taken it by now.

Movement caught my eye and Jeanie appeared in the doorway of the kitchen without Nicole. I always felt better with my sister acting as a buffer between Jeanie and I, especially when I was in trouble. But I put on a brave face as Jeanie wearily sidled up the counter.

"Lexie, I need you to tell me how you met Gavon McKinnon."

I sucked in a breath. "I met him on my Magic's Eve."

Her eyes widened, but she didn't respond immediately. She seemed to be tempering her response. "And what happened then?"

"He...well, he gave me a book. A magical primer. He said it would help me learn how to use my magic."

"And was he very concerned with that?" Jeanie asked, almost too calmly. "You learning how to use magic?"

"Not at first. Jeanie, who *is* he? And why are you so—"

She held up a hand to silence me. "I'll answer your questions. I just need to know what he's done."

"He hasn't done anything except show me how to use my magic, something neither you nor Nicole ever bothered to do." I shouldn't have added that last part, but I'd reached my limit on lies from Jeanie.

Jeanie squeezed the bridge of her nose. "Lexie, that wasn't my... Why didn't you tell me you'd met him?"

"Why should I have?" I said, folding my arms over my chest. "He didn't do anything but help me."

"Lexie, he's dangerous."

"Because of his Warrior magic? I have it too, you know."

"Not be—" She glanced at me. "How do you know what that is?"

"Warrior magic? The Separation? The tear? He told me all about it," I said, secretly pleased I'd learned so much of something Jeanie had kept from me. "When he took me to New Salem—"

She jumped out of her chair so fast that it toppled over behind her. "*He took you there*?"

"Y-yes," I said. "After Thanksgiving, when Gram—"

"Oh God, when you were gone...no wonder I couldn't find you." She ran a hand over her face and cursed. "Lexie, this is *bad*. What did he do to you?"

"He didn't *do* anything," I said, standing up. "Actually, he *healed* me. I'd lost control of my magic and collapsed, and so he took me to New Salem to heal me. Then he took me right home." I folded my arms across my chest and pursed my lips. "He was worried that *you* would worry about me."

"I'm so sure he was," Jeanie said with a bitterness I did not miss.

"What's the big deal?" I said, raising my voice. "It's not like he's trying to take over the world or anything. The guy reads investing strategy books—"

"Oh, really? You think you know him so very well?"

"Yeah, I do—"

"Lexie, he's one of *them*. He's their *leader*."

"There's no such thing as the Separatists! That was three hundred years ago!"

"Oh really? Then why is your mother dead?"

Whatever was on my tongue died, and I could only stare at Jeanie with my mouth agape.

"Gavon McKinnon showed up right outside our compound," Jeanie said. "He befriended your mother—our whole family. Promised that he meant no harm. Then when he found out your mother was having a Warrior, he..."

I opened and closed my mouth. That couldn't be right. Gavon wasn't that person. Gavon, the man who knew gravity was due to inertia and loved old books. Gavon, the man who had seemed so concerned with making sure I was healthy. Gavon, who wanted me to mend fences with my sister.

"There were a *thousand* opportunities for him to hurt me, and he never did. In fact, he kept healing me!"

"Lexie, you have to believe me, he is bad. I don't know what he's after—"

"Is that why Gram wouldn't let me into the clan?" I asked. "Because of Gavon? Because he wanted me dead? Or because he wanted me to join *his* little club?"

"No, Lexie—"

"You know, maybe that's not such a bad idea," I said. "Gavon's the only person around here who seems to understand me."

"Lexie, you have to believe me that—"

"Why should I? You and Nicole have done nothing but *lie* to me. For what? Because some old woman in Massachusetts who doesn't seem to give one crap about me said so? And Gavon's *never* lied to me—"

"Every word out of his mouth has been a lie, Lexie, you *have* to understand."

"No, *you* have to understand. All you do is yell at me and tell me I should *control* my magic. How could I have controlled something I never knew existed? You didn't do a *damned* thing to help me since I got my magic—"

"Alexis, *watch your mouth*—"

"And Gavon's had all the answers—"

"He's *using* you—"

"For what?" I said.

"He's *dangerous!*"

"Yeah, well, according to Gram, so am I," I said, throwing my hands up. "I heard your little conversation. She's *scared* of me. Scared I'm going to dethrone her or whatever."

"She's not... That's not..."

"Maybe if Gram got off her high horse and actually *talked* to me, she'd know that taking over her spot as the chief whatever of a group of magicals who never bothered to show up my entire life is the *last* thing I ever want to do. In fact, I don't even *want* to be in her stupid clan."

"Don't say that, Lexie," Jeanie said. "That's your family."

"No, that's *your* family."

I stood and walked to the kitchen door, needing to get out of this house and process this conversation in private.

"You aren't allowed to leave this house, Alexis. You're—"

"Don't you *dare* try to ground me," I shot back. "*You aren't my mother.*"

Jeanie's face went slack and her eyes widened.

When no more words came, I transported myself to the sparring beach.

I was shooting fireballs before my feet touched the sandy ground. Adrenaline and anger were coursing through me and I released ten before I stopped, welcoming the dip of magic and the quick rejuvenation. I was healing faster now; I almost didn't need Marie anymore.

I plopped down on the sand and stared at the waves crashing in the moonlight, echoes of the argument with Jeanie running through my brain.

I wasn't surprised that they thought Gavon was something he wasn't. He'd been too evasive, too clearly trying to hide his presence in my life from them. But I'd never gotten an uneasy feeling from him, I'd never felt like he wanted to hurt me.

I glanced around, expecting to see his purple puff of smoke any second, but then realization washed over me. Gavon hadn't been coming the past few nights. Either something had happened to him, or I'd done something to screw up our good thing.

I had nowhere to go. Nicole would probably take Jeanie's side.

Even if Marie had her magic, she wasn't going to help me anymore.

Frustrated tears spilled down my face and I hastily wiped them away. I was a Warrior. We just did what needed to be done. If I needed to figure out a way back to that tear, I'd do it. If Gavon was in trouble, I'd help him however I could.

I stood and brushed the sand off my pants and closed my eyes, concentrating on finding the compound with my magic. As soon as I found a deserted spot, I sent my body to join my magic, landing on the rocky soil of the shoreline.

"*Crap on a stick, that's cold!*" I screamed into the snowy air. I charmed my hoodie to warm me, but my skin was still frozen by the wind and ice shooting off the water. I threw the hood over my head and wrapped my arms around myself, immediately regretting the decision to come here.

The storm was dying around me, the icy pelting turning into a soft drizzle until there was no more precipitation. A magical dome had been erected around me, protecting me from the elements. But the dome was dark gray...and I didn't have to guess who'd created it.

"Fancy seeing you here," Cyrus said, as if it wasn't surprising at all. "Has Gavon not taught you how to keep the rain off of yourself?"

I closed my mouth and swallowed the screaming desire to run as fast as I could in the other direction. I was a Warrior, after all, and we didn't run away from our problems.

"What's happened to Gavon?" I asked, my voice echoing in the magical dome.

"Happened to him? Oh, dear girl, nothing at all. Guild business has been keeping him away."

He's their leader, Jeanie's voice echoed in my brain, but I shook my head to clear it. "So he's not hurt?"

Cyrus laughed, and the hairs on my neck stood straight up. "Who would hurt him, dear?"

You. "It's not like him to be away for so long."

"I can take you to talk to him yourself, if you'd like."

My head was screaming *danger-danger-danger*, but I was torn by indecision. I could walk around the beach forever, looking for that tear. There was no guarantee it hadn't been charmed by Gavon to be hidden from people. And although Cyrus was slimy as a snake, he was my ticket to New Salem.

"Well?" He held out his hand.

Finally, my smarter half took over, and I shook my head. "Just...tell him that I'm ready for our next lesson. I've got to be getting home."

"Ah, well, I tried."

Twenty-Four

It was dark and cold when I awoke. I had no memory of what had happened in that magical bubble. Or how I'd ended up lying face-up in this room. Or why the hell my head ached as I sat up.

I was in a cell of some sorts. My hands slid over damp, slimy stone as I pushed myself up. From what I could see in the dim light, the small room was made entirely of stone except for a small, barred window.

Something else was wrong—my magic was gone. Panicked, I struggled to find the hum beneath my skin, but couldn't find it.

"Good morning." Cyrus's voice boomed in the cell, and I glanced around looking for the source. The cell door was shrouded in darkness, but I heard it squeak open and my kidnapper appeared in a small trickle of light.

I had a million questions, but I kept my mouth shut. If I could find Gavon, maybe this would all be okay.

"I do apologize for the headache, but I doubted you would

come willingly," Cyrus said to my silence. "And since you've got an important day today, I wanted you to put your best foot forward with the Guild."

That, I had to respond to. "Wh...what's happening today?"

"Your introduction day," Cyrus said. A far off reminder, Guild politics, introduction day was....

"I don't want to be inducted!" I cried, springing to my feet then groaning and bracing against the cell wall as my headache thudded in my skull.

"Dear, you're a year away from that," Cyrus drawled. "At *least.* Your introduction day is simply...showcasing your powers for the Guild to consider you for membership."

"Whatever," I snapped, my hand coming to cover my heart. "I don't want *that.* I don't want to be part of your stupid Guild, and I don't—"

"You *don't* have a say in the matter," Cyrus said. "Your father promised you to us when you were born."

A thud fell in the back of my mind.

"F...father?"

Cyrus stepped into my cell, practically salivating at my shock. I hated him more. "Come now, don't tell me it's a *complete* surprise? You never knew your father, and suddenly upon Magic's Eve, you receive a visit from an older man who takes a particularly *fatherly* interest in you and you don't even question? Not to mention you both have that *particular* shade of Warrior Magic?" Cyrus laughed softly. "Gavon said you were the smart one."

I had considered it, dreamed and hoped about it. It had been staring me in the face since the moment I met him, and despite all the lies Jeanie had fed me, I knew the truth.

But somehow...this felt wrong. Gavon wouldn't promise me to the Guild.

Except that explains why he's been training you all this time, the voice in my head said.

Were Jeanie and Nicole right?

It didn't seem possible. Not Gavon.

Cyrus chuckled, presumably at the confusion on my face. "We've been waiting for this day since your birth. Since your two sisters were duds—a potion-maker and a healer, how embarrassing for him."

Shock turned to anger. "Don't you *dare* talk about my sisters like that."

His hand connected with my cheek and I flew off the stone bench.

"*You will not talk to your Master like that*," he bellowed, his voice echoing in the chamber. "Gavon was kind—most in the Guild would have killed the potion-maker at birth and impressed the healer into training. But I will not be so gentle."

"M...master?" I whimpered, slowly removing my hand.

"When you are introduced tomorrow, you will become my apprentice," Cyrus said, standing straighter and turning to leave. He paused in the doorway. "That is, if you survive the introduction match."

The door slammed shut, and I couldn't breathe.

Master? Introduction?

Gavon *was* my father.

I'd known, but I hadn't let myself believe I'd be so lucky. He was everything I'd ever wanted a father to be. In the back of my mind, I'd envisioned him putting his arm around me and explaining all the reasons why he'd been absent the last fifteen years and they would make perfect sense. I would forgive him, and he and I and my sisters would move in together and...

A tear slipped down my cheek, followed by another.

And instead of my made-for-TV movie ending, I got a rude explanation by a man who seemed intent on killing me.

If you survive.

More tears fell, and I couldn't stop them. I was going to fight in a match, and there was a very real possibility that I wasn't going to live to see the end of the day. I tried to remember what I knew about dueling, but my mind was too scattered with fear, not to mention the headache that would not go away.

I sniffed loudly, wishing I wasn't so weak. I was sure Cyrus stood just outside my cell. Maybe he drew power from my tears. Or he was just a sadistic bastard.

Either way, I hastily wiped my cheeks and forced myself to get a grip. Gavon had said—

Gavon.

Had the past few months been training me for this? Father or no, he'd taught me a lot. I wasn't passing out after every spell, and I'd held my own for a bit against James. For a while.

"Warriors don't whine. We just do," I whispered to myself. "A calm magical is a useful magical."

A tepid calm washed over me as I exhaled, and I allowed

myself little hope that maybe my death wasn't a foregone conclusion after all.

Several hours later, Cyrus opened the door to my cell, enjoying my tear-soaked cheeks and disheveled look. Well, if he thought I was going to roll over and die, he had another thing coming. I'd spent the last however-long-I'd-been-locked away pumping myself up to kick some magical ass. Perhaps my confidence would all go away in the first minute of sparring, but up until then, I wouldn't give him the satisfaction of seeing me upset.

"Shall we, Apprentice?" he said.

I wasn't his apprentice yet, but my cheek was a throbbing reminder not to piss him off, so I didn't correct him. Wordlessly, I stood and walked out of the open cell. As soon as I passed the threshold, the hum of magic returned.

"What the hell?" I gasped, looking at him then back at the cell.

"Iron," Cyrus said, with almost a bored expression. "The only metal that can contain magic." As if to prove a point, he dangled a pair of manacles in his left hand, a silent warning. But he needn't have worried. I had no idea where I was or how far away from Gavon, so my best bet would be to follow without protest.

Cyrus' basement prison led into a house equivalent in size and opulence to Gavon's, although Gavon's seemed a bit nicer, more inviting.

We stepped outside the house and I stopped short.

There was an old carriage waiting for us...but instead of horses, there were two horse-sized dragon-looking things. They screeched and clawed at the ground, spitting fire that sparked out before it caught anything around them.

"Are you unfamiliar with wyverns?" Cyrus said, turning and observing me. "My lord, what *has* that father of yours been teaching you?"

Instead of answering, as I didn't trust my voice not to betray emotion, I continued walking toward the carriage, swallowing my fear of the winged beasts. My skin tingled with unfamiliar magic, and I looked down. I no longer wore my hoodie and jeans, but a white shirt that billowed to my hands, a leather vest, dark cotton pants, and leather boots that would make Callista jealous.

"The official Death Eater uniform?" I asked, glancing back at Cyrus.

Cyrus squinted at me quizzically. Guess he'd never read Harry Potter.

"You must present well, Apprentice. Or the Guild might consider killing you before you even get to the fighting ring."

"Noted."

The village looked like something out of a period movie, all dirt roads and thatched roofs. A sewage smell permeated the air, blown by a cold wind that cut right through my cotton shirt. The villagers wore the same sort of clothes as I did, but they didn't seem bothered by the cold.

I'd thought it odd we didn't just transport into the ring, but as the villagers gathered to gawk at me, I realized I was part of a one-person parade. Cyrus hadn't been lying that I was well-known.

Villagers, mostly dirty and missing teeth, bowed as I rode past.

"Welcome, Mistress McKinnon."

"We are pleased to see you well, Mistress McKinnon."

"Best of luck in today's match."

I nodded dumbly at them, curiosity getting the better of me. "How do they know me?"

"When you were promised to us, you were promised not simply as a member of the Guild, but as a potential Guildmaster."

My head swiveled around. "*What*?"

"Gavon wanted a child raised in your world to lead us," Cyrus said, as if he were discussing the weather.

I almost didn't want to ask. "Lead us to what?"

"The reclaiming of our lands," Cyrus said. "To complete James Riley's dream of enslavement of the Nonmagicals."

My jaw dropped. "And what makes you think I'm okay with that?"

Cyrus's gaze slid over to me. "My dear, I don't think you'll live past today, so it doesn't really matter."

Despite my fear, I glared at him and turned to a nearby villager who'd come up to greet me.

"Thank you. I plan on winning," I said, not missing how Cyrus's mouth turned down.

We meandered slowly toward a large stone arena, piece of which littered the dirt road. The stones grew progressively larger, scorched and jagged as if blown off the arena by a great deal of magic.

The carriage stopped in front of the looming stone structure, and Cyrus stepped out of the carriage, offering his hand, but my gaze fell on the ten magicals assembled behind him.

They were all in their sixties or older, and I could tell they were powerful by the way the hair on my arms stood upright. But what scared me most of all was they were Warriors.

It became clear to me why John Chase had wanted specialties eradicated, especially Warriors. Wielded by the wrong person, by these people, the results could be catastrophic.

But if they were Warriors, why did they need me?

Cyrus's magic wrapped around my legs and yanked me off the carriage, and then pressed against my back, forcing me into a low bow.

Then, horrifically, the magic pushed into my mouth and down into my lungs and I spoke. "It is my honor to meet you, esteemed Council."

I stared at the ground, nauseated but refusing to retch in front of whoever this esteemed Council was.

They seemed pleased with my humiliation, and vanished in a multicolored puff of smoke.

"It's a shame Gavon hasn't taught you basic manners," Cyrus said, adjusting his fine leather gloves.

My own hands tingled from the cold, but my new Death Eater uniform hadn't come with gloves. Or, as I found when I searched my hips, pockets.

I settled for crossing my arms over my chest and digging my fingers into my armpits, as I scurried after Cyrus into a dark tunnel. The wind was even worse, tossing my hair around and cutting right through my shirt.

It was at this point I remembered I had magic, as did everyone else in the village. My thick cotton shirt suddenly became as warm as a winter coat and I managed to magic my hair into a long braid. Cyrus tossed a look behind me, as if he somehow expected me to freeze to death. I returned his look with gusto.

The tunnel opened into the arena, which resembled the Roman arenas I'd seen during history class. Stone stands rose to the skies around an oval playing field. I could see remnants of magical circles etched into the stone ground, which was already missing several pieces.

"I only suppose I don't have to give you a primer on dueling," Cyrus said.

"What would it matter if you think I'm going to die anyway?" I shot back.

"If you don't," he said with a sneer. "I'm going to enjoy breaking you of your nasty disposition."

"Good luck."

His eyes flashed, and his magic pressed around my throat, closing my windpipe. I gasped, suddenly missing the precious air I'd taken for granted my whole life. But even as spots danced in my vision, I refused to even *look* in his direction for help.

"*Cyrus.*"

Air returned to my lungs, and I collapsed to my knees, gasping. But I didn't dare look up. I couldn't, not when I still had so many questions.

"You don't get to interfere with my apprentice, Master

Gavon," Cyrus said, adjusting his gloves again. "Even if she is your daughter."

At that, I couldn't not see his reaction. His eyes flashed angrily, then quickly diverted to me, before his gaze settled squarely on Cyrus.

"I am familiar with the Guild's rules," he said stiffly. "May I have a word with her before the match?"

My heart flew to the sky. Gavon was going to save me!

"I don't believe so," Cyrus said, dashing my dreams. "The match is soon, and she'll need her focus. Besides," he smiled in my direction, and I bared my teeth at him, "she'll need to learn how to get on without you eventually."

I waited for Gavon to argue and to do some kung fu magic stuff to Cyrus's stupid face. But he simply nodded his agreement and, with a swish of his cloak, he was gone.

I heard another thud somewhere in the back of my mind.

Gavon wasn't going to help me.

Jeanie was right. Cyrus was right, too.

I was nothing but the product of some plan. My poor mother had been an unwilling participant in his evil schemes. If Marie or Nicole had been born with Warrior magic, I wouldn't even be alive.

"Dry your tears, Lexie," Cyrus whispered in my ear. "The worst pain is yet to come."

Twenty-Five

Cyrus led me out of the arena and down another hallway, then stopped in front of a small room. His magic wrapped around me once again, and pushed me inside. Before I could argue, the door slammed shut and locked, leaving me, yet again, alone in a cell.

I glared at the door, hoping Cyrus could feel my anger through the door.

But after a moment, my anger dissolved into the nagging fear that had been just below the surface.

Gavon wasn't going to help me, that was fairly clear. There was a small chance—minuscule, really—that Jeanie would come for me. But even if she did, what could she do? She barely used magic as it was. And forget the rest of the Carrigans. Thanks to my little Thanksgiving outburst, I was dead to them.

I was truly on my own. And really, I wasn't all that sure I could save myself.

I went to the single window in the room. I couldn't see much from this angle, but I could see some stands that had filled with people, and I heard an echo of the crowd. Duels must've been the only entertainment in this place, and I'm sure watching the Guildmaster's daughter get blown to bits would be great fun.

The door behind me opened and my pulse went into overdrive. "It's time, Apprentice."

I didn't want to give him the satisfaction of knowing how out-of-my-mind terrified I was, so I squared my shoulders and followed him out of the cell. When we reached the arena, I couldn't help a gasp of surprise.

There weren't just a few people, there were *hundreds* filling the stands, and even more milled around the top level looking down. Most of them were unwashed and unkempt, a far cry from Gavon or even Cyrus. In the center of the stands, there was a box of sorts where some of the magicals I'd met earlier stood. They ignored the masses completely; one whipping out a handkerchief to cover his nose when a peasant walked too close.

"Is everyone here a Warrior?" I asked, unable to help myself.

Cyrus snorted and for a moment, I thought he might ignore me, then he said, "Obviously not. These peasants are the weaker sort. Enchanters, Charmers, a few Empaths. The occasional Healer."

It didn't escape my notice that he hadn't mentioned potion-makers. I didn't want to know what they did to those.

My curiosity ended as two figures materialized at the other end of the arena and a cheer broke out amongst the spectators. Neither Gavon nor James wore a happy expression.

"Shall we?" Cyrus said, as if I had a choice.

His magic pushed me toward the center of the ring, where we met Gavon and James. Despite all the evidence to the contrary, I still hoped Gavon was working some magic to get me out of this. As we approached each other, I searched his face for a sign that he was going to let me go, even though my hopes dwindled.

"You see, Apprentice?" Cyrus said, as we approached. "I've given you a gift. You will duel with someone familiar."

I glanced at James and read anger, jealousy, and a desire to blow me to smithereens. I didn't see how this was a gift.

"Master Gavon." Cyrus tilted his head. His magic forced me into a bow again.

"Master Cyrus," James said, bowing low of his own volition. Gavon said nothing but there was blistering anger in his eyes. That, at least, was something in my favor.

"*In mortem*?" Cyrus asked leisurely.

Gavon's eyes grew wide, the first bit of real emotion I'd seen from him since I'd arrived in New Salem. "That's uncalled for an introduction match."

"As the potential master of the indroductee, I'm within the Guild's rules to—"

"*I know the damned Guild rules*," Gavon snarled. I waited for him to argue, but yet again...nothing.

"Then it's settled," Cyrus said, placing a hand on my shoulder. "After all, if she doesn't prove herself worthy to lead us, it's just as well. She's of no use to us then, don't you agree?"

Gavon gnashed his teeth together and said nothing. Somehow,

I was still waiting for him to deck Cyrus in the face, or to do something. Magic me out of there. Go nuclear. *Something.*

But he jerked out his hand, a murderous look on his face, and Cyrus gently accepted it. A jolt of electricity shot through my heart as they shook, and I knew the outcome of the duel was set.

Cyrus released Gavon's hand and led me back to my end of the ring. I struggled to control my magic, but my heart was racing too fast, my mind too preoccupied with probably dying in the next few minutes. I couldn't even remember a simple protective spell.

"I suppose this is goodbye," Cyrus said, snapping me out of my panicked reverie.

"Go to hell," I spat back at him.

He reached for me and I flinched, but he simply took my chin gently in his hands. "Say hello to your mother for me."

I'd already been on the verge of falling over, but his parting words nearly sent me to my knees.

"*Welcome to the five hundred seventy seventh introduction match to our Guild—James Riley against Alexis McKinnon...*"

"Carrigan," I corrected, glaring at the announcer.

Per the Guild rules, the Master of the potential introductee has requested in mortem. *The fight will end when either one of the participants are dead—*"

"*What?*" I screamed, taking a step back.

I'd thought that this was a one-way street, that they'd be trying to kill *me*. But if I wanted to walk out of this place alive, *I* would have to kill James. Who might be a turd blossom, but was a kid like me.

I looked across the ring at James and was unsurprised to see him...well, unsurprised. The asshole actually looked *happy*.

Probably because he knew I was toast.

"Duelers, please take your marks."

I couldn't do it. I couldn't be a murderer. Even if it meant I'd survive by killing him.

"*Begin!*"

Magic erupted around us, but the purple end was near James this time. Over my head was a dark gray magic, Cyrus's magic. I knew that if I survived this match, I wouldn't survive Cyrus' apprenticeship.

James's first spell came at me like a freight train, blasting me backward into the wall of the dome. I slid to my knees, shaking my head, just as another came hurtling toward me. I shifted out of the way on pure instinct.

"What the hell is your problem?" I screamed. I knew we had to kill each other and all, but he could give me a *little* time to breathe.

James didn't respond, flinging another scorching spell at me. This one I barely escaped, feeling the edges of my cotton shirt grow warm with the closeness of the flames.

Talking wasn't going to work with this guy. He had a chip on his shoulder and the only way that I was going to get out of this was—

To kill him. And although I had some major hangups about becoming a murderer at fifteen, the alternative was also pretty terrible. I really wasn't ready to die.

His next spell landed during my momentary distraction. The magic bruised and bloodied me before leaving me on the ground. I lay for a moment, as there was nothing else I could do.

"Had enough?" James stood over me, a swirling ball of green in his hands. "Shall I kill you now and get it over with?"

"Why do you want to kill me?" I asked, lifting my head off the ground.

"Because you're a threat," he snarled and released the spell.

I deflected it with one of my own, sending it flying into the stands, scattering the spectators.

"I'm not a damned *threat*," I spat, coming to my feet. "I don't even want to be here. You can have the little Guildmaster thing for all I care."

"This isn't about the *Guildmaster*," James growled, and released another spell, which I deflected again, much easier than before. He was growing angry, and was losing control of his magic, the same way I had. But his gaze kept darting to Gavon, whose white knuckle grip on his ornate chair was visible, even from here.

Oh.

I could work with this.

"Bet it killed you when I showed up, huh?" I asked, firing off a spell that knocked him down. "Gavon's own kid taking his attention."

James's snarl told me my blow had landed. The angrier I could get him, the less likely he'd be able to kill me, and the more time I could use to figure out how to leave this ring without needing to take his life.

"Where are your parents, huh?" I asked, dodging another blow from him. "You can't have mine."

"He's not *yours*." James was red-faced now, anger radiating off him. In fact, I could now see his magic. Glowing green and fierce, it surrounded him, gathering and pulsing with rage. And like a rubber band about to snap, I had pulled him tight.

Perhaps getting him angry wasn't the best idea after all.

"You're going to regret ever setting foot here," James said. And he released his life-ending wave of magic, headed straight for me.

"*Stop!*"

The green wave disappeared just before it hit me, and James collapsed to the ground. Just as suddenly, my own magic disappeared, and with it, my strength to stand. I tumbled to my knees, lightheaded and realizing how much of my strength had been thanks to magic.

But then I felt it, that familiar warmth spreading from my heart to my fingertips.

"Marie...?"

"I'm here," she said. As her healing magic replenished that which I'd lost, I began to think a little clearer.

Wait a minute...

"Marie!" I cried, springing to my feet. The change was too much and I swooned, leaning into Marie and someone else.

"Stay here," Nicole whispered, clutching me tightly to her. "Let Gram handle this."

"*Gram?*"

My shock overpowered my exhaustion, or Marie's healing had kicked in, because I stood upright and stared at the center of the sparring arena. My grandmother stood with eight other family members I only briefly remembered talking with, and Jeanie. She was speaking with Gavon, who wore a mask of indifference. But I saw it—the small spark in his eyes.

"W-what's going on?" I said. "How...what are you doing here?"

"D—"

"It's a long story," Nicole snapped, cutting Marie off with a look. "The bottom line is that you're safe now. Gram's working it out."

"But they said—" I said, glancing around at James, who was still lying in the dust. I hoped he wasn't dead. "They said it was to the death."

"He's not dead," Marie said quietly. "Just depleted."

I hoped they didn't have healers in New Salem. James deserved to heal the old-fashioned way.

"But the duel—"

"We found a loophole. You can't belong to this Guild until you formally renounce your membership to our clan," Nicole said. "You can't belong to both."

"But Gram said—"

"She claimed you," Nicole said with a smile.

I closed my eyes, thanking my lucky stars that I'd never figured out how to formally distance myself from the clan. I would also grovel and beg for Gram's forgiveness. Maybe even attempt a hug, if she'd let me.

"And since the rules of their Guild expressly forbid granting membership to someone ineligible, this match had to be ended," Jeanie said, appearing in front of me. "Are you all right, honey?"

I leaped from Marie into Jeanie's, words of gratitude and apology tumbling out of my mouth quicker than I could say them.

To my relief, she returned the embrace and kissed me gently on the top of my head.

"You're all right now," she said. "But next time, don't run off, okay?"

I nodded fervently, until my gaze landed on Cyrus on the other side of the arena. I took comfort in the look of pure fury on his face, while Gavon calmly spoke with the so-called "esteemed Council." None of them looked pleased with the situation, but their looks of displeasure were mostly directed toward Cyrus.

"What's he saying?" I asked.

"None of—"

"Jeanie, just stop," I whispered. "I know everything."

She sighed heavily and locked gazes with Gavon for a brief moment. Before I knew what was happening, Gram's magic surrounded us, transporting us back to the tear. It was with no small amount of relief that I crossed through it, grateful to hold Jeanie's hand.

Twenty-Six

"In the kitchen," Jeanie said when we arrived back home. "All of you."

I swallowed nervously, following Marie's golden hair into the kitchen. I sat on a barstool and looked at my hands, ready for whatever Jeanie was going to throw at me. Marie placed a hand on my shoulder and continued healing me. Or perhaps it was just a show of support.

"First of all," Jeanie said, plucking a soda from the fridge and setting it in front of me. "Are you all right?"

I nodded, even though "all right" was the farthest thing from what I was.

"Good," Jeanie said.

"About what I said..." I whispered but she waved me off.

"There's a bit of blame to go around," Jeanie said, sitting down. "I thought it was best not to tell you the whole truth because...because I didn't want you to have that burden."

"Which burden is that?" I asked a little hotly. "The fact that I've had magic since I was born, or that my father was the leader of an evil gang, or perhaps that I was only conceived to be the next leader of that gang?"

Jeanie went back to the fridge to grab a beer and sat back down. She looked a lot older than her mid-thirties.

"I'm sorry," I said. "It's just...it's a lot to take in at once."

"You have one thing wrong," Nicole said, joining Jeanie with a beer in hand. "You weren't wholly conceived to be the leader of that gang. Mom..." She closed her eyes and took a long drink of her beer. "Mom loved Gavon. Until the end. And she loved you."

I was too afraid to ask my next question, so I shifted topics. "I've had magic since I was born, haven't I?"

Jeanie nodded slowly. "Gram put a grounding spell on you, but you were so powerful, even when you were born, she wasn't sure it would stick if you knew about your magic. A few times, growing up, I thought I saw a bit of magic from you."

Fifteen years of being cooped up by a grounding spell. A simple grounding spell. Of course Gavon would've known how uncontrolled it would be after fifteen years of disuse. No wonder he'd shown up when he did.

"Why...why wouldn't they let me go up to the compound?" I said. "All of this, if I'd just had *someone* to show me what to do—"

"Because Mom was worried Gavon was still around, that he'd come for you and... Well, she was worried that if she let you into the compound, he'd come, too. She was trying to protect the clan."

"So is that why we're...we live here and not in Salem?"

Jeanie sighed heavily, and I thought I saw tears in her eyes. When she spoke, her voice was strained. "It came out of the blue, you know? I was in college, out at a bar, and I get a phone call from Gram that Mora was...Mora was dead. We knew what Gavon was, but Mora was so stubborn. She swore he could be trusted, and she married him without telling Mom, got pregnant. Then...then..." She swallowed. "After she died, Gram thought it best to let Gavon take the three of you."

There was a sharp intake of breath, but it hadn't come from me or Marie, it had come from Nicole.

"You can't be serious," she whispered. "She...she was willing... *Do you know what they would've done to me over there?*"

"I knew," Jeanie said with a hardness in her gaze. "And that's why I told her I'd take you. All of you. Mom told me that if I did, I'd be on my own, at least until Lexie grew into her powers and we made sure Gavon wasn't still interested in her. I wasn't...I wasn't even allowed back at the compound until you came of age."

I stared at my aunt in a new light. She'd given up everything—her family, her friends, her world as a magical in the compound. My own life could've turned out very differently had Jeanie not stepped up. I would've grown up in New Salem, been a puppet for Gavon's Guild. I wouldn't even have known Gavon—Cyrus would've taken me. And who knew how I would've turned out under that psychopath's tutelage?

"I'm sorry for ruining your life," I whispered.

"No, sweetie, this is *not* your fault," Jeanie said firmly.

"But it is! It's because of me—"

"We're all Gavon's children," Nicole said, although she spat out the name of our father. Silence fell on the table.

"I should've told you about him sooner," I said after a moment. "I just..." Thinking about how safe and comforted I'd felt with him brought tears to my eyes. Was it because he was my father, or because he'd wanted me off my guard? "He was so helpful. I felt like he *got* me, you know? I had all this power and I had no idea what to do with it and nobody was helping me and—"

"I'm sorry," Jeanie said. "Lexie, I had no idea...I'm not a strong magical. I never practiced like Mora did, or Mom. And when you came along and you just...I had no idea what to do with you."

She didn't say it, but the power imbalance between us was clear. Just as Marie had always been more powerful than Jeanie, I, too, was way out of her league. No wonder she'd been trying so hard to find me a better teacher.

But I couldn't be angry with her for being less than she was, not after she'd come for me. Not after she'd been the only person standing between me and Cyrus my whole life.

"Besides that, we didn't give you any reason to be suspicious," Jeanie said. "I know how easily he worms his way into your life." Her face grew dark. "Remember, he was married to your mother for almost a decade...lived at the compound with the rest of us. He was especially interested in Uncle Ashley's old book collection."

I swallowed, hating myself for what I was about to say. "He gave me some old magical books. Primers and history books. You should probably take them."

"I think the books are fine," Nicole said. "I've still got the potions books he gave me and they're...well, mostly innocuous."

I shook my head, another fairly obvious puzzle piece fitting into place. Of course Gavon had known which book I'd used to make my ill-advised healing potion.

"What kind of books did he give you?" Jeanie asked.

"History books, and...a dueling primer," I said. "I thought it was to help me learn how to spar better. Maybe it was...I don't know." My gaze fell on Marie, recalling her strange behavior after she'd begun to heal me. "Did Gavon do something to you to force you to heal me?"

Jeanie and Nicole's gazes swept over to Marie, who seemed the least concerned of all of us. "Force me?" She barked a laugh. "He didn't have to force me. I was glad to do it."

"*You* spoke to Gavon?" Nicole gasped, a mix of horror and disgust. "How could you not *tell* us he was here?"

Marie shrugged, tilting her chin higher. "Because he has money. He said if I helped Lexie, he'd give me money so I could move out."

I wasn't sure which stung more; that Marie had effectively been bribed to heal me, or that she'd lied to my face about our father when I asked her.

"How could you!" Jeanie said. "You, more than anyone...you should've told us—do you have *any idea* the danger you put Lexie in?"

Marie's face grew red. "He said he was just trying to help you get your magic under control, I didn't know that he was training you to fight in a duel!" She swallowed and lifted her chin. "And honestly, I don't believe he's all that bad."

"He let Mom die—"

"So you say, but I think there's more to the story—"

"Says who? Gavon?" Jeanie snorted.

I groaned and sank my head to my arms as the fight between the three of them escalated. My brain began to point out the inconsistencies in his behavior—how he hadn't wanted to train me at first, how he'd resisted giving me a healing potion to speed up my recovery. He'd been more concerned about my emotional wellbeing than making sure I was a fighter.

But then again, he'd sat there while I was nearly annihilated by his crazy apprentice.

But then again...my head began to hurt.

"Marie, do you even know how much danger you put this family in?" Jeanie yelled.

"Obviously we would've been in the same amount of danger regardless, because if you'd told Gram, she would've excommunicated us!" Marie sat down. "I remember Dad, okay? And I don't believe he's capable of what you all say he is."

"Yeah, and I remember the day he didn't show up and let Mom die," Nicole shot back, fire in her voice.

"Wait...what?" I glanced between the three of them. "What do you mean? What happened when Mom died?"

"Oh yes, why don't you tell her what really happened?"

My blood ran cold and I sprang to my feet.

Cyrus stood in the doorway of our kitchen. There was

something so familiar about his face, about how he walked into the kitchen as if he owned it. My magic crackled at my fingertips, recovered from the duel, or perhaps egged on by some other force.

But as soon as it started, the magic was gone.

"You can't have her," Jeanie said, and I realized she'd taken my magic.

"Jeanie, give it back!" I cried, knowing that she was powerless against him.

"Marie, take your sisters and run!" Jeanie said, yellow magic gathering at her fingertips.

Cyrus chuckled. "As if you would be any match for me. Your sister's magic was pathetic, too."

Jeanie looked back to Marie, who stood frozen in fear. "*Marie,* get your sisters out of here!"

"Jeanie, give me my magic back," I said, torn between watching Cyrus and needing Jeanie to see reason. She couldn't possibly--

"There's more than one way to reverse a grounding spell," Cyrus said.

It happened in painful slow motion, every millisecond burned into my memory. The spell that gathered in his hand, dark gray like a thundercloud. The sharp intake of breath, the way I searched for my magic to protect her, to deflect the spell that crossed the kitchen.

When my magic roared within me, I knew it was too late.

"Jeanie, no!"

I stared at my aunt, her eyes half-open and the blood trickling from her forehead as the magic pooled in my hands. Marie screamed as she tried in vain to replenish the life that was gone.

"And what are you going to do, potion-maker? Throw your iron dust at me?"

I moved on instinct, surrounding both of my sisters with magic and transporting them to Gram's front yard where I knew they'd be safe. But I'd never be safe as long as this psychopath was around.

"You know, it's just a shame I have to kill you, Alexis. You would've made an incredible Warrior."

I cut off his monologue by switching off the lights in the kitchen, the only thing I could think of to distract him, and disappeared, reappearing on our sparring beach.

There was a chance—a small one—that the charm Gavon had placed on this spot would activate, and he'd know I was there. The only question was, would Cyrus kill me first?

"Oh, how poetic." Cyrus was behind me. I spun around and nearly lost my footing on the shifting sands beneath my feet. "He's quite busy cleaning up the Guild business, you know. They weren't very pleased that you didn't complete your match. Curious how someone outside our Guild could've known about the membership clause. Curiouser how that clause ended up in our bylaws in the first place."

I took another step back. "He'll come."

"That's what your mother said, too," Cyrus said.

And I knew she had. A memory filtered into my consciousness, one that felt as familiar as rewatching a TV show from my childhood. Cyrus and I had been on a beach together, not this one, but a colder, rockier beach where the waves smashed against the shore. There had been lightning and thunder, a rare fall storm for Salem.

The memories of that night and this one crashed together in a poetic symmetry. It had seemed impossible—Gavon had said he'd charmed and hidden the tear to keep anyone else from coming through. But there he was, a stranger in my living room.

No, my mother's living room.

Then, as now, I had transported away from the house to save my children—no, my sisters.

I had drawn him to our sparring beach, but not our sparring beach, the one Gavon and my mother had practiced on in Salem.

This was a magical memory—my first. The night my mother died, the night I'd been born. Cyrus had tried to kill her, and she'd defended herself using my magic.

And when the connection between her and I had been cut, she'd died.

The realization drew forth more memories: sparring with Gavon. But it wasn't me—it was *her*. He'd taught her how to defend herself. All my instincts, they had been honed when I was in the womb. She'd been able to tap into my magic and Gavon had taken advantage, teaching her how to fight. She'd loved him, and she'd felt safe with him, the same way I had.

But the night of her death, she'd stalled as long as she could, waiting for Gavon to show up and protect her family. And when he didn't, she'd sacrificed herself.

I couldn't help the sob that escaped my lips as the memories of love and betrayal swam in the back of my mind, made more complicated by my own knowledge of Gavon.

"Oh, don't cry, Lexie," he said, drawing up a deadly-looking spell. "You'll be back with her soon enough. Then your sisters will join you."

My magic throbbed beneath my skin, remembering what it was to fight with skill and practice, and I let go of control, deflecting and attacking with the grace of a practitioner much more advanced than I. My body danced as effortlessly as Gavon's had, and I drew up three spells of my own, not to kill, but to confuse.

"I do like a challenge," Cyrus said. "Unfortunately, I don't have time—"

I released a blast, if only to shut him up, and he blocked with a spell of his own, but the force had knocked him back a few feet. When I saw the confusion on his face, I knew he'd underestimated me, which meant I had him.

I exploded in purple and fury and power. The spell crashed into Cyrus, pummeling him mercilessly until he fell to his knees. Blood dripped from the corner of his mouth, and he panted, struggling to gather his magic. Somehow I knew, perhaps through the magical memory, that I was going to use the rest of my magic to destroy him, and I was going to die.

Goodbye Nicole. Goodbye Marie.

With a loud crack, I released my final magic, the last of my life bleeding from me in slow motion. Cool sand met my face as I fell to the ground, the spell engulfing Cyrus as I closed my eyes as someone screamed my name.

Twenty-Seven

"I'm not losing her, Marie."

"Daddy, she's gone."

"No!"

I awoke slowly and miserably. Every single inch of my body ached, my mouth was as dry as a cotton ball, and my head thudded. There was a glass of water within reach, but even moving my arm was difficult. Eventually, I mustered enough strength to pull it to me, gulping down the precious fluid before lying back down.

The door cracked open and Nicole walked into my room. "I thought I heard you stirring."

"W-what happened?" I whispered.

"I... Where do I start?" Nicole said, wiping a tear away from her eye.

I lay back against the pillows and closed my eyes, knowing what she was thinking. "Jeanie's dead."

Nicole nodded. "There was... She was gone before..."

I wanted to cry more than anything in the world, but I couldn't. Maybe in a few days, when I was physically recovered, I could let loose the wails and sobs of misery that hurt even in my numbness.

"Marie went back to the house once she realized what you'd done," Nicole said bitterly. "She said she found you on the beach with Cyrus. She said she thought...she thought you'd died."

I had died, or I'd wanted to. Or was that just the magical memory? I suddenly wasn't looking forward to feeling well enough to cry.

"She found a spark," Nicole said, wiping away a tear. "Something tiny, but it was enough. She's...she's been healing you for the past few days."

"D-days?" I sputtered.

"She's sleeping off another session," Nicole said. "It's been difficult on her to heal so much. She can't... I'm glad you're awake." She walked over to the dresser and plucked a glass of brownish liquid from the shelf. "Drink this."

I knew it was a healing potion before I even tasted it. "You made a potion for me?"

"It was in one of my old... Well, I did my best," she whispered.

Gavon must've taught Nicole how to make potions. Gavon had been in Nicole's life. Had been her father for at least six years. And then she'd had to live with the fact that he'd betrayed our mother and...

"*Most in the Guild would have killed the potion maker at birth,*" Cyrus had said.

Was Gavon continuing the facade with my mother or did he truly care about Nicole? Why would he teach her potion-making if he thought her to be insignificant in his grand world domination schemes?

The more I knew about the man who'd fathered me, the more confused I became.

Nicole's potion was far superior to the one Gavon had made for me, and by the second sip, I was already feeling half-human.

"Thank you," I whispered over the rim of the glass.

"Don't scare me like that, Lexie," Nicole said, climbing into bed next to me.

I gulped down the rest of the potion and placed the glass on my bedside table. She wrapped her arms around me and rested her chin on my shoulder.

"What happened to...to Cyrus?"

"He's gone. You don't have to worry about him anymore."

I didn't believe her for one second, but I didn't say anything. I was barely fifteen—he had at least thirty years of magical training on me. And he would be back to finish the job. Which begged the question...

"Why are we here? Why aren't we at the compound with the family?" Except, for some reason, I couldn't quite remember where the compound was. Memories of a woman, Thanksgiving, an argument...

"Lexie, Gram...she's..." Nicole covered her face and sobbed.

"They've kicked us out of the clan, haven't they?"

Nicole nodded and wiped her face. "Gram came...came

for...Jeanie and told me...she said that she couldn't afford to lose any more clansmen. That was her...her first priority."

"But we're her *grandchildren—*"

"We're a liability," Nicole whispered.

"I'm a liability," I corrected.

Nicole's eyes filled with tears again, and I closed my mouth, keeping my outrage at bay for her sake. I was torn between admitting it was smarter to keep the family away from us and our strange parental problems and the aching hurt that came with knowing our own family had forsaken us.

Father or no, Irene was our grandmother, Mora was her daughter.

My magic stirred in my chest, dredging up the memory of my mother's last day. I didn't want to tell Nicole that I knew *every detail* of how our mother had faced Cyrus, how she'd used my magic to fight him. It was no wonder I knew how to use attack spells; she'd been an artist. Her magic ebbed and flowed like water on the beach, but the most shocking thing was how calm she'd been. She'd known that she was going to die, but she was fearless.

A tear slipped down my face for the woman that I would never know. I'd always pictured her to be this blonde, kind woman, a nicer version of Marie, but she was...she was a badass.

Questions burned me—how could she have wielded my magic, what was Gavon like before Cyrus showed up and ruined everything?

Why hadn't Gavon shown up to save her?

Why hadn't he been there to save me?

What were we going to do now?

I looked at Nicole, devastated and heartbroken, and decided that questions would come much later—when we were stronger and had our feet under us.

I wrapped my arms around her and stayed silent as she cried on my shoulder.

I went back to school a week later. The story circulating in my first class was that I'd been in a bad accident and my aunt had been killed, so I got a lot of mournful looks from my classmates and pats on the shoulder. The only positive I could see was neither Callista nor Joel (they'd apparently made up) found it within themselves to step on me when I opened my locker. Mills had pulled me aside to assure me that I had all the time I needed to make up the essay tests I'd missed, and if I needed to talk, he was there. I appreciated his offer, but I couldn't say anything to him.

There was no one in the world I could talk to—no one I wanted to, anyway. I'd barely seen Marie since she'd stopped healing me. Sometimes I'd see her at school, a pale-faced shell of my sister. Once or twice, I offered to listen to whatever guilt she was feeling, and she angrily rebuffed me. But I could see it in her eyes and I continued to try to get her to talk.

Nicole, on the other hand, had bottled up her fears and insecurities so tightly they were leaking out of every half-smile and fake laugh. She told us she was quitting school and getting a better job, but I knew she'd never be able to afford the mortgage payment. Not that if any of us really wanted to live there anymore, not with the memory of Jeanie.

I hated how much I'd taken my aunt for granted, how little I'd really known about her. She, like my mother, was this new person to me. I'd always thought we'd been forced upon her, but she'd taken us in. She was arguably the *least* qualified person, but she'd done it because she loved us.

And now I'd never get the chance to thank her for her sacrifices. So instead, I promised her that I'd protect what was left of our family.

Even though *he'd* given them to me, I dove into the magic books hidden under my bed. I wanted to be as good—better—than my mother was. Maybe then I could be prepared when Cyrus came back.

I wasn't sure what he was waiting for, maybe to catch me off-guard, but the longer he stayed away, the more paranoid I became, until I started prowling the beaches of Salem for the tear. I was going to try to close it, or charm it with one of those magical intruder alert charms that *he'd* always been using.

Once or twice, I thought I saw someone I knew, or I passed a house that seemed familiar, but I ignored the tug toward Clan Carrigan. If Gram wanted to have a conversation, she could find me. As far as I was concerned, they were as dead to me as I was to them.

It was a Thursday afternoon when I finally stumbled across the tear. I was walking along a desolate stretch of beach, trudging through snow and mud, when my magic began to sizzle and pop against my skin. I closed my eyes and let my magic loose, and it circled and felt *his* magical charm around the tear. Our magic was so similar that the charm unwound and a bright, crackling light appeared in front of me.

I released a breath and waited.

When the sun set and I knew Nicole would start to worry, I went home, but the next day, I was back. I sat in front of the tear and watched it. The third day, I brought a magic book with me to try to locate that magical charm Gavon had levied on the tear. The fourth day, after I tired of reading, I practiced attack spells on the Atlantic.

"*Yah*!" I screamed, flinging another powerful spell out. It was paltry, nothing like when I'd been fighting for my life. But after releasing thirty of them, I started to feel a little woozy. I sat down on the rocky beach, glad that it felt nothing like the beach back home. I wasn't sure I could ever go there again, the same way I was avoiding walking into Jeanie's bedroom.

"I'm not sure that throwing spells across the ocean is such a smart idea."

I jumped to my feet, shocked that *Marie* of all people stood behind me. She wore a thick winter coat that I was pretty sure she'd stolen from some posh Bostonian and a pair of fur-lined boots. She didn't bother to sit, but she pulled off her black gloves and stuffed them in her pocket.

"Come here."

I crossed the space between us and let her heal me, although I was rather fond of ending the day drained. It made dealing with the memories in our house a lot easier to stomach.

"Why are you coming here?" she asked.

"Want to make sure he won't come back."

Marie snorted. "Which *he* are you talking about?

I didn't answer her question. "Did Nicole send you?"

"Nicole has no idea where you are, remember?"

"So why are you here then?"

"Because you've been obsessing over this tear for weeks, and it's time you come home. It's Christmas Eve."

The reminder of our first Christmas without Jeanie threatened to overtake my stoic mood, so I swallowed. "I want to make sure no one comes through that tear."

"Are you making sure, or are you hoping someone does?"

I looked at my hands. I was waiting for someone to come back. I wanted answers.

"What was it like with him?" I asked, squinting at the tear as a large lightning bolt cracked out of it.

"I don't remember much of it," Marie said. "But I remember things were...good. Happy. He was a great dad."

The pain in my chest turned into lead. "Do you think it was all a lie?"

Marie was silent and chewed on her lip for a moment. "Look, he left. He let Mom die. He almost let *you* die. So it really doesn't matter what life was like. He's just..." She sighed again. "He's just a ghost. And one you don't have to worry about anymore."

"I wish—"

"No," Marie snapped. "You lived fifteen years without him. You don't need him around anyway."

I looked out on the black ocean again. "I want him around, though. I felt like...like he..."

"You don't need him," Marie repeated, wrapping her arm around my shoulder. "You have me and Nicole and...well, that's all you'll ever need, okay?"

I leaned my head on her shoulder. "Does that mean you'll stop being so mean to me?"

"I am never mean."

I actually laughed. It was the first time in weeks.

"I don't want you coming back here again, okay?" Marie said softly. "We all need to find a way to move on. And we can't do that without you."

I nodded and allowed her to pull me to stand.

They did need me, but not to move on. There were people out there who wanted me and my sisters dead. I was now the leader of our little three-person clan, and it was up to me to keep our family together. And since the rest of my family had forsaken us, it was up to me to keep us alive.

After all, Warriors don't whine, we just do.

Acknowledgements

As always, thanks first go to you, the reader, for picking up my magical book and reading it to the end. If you've got a spare minute, I'd appreciate it if you'd leave a review on Amazon, Goodreads, or your favorite eBook store. Even a short review is incredibly helpful to an indie author like me!

Next, thanks go to my bevy of brilliant beta readers. Karlin, thanks for being such an awesome supporter from Lyssa to Lauren to Lexie. Tamara, Alice P., Ali L., Arpita, Emma, thank you for offering your help and insight!

Dani, as usual, you're the best.

And finally, thanks also go to my typo checkers, Lisa, Brett, my mom, and Apple's text-to-speech function.

Lexie's adventures continue in

magic & mayhem

April 2017

About the Author

S. Usher Evans is an author, blogger, and witty banter aficionado. Born in Pensacola, Florida, she left the sleepy town behind for the fast-paced world of Washington, D.C.. There, she somehow landed jobs with BBC, Discovery Channel, and National Geographic Television before finally settling into a "real job" as an IT consultant. After a quarter life crisis at age 27, she decided consulting was for the birds and rekindled a childhood passion for novel writing. She sold everything she owned and moved back to Pensacola, where she currently resides with her two dogs, Zoe and Mr. Biscuit.

Evans is the author of the Razia series and Empath, both published by Sun's Golden Ray Publishing.

Check her out in her internet home
http://www.susherevans.com/

Or on Twitter
@susherevans

Also by S. Usher Evans

The Razia Series

Lyssa Peate is living a double life as a planet discovering scientist and a space pirate bounty hunter. Unfortunately, neither life is going very well. She's the least wanted pirate in the universe and her brand new scientist intern is spying on her. Things get worse when her intern is mistaken for her hostage by the Universal Police.

The Razia Series is a four-book space opera series and is available now for eBook, paperback, and hardcover.

empath

Lauren Dailey is in break-up hell, but if you ask her she's doing just great. She hears a mysterious voice promising an easy escape from her problems and finds herself in a brand new world where she has the power to feel what others are feeling. Just one problem —there's a dragon in the mountains that happens to eat Empaths. And it might be the source of the mysterious voice tempting her deeper into her own darkness.

Empath is a stand-alone fantasy that is available now in eBook, paperback, and hardcover.

Also by S. Usher Evans

THE MADION WAR TRILOGY

He's a prince, she's a pilot, they're at war. But when they are marooned on a deserted island hundreds of miles from either nation, they must set aside their differences and work together if they want to survive.

The Madion War Trilogy begins with The Island and The Chasm, available in eBook, paperback, and hardcover. Book 3, The Union, will be available Valentine's Day 2017.

Find all these books and more at
www.susherevans.com

Made in the USA
San Bernardino, CA
03 May 2017